Praise for the novels of Laura Caldwell

"The latest magnificent McNeil legal thriller...
With her father back in her life after years of not being there
for her, last year's Sam fiasco (see *Red Hot Lies*), and now the
Theo incident; Izzy wonders whom do you trust when you
cannot trust a loved one. This is a terrific twisting tale."
—*Mystery Gazette* on *Question of Trust*

"Forget John Grisham; Laura Caldwell is the real deal."
—*Mystery Scene* on *Claim of Innocence*

"Caldwell's trial scenes, breezy but effective, are key to the
unmasking of the real culprit. Izzy's successful juggling of
personal and professional roles should win her more fans."
—*Publishers Weekly* on *Claim of Innocence*

"Smart dialogue, captivating images, realistic settings
and sexy characters...The pieces of the puzzle come together
to reveal the secrets between the sheets
that lead Izzy to realize who the killer is."
—*BookReporter.com* on *Red Blooded Murder*

"*Red Blooded Murder* aims for the sweet spot
between tough and tender, between thrills and thought—
and hits the bull's-eye. A terrific novel."
—#1 *New York Times* bestselling author Lee Child

"Izzy is the whole package: feminine and sexy, but also smart,
tough and resourceful. She's no damsel-in-distress from a
tawdry bodice ripper; she's more than a fitting match for any
bad guys foolish enough to take her on."
—*Chicago Sun-Times* on *Red Blooded Murder*

"Told mainly from the heroine's first-person point of view, this
beautifully crafted and tightly written story is a fabulous read.
It's very difficult to put down—and the ending is terrific."
—*RT Book Reviews* on *Red Hot Lies*

"Former trial lawyer Caldwell launches a mystery series
that weaves the emotional appeal of her chick-lit titles
with the blinding speed of her thrillers."
—*Publishers Weekly* on *Red Hot Lies*

Also by Laura Caldwell

The Izzy McNeil Novels

Red Hot Lies
Red Blooded Murder
Red, White & Dead
Claim of Innocence
Question of Trust

Look for these other books by Laura Caldwell

Long Way Home: A Young Man Lost in the System
and the Two Women Who Found Him
The Good Liar
The Rome Affair
Look Closely
The Night I Got Lucky
The Year of Living Famously
A Clean Slate
Burning the Map

FALSE
IMPRESSIONS

LAURA CALDWELL

HARLEQUIN®
entertain, enrich, inspire™

Recycling programs
for this product may
not exist in your area.

ISBN-13: 978-0-7783-1373-1

FALSE IMPRESSIONS

For questions and comments about the quality of this book please contact us
at CustomerService@Harlequin.com.

www.Harlequin.com

Printed in U.S.A.

This book is dedicated to Katie Caldwell Kuhn,
who knows nothing of false impressions,
only of real love.

Prologue

Watching Madeline Saga from outside her gallery had become an obsession. Just like Madeline also had an obsession—art.

Madeline was in her gallery all day. Then she would return at night, often wearing different clothes, more casual than her usual fare, her silky black hair pulled back loosely.

There was always a breath held for a moment, when Madeline opened the building's door and disappeared. It only lasted for a minute. Likely Madeline was simply talking with one of the doormen, who were there twenty-four hours. Then, through the gallery's glass walls, Madeline could be seen switching on lights and walking her gallery. She would pause to stare at the paintings and sculptures as if studying them for the first time.

She would disappear again—this time into the back room, sometimes for minutes, sometimes for hours. The torture of waiting could be exquisite. When she finally left, there was always the flattening of mood, the sadness that crept in.

But Madeline would be back. Madeline could be watched again. Soon.

1

"I need you on something, Izzy," Mayburn said, looking serious, his brown eyebrows pushed together.

"Can't," I answered without asking what the assignment was. I leaned back to give the waiter room to place our plates.

Mayburn continued to talk as if he hadn't heard me, as if the waiter wasn't between us. "It's a part-time gig. Just part-time."

I waited until the waiter finished.

"That's nice," I said to Mayburn. "But since I have a full-time job now…" My friend Maggie Bristol, who was also my boss, was pregnant and due in nearly a month. She needed me to take more responsibility at the criminal defense firm of Bristol & Associates, so I had little or no time for a freelance private investigation gig.

"You *have* to do it." Mayburn bit into a lobster roll, then looked around the restaurant on North Sheffield. "When did all these damn fish places open in Chicago?"

"You don't like your lobster roll?" I tasted my crab cake, which was delicious.

"It's not that I don't like the food." He gestured around with his sandwich. "But when did every second bar start looking like a boathouse from northern Michigan?"

I glanced around. Kayaks, rowboats and oars hung from the ceiling, accented by netting and fishing poles.

"Anyway," Mayburn said, putting his lobster roll on his plate. "This is an assignment only you can do."

"Put Christopher on it," I said. My dad worked occasionally for Mayburn, as well. Somehow the part-time private detective work that I did with them had become a family affair.

"I did get Christopher on it. Sort of. Research. But I need you at the front of the house."

"What house? Does this have to do with Lucy?"

The love of Mayburn's life, Lucy DeSanto, was a lovely woman, someone I admired for her kindness and her devotion to her family.

"It's not Lucy," he said.

"Then who's the client?"

Mayburn pushed aside a bottle of hot sauce. There were two more still on the table. He lifted one—*Mojo Hojo Caliente*—then another—*Crazy Billy's Brain Damage*. He pushed them away.

He looked at me. "It's the Saga."

"Madeline Saga?" I couldn't keep the surprise from my voice. "From what you told me about her, I guess it's good that you're pushing away the hot sauce. Stay away from the heat."

"Ha. Yeah." According to Mayburn, he and Madeline had engaged in a very sexy and tumultuous relationship. Mayburn was the first to admit that the tumult was his own. He'd always feared she didn't love him as much as he did her, that her true love was art and her gallery.

"Does she still have her own gallery?" I asked.

He nodded. "She moved it from Bucktown to Michigan Ave. But now she might lose it."

"Why?"

He glanced around to see if anyone was listening. "She found out that some of the paintings she's sold were forged. But they were not fakes when the gallery acquired them."

I returned a bite of crab cake to my plate and sat back. "Whoa." I didn't know much about art, but that didn't sound good. "What did the cops say?"

"She hasn't contacted the cops."

"Why? Something was stolen from her, right? The paintings would have to be stolen before they were replaced with fakes."

"Right, but the CPD doesn't have an art crime division. Almost no local police departments do. And it can take decades for a stolen piece to show up on the market again. Plus, Saga doesn't want anyone to know this is happening. Reputation, for an art gallery owner, is everything."

"What about security cameras? Did she have them?"

"Yes and no. She didn't at the Bucktown gallery, but when she built out the new space, they were installed. I've analyzed the video for her. Nothing strange. Just Madeline in and out all the time, people she had working with her, customers."

I continued eating my crab cake.

Mayburn looked deeply troubled. "The worst part," he said, "is that whoever is stealing the paintings is trying to hurt her."

"What do you mean? Was she attacked?"

"Not yet. But things have been weird—finding

doors open at her house that she swore she'd closed and locked. Things that seem moved around in her office, although she can't be sure. And then there's the fact that anyone who knows Madeline knows that taking her paintings away would cause her great pain."

I noticed he referred to the paintings as if they were her children. "Sounds complicated."

"It is."

I thought about it. "You know what's interesting? A lot of jobs you've had me on have dealt with your love life."

"What do you mean?"

"A lot of these cases have had to do, in one way or another, with Lucy or Madeline."

"Look who's talking!" He was clearly annoyed. "You came to me last year because of Sam, when he up and disappeared. And then last year? You had me on Theo's case. Both involved were your boyfriends. One was your fiancé, if I remember correctly."

Zing. That hurt. The relationship with the fiancé—Sam—was done, fault of no one. And the boyfriend—Theo—had taken off to Thailand.

Mayburn saw my look. "Sorry," he mumbled. He picked up his sandwich and began eating again.

"It's okay," I said. I put my fork down. "So this thing with Madeline Saga, you really need me?"

"I do. I need you to work as her assistant in the gallery."

"I know absolutely nothing about the art world. You sure you want to throw me into this?"

"I need someone on the inside. We need to figure out who would have access to the paintings and any pertinent info on those paintings, plus we need ideas of anyone who might want to hurt Madeline."

I thought about Maggie. I could talk to her. "How long would you want me?"

"Shit, I don't know. Two weeks. Max." He looked across the restaurant, past the net curtain festooned with shells. "God, it would just kill me if something happened to Madeline or her business."

"Kill you?"

He shot me an irritated glance. "Hey, I might not be in love with the Saga anymore, but…" He took another bite of his lobster roll. He chewed, shrugged. "I just want her to be happy, okay? It's like…I don't know. This is hard to explain. But Madeline draws energy from everyone around her. Really. Everyone. And even though I don't see her much, she'll sense if I'm gone. She's like that. And I want her to be content, settled, before I can totally move on to Lucy."

"It still sounds complicated."

"It is." A pause. "Which is why I need you. For two weeks at the gallery. Cool?"

Because he was a friend now, because he had helped me out of more than one bind, I nodded.

2

If I was going to take a temporary gig with Mayburn, I had to talk to Maggie.

The next day, in a cab after visiting a new client (a prominent doctor accused of writing prescriptions for cash), I called Q. "Where is she?"

"Trial," he said. "The Cortadero case."

Q had been my assistant at Baltimore & Brown, the big civil firm where I'd formerly worked. We had long ago dropped the pleasantries and adapted the skill of being able to talk in shorthand. Now Q and I worked together at Bristol & Associates.

"Nice! Good for Maggie," I said, smiling. Then I paused and frowned. How had I come to a point in my life and my law practice where I was praising my boss for trying a case on behalf of a Mexican drug cartel? *Alleged* cartel, I corrected myself.

"Closings today," Q said.

"Nice!" I said again. Now, that was truly something to get excited about—a closing argument by one of the best lawyers I knew, who also happened to be my best friend. I leaned forward and asked the taxi to change directions and take me to 26th and Cal.

The epicenter of Chicago's criminal/legal world was

at 26th Street and California Avenue. It housed, in addition to a dozen jails, the busiest criminal courthouse in the country.

The cab driver, who was talking on his headset in a language I did not understand, said nothing in response to my request. Instead, he calmly swung the cab around in the middle of LaSalle Street, crossing three lanes of traffic. The move drew a few perfunctory honks from other drivers, but mostly everyone went on talking in their own earpieces or singing to the radio. Chicagoans didn't get particularly aggrieved by poor or even aggressive driving. Everyone seemed to realize we were all just trying to get somewhere, that was all.

The driver headed west. Outside, the January sky was moody and heavy, but with teasing glimpses of a distant sun-lit blue sky. But as we approached 26th and Cal, the weather made up its mind—distinctly cold and smothered with gray.

I hurried up the steps when we reached the courthouse. Inside, I flashed my ID, calling, "Hey, Tommy!" to a sheriff I knew well by now. I hurried up to the fifth floor and found the grand courtroom where Q said Maggie would be.

Inside, it was quiet and still. The only inhabitants were Maggie, standing at the counsel's table, and two guys who looked like state's attorneys. (You could tell—it was something to do with the inherent cockiness they exuded, mixed with friendliness. And why shouldn't they have such an attitude? The state won the vast percentage of criminal cases in Cook County.)

Maggie was eight months pregnant, but as I walked toward her, I noticed that she barely looked as if she was nearing childbirth. She had a round bump, but she was still tiny everywhere else.

"Great cross," I heard Maggie say to one of the guys. "Really. And that shit you pulled with Officer Cooper? Hysterical."

Maggie was complimenting the state's attorneys, which could only mean one thing—the jury was out. I took a breath, waved and walked toward her.

Ah, the sweet, sweet—*sweet*—time between when a jury is sent to deliberate and when they return with a verdict. The law, which has names for nearly everything—*voir dire, res ipsa loquitur* and so forth—has no name for this odd bit of time. It's not exactly purgatory. It's not limbo, either. It's something much more… hopeful. When a jury is out to consider the verdict—to mentally duke it out in an airless back room when the attorneys' jobs are over—anything is possible.

Which meant it was a good time to ask my boss for time to work a new job. I couldn't really explain too much. Mayburn had a strict policy that I not talk to anyone about my private investigative jobs with him. I'd been forced to tell Maggie once before. But now, I planned to simply mention I had a gig with Mayburn, say little else and hope for the best.

If I thought Maggie would have an issue with my time out of the office, I was wrong.

"Oh, thank *God*." She clapped. We were seated at her counsel's table now, the state's attorneys having gone to their lair in the other part of the building. "I'd love for you to work outside the firm for a bit."

"Really? You told me I needed to take more responsibility, and I know we don't have a lot of time to spare…."

"No, we do!" Maggie said. "What I meant when we talked was that *eventually*—like, when I go into labor—you'll need to take more responsibility, but in the meantime, have at it. *Enjoy* yourself."

"Really?" This was the second time in the last year that one of my lawyer friends had suggested enjoying my professional life. Not everyone in the law enjoyed it, not even close, so I liked the reminder.

"Absolutely," Maggie said. "I need you to take time off and do whatever you want because when I have this baby—" she gestured toward her belly "—I need you to essentially manage the firm. Marty is going to come in for a while." Marty was Martin Bristol, Maggie's partner and grandfather. "But he's pretty much retired, and you know more about our cases now than he does."

I nodded fast and swallowed hard now that she was getting specific about my upcoming responsibilities. A mood passed over me, almost a sense of dread.

"You're nervous," Maggie said.

"I guess I'm overwhelmed by the thought of managing a firm. One that I didn't even work at a year ago. Not to mention the fact that I haven't been practicing criminal law even a year." I heard the anxious tone in my voice. "But I want to help, too. In any way. So I'm in." Maggie and I had been there for each other since we met in law school.

"You have been contributing," Maggie said. "You've been great."

"But since I'm not a mom myself, there's no advice I can give you." Truth was, I still didn't know if having kids would ever be for me.

Maggie rolled her eyes again. "Thank *God*. Because I am so sick of mommy advice. It's overwhelming."

She put her hand on her pregnant belly, draped in an empire-waist black dress. "But it's reassuring to know *you're* going to be at the office when I'm not."

"Are you just trying to make me feel better?"

"Hell, no. I would be a nut job if it weren't for you." She paused, her eyes looked directly into mine. "So take the time you need. *Now.*"

"Okay, good," I said. "Thanks." I nodded at the bench. "How was your judge for the case?"

"Good. But if we lose we are so screwed. You know what they call him?"

"What?"

"Father Time."

"Long sentences if there's a guilty verdict?"

"Yep. Looonnnng." She sighed. "So, since you're not going to be at the firm much in the meantime, where are you going to be?"

"Michigan Avenue. That's about all I can tell you."

"When do you start?"

"Tonight, if it's cool with you."

"Go get 'em, Iz."

3

Much had been made of typography, but Madeline Saga had always viewed such art from a bit of a distance, never able to get too attached to an image comprised of letters or words. She usually felt that either the words selected or the final images were weak. She recalled a piece she'd seen in a Chelsea gallery, where one word appeared across the top of the canvas—*FIRE*. Throughout the rest of the canvas, the same word was turned over and over, sometimes right side up, other times facing backward. The repeated word formed a bloodred rose. Madeline supposed she understood the juxtaposition between the vaguely alarming word and the sweet flower. A rose was sometimes a sign of love, and love could be very electric and volatile—like fire. Madeline knew *that* well enough. But still, the result was too feeble for her. She'd often thought that maybe she wasn't a literary person, maybe words just weren't her thing.

But now, sitting in her office behind the gallery, it was different.

She looked at her computer screen, at her own gallery's website and an image she had placed there—a photo of Dudlin's *Eight Days,* a sketch she'd sold after she moved to this new gallery space.

Eight Days was displayed on the gallery's Past Works page. She liked to visit all the works she'd once owned, liked to see the comments below them, to behold what the world was saying about the pieces she'd sold or collected.

But not now. She'd read these particular comments too many times.

The words blurred until she forced herself to slow the panicked movement of her eyes and read one word at a time—each word, in black, appearing in a separate horizontal row. They were just words, just comments, but they struck her as a kind of typographic art. Perhaps she finally understood the power of that type of work.

Madeline dialed up the brightness on her computer, alternately gazing at the image of *Eight Days* and the comments under it, the white spaces littered with terrifying insinuations. Some targeted the artist, and those angered her. But what scared her were the ones pointed toward her.

The computer screen seemed to pulse as she stared at it. The screen seemed to gain heat. Finally, she hit the print button and waited for the two pages to come out of the printer—one showing the Dudlin piece that she'd sold, the other the comments beneath it.

She stared cautiously, suspiciously, at the printer. Recently, she'd come into her office in the morning and found pages waiting in the printer tray. Always they were pages she'd viewed before—art from some of the artists she'd worked with, pieces sold by other galleries—and yet she didn't recall printing them.

Startled. Haunted. That was how she felt when she

saw the pages waiting for her. She'd mentioned this to a few people, who'd suggested perhaps she'd had a glass of wine too many or smoked too much pot. But although Madeline did drink and sometimes smoked, she never did so to excess. Spirits and drugs didn't ignite her like they did other people.

Now, not wanting to think about the mystery of finding those pages, needing to get away from her office, she took the pages she'd printed and walked into the main space of the gallery. On a far wall hung a massive canvas, depicting a woman at two different times of the day and in two different eras.

The first was a morning image harkening back to the early 1900s. The background was painted the pink-grapefruit color of morning and showed the woman in a cream-colored nightgown, thick and comforting. The second image was of a blue-black contemporary evening, the woman now wearing a white negligee, her skin golden against the sheer white fabric, her nipples black beneath it.

In front of the painting, far back enough to gain perspective, Madeline had placed a navy-colored chaise lounge, made to resemble the one in the evening part of the painting.

She sat on the chaise now and glanced at the printout depicting *Eight Days,* which was a charcoal sketch of four street images. The sketch had been glazed with resin, giving it a vivid, sparkling finish that seemed to awaken the street images, seemed to call them to life.

Madeline flipped her long black hair over her shoulder and switched the sheets of paper in her hands so she could read the page with the comments.

Since some art aficionados thought Sir Arthur Dudlin had been lazy in using simple charcoal and then "tossing" glaze on it, Madeline hadn't been surprised when she'd read the first comment months before. *Dudlin,* it said, *gentleman though he was, faced the greatest challenge to an artist—age. And he did not fare well.*

"Poor Dudlin," she had said when she first saw that note, then scoffed. She had known the artist well at the end of his life, had an immense respect for him. She'd even been the muse for another one of his sparkling charcoals. She had been irritated at how discourteous that comment had been.

But it was the more recent comment that plagued her. As she read it, she felt something roil through her stomach—something hot, something angry. One hand held the pages, the other was on the navy chaise longue as if to brace herself for another reading, hoping she had been too hasty and judgmental the first few times around.

The comment was from someone else, who posted anonymously under the name *ArtManners.*

Dudlin, it read, *not only aged at the end of his life, he went into a different profession—that of manager. He didn't create art any longer. He issued directives to his assistants, who replicated his glazed charcoal pieces, then allowed the master to pass them off as his own.*

She braced herself for the next few lines. *Check your Dudlin if you have one. Especially if you bought it from this gallery.*

There were two more lines, but she couldn't bring herself to read them again.

Madeline put the pages at the foot of the chaise and

scooted back until she was reclining, far away from the comments.

Thankfully, no one was in the gallery.

Thankfully, John Mayburn was sending Isabel Mc-Neil.

4

"Nice to meet you," I said, shaking the hand of Madeline Saga. She was, as Mayburn had described her to me, a tiny, luminous Japanese woman with skin that seemed almost pearly. Her intent brown eyes were strangely bright, almost as if they could actually feel, as if they had senses other than sight.

"Lovely to meet you, too," she said in a quiet yet strong voice.

I looked around the gallery. It was almost triangular in shape, housed in a corner of the Wrigley Building on Michigan Avenue. Inside, the space had blond wood floors, white walls and white columns.

"This is wonderful," I said.

"Thank you. Very much." She looked around the room as if appreciating it herself. "Let me show you around."

With every step, the gallery was a surprise. First, she showed me a miniature stamp, decorated in an Indian sort of pattern, surrounded by a matte a thousand times bigger than it was, taking up half of a wall. Next, she pointed out a sculpture that looked like ice cubes with silvery insides, next to an ice bucket with real ice inside. "An installation," Madeline said.

"Interesting," I said, looking at it.

"What strikes you?" she asked.

"I'm not sure. I guess it's the combination of the real and the not real."

"But do we ever know?" Madeline asked in a musing voice. Then she added, "Nearly anything can be art. Most art simply shows different ways of looking at life, or a part of it."

Next was something more traditional and I adored it on sight. It showed a woman in side-by-side panels. It was clearly the same person, but the woman was portrayed in two different time periods. She was living two lives. I had felt very much the same over the last year and a half.

"And then that piece of furniture?" I asked Madeline. I pointed again.

"Ah, the chaise?" Madeline asked, her voice sounding lighter. "What do you think of it?"

Her questions made me feel unsure. Aside from an art history class in college and visiting the Chicago museums every once in a while, I knew nothing about art or technique. And now here I was with a woman who had two master's degrees, one in studio art, the other in art management, both from prestigious New York schools. She owned an art gallery, and according Mayburn, "lived for art and sex."

And yet Madeline looked at my face expectantly, with an eager expression.

"The chaise looks exactly like the one in the painting with the woman in the negligee." I pointed at it.

"Yes." Madeline wore a small smile. "I had the chaise made just as soon as the artist and I reached a deal for him to sell. He loved the idea. It's an honor for me to be able to contribute."

"I know very little about art," I said, "but I was thinking that your gallery is full of wonderful surprises—the matte that's so much bigger than the stamp, the real ice cubes that you must have to refresh, the exact piece of furniture from the painting."

"Isabel," she said, gently interrupting me. Although I'd told her to called me Izzy, she hadn't taken to the name. And *Isabel* sounded wonderful coming from her lush mouth, ripe with a purplish gloss. "Isabel, you say you do not know art. But you know love. I can tell that."

I paused, about to ask her what she meant. But then I let the answer float up. "Yes," I said. "I know love."

"Well, then." She softly grasped my upper arm. "You know art."

I didn't know precisely what to say. Or to think. I could only notice that even through my suit coat, I felt something electric. Or was it just what Mayburn had said about the Saga drawing energy?

We walked around the gallery some more, often in silence as Madeline gave me time to look at each piece. Sometimes, she asked my opinion ("or just your *feeling*").

Once, when we reached a sculpture, she said, "An Italian designer. What do you think of it?"

The piece was about two feet tall by two feet wide, a delicate iron tree painted in a shiny black, its leaves green jewels.

"I think it's stunning."

She smiled, gave a single nod.

Madeline kept showing me around the gallery, and I watched as she talked about the art. As she spoke, her face seemed to acquire a peach glow and her eyes brightened. She was, I thought, an incredibly sexy woman. I could see why Mayburn had been mad for her.

But then suddenly she stopped. "May I show you something?" There was a different tone to her voice now.

"Of course." I looked around the gallery, wondering what surprise was in store next.

But Madeline turned and began walking toward the back. She wore high, nude-colored patent heels that made only the lightest *tap, tap, tap* on the floor. I followed her, noticing that my own heels seemed to *clump, clump, clump* compared to hers.

The space behind the gallery, like that in front, had high ceilings and white walls. But where the front had been spacious, back here it was tidily packed. Slotted shelves held framed paintings and stretched canvases. Undisplayed, the artworks seemed diminished, whereas out front the art was allowed to breathe, to be surrounded by space and light, letting it shine, letting its viewer see it in many different ways.

In front, the sculptures might sit atop a pedestal, as the jeweled tree had done, lit perfectly. Here, a small sculpture made of bronze bricks sat on a file cabinet. Another sculpture was on top of the refrigerator.

Off to the side was a small office. On a table in the center of the room was a white laptop. We sat and Madeline pulled her chair close to mine, her laptop in front of us. She pulled up a website.

"It's your gallery site," I said.

"Yes," Madeline said. "I have photos of nearly all our artwork on the site. I like to make it as interactive as possible. One of the features is the ability to comment freely on any piece of art."

She clicked to a page of tiny images, all showing various artwork. She clicked on one—gray on a white canvas, depicting four sketches of some urban landscape, the whole thing glossed to a high sheen.

"It's a very interesting piece by Sir Arthur Dudlin," Madeline said. "I can tell you more about it later. But this is what I want to show you. The comments I received."

I read the first one—something about the artist getting older but not better.

I stopped reading and looked at Madeline. "Do you have approval on the comments, so you can authorize them before they appear?'

She shook her head. "I despise censorship. I feel with deep conviction that response to art is as important as the art itself."

Madeline showed me the next comment. *Dudlin not only aged at the end of his life.... Check your Dudlin if you have one. Especially if you bought it from this gallery.*

I stopped reading and pointed at the sentence about checking a Dudlin artwork. "Is this the first indication you had that something might have been forged?"

"The first public one," Madeline said, her voice thin. "But it's the last few lines that disturb me most."

I looked at the last two lines. *Madeline Saga makes everything she touches rotten. She obliterates.*

"Obliterates," Madeline said. "*Obliterates.* I don't understand that. I try to bring things to life. I bring art to the world."

"Do you have any idea what they mean in context with you?"

"No." She sounded bereft. I wanted to comfort her, but I had no idea how one would do that with Madeline Saga.

I looked at the comment again, then at Madeline. "I think it's time to enable your approval settings on these comments."

Madeline's face was distressed.

"Let me run it by Mayburn." I texted him what I wanted to do, and he agreed.

But Madeline didn't move when I told her that.

"Do you want me to handle it?" I asked.

Finally, Madeline nodded, gave me her passwords and watched in silence as I adjusted the controls of her website comment section and deleted those about the Dudlin.

I was just about done when the sound of a bell startled me.

"That's the front door," Madeline said softly. But she still gazed at the space on the screen where the comments had been; she was staring into it as if it were a long tunnel, one where she could somehow see many things. And those things—whatever they were—were deeply disturbing to her.

"Let me go see who it is," I said, since Madeline wasn't moving. I was glad to have something official to do for my new job.

She looked at me. "Thank you," she said earnestly, as if someone hadn't helped her with anything for a long time. "But no, I'll come with you. And Isabel, I don't mean to be difficult but…Mayburn has suggested that you've had a lively few years."

I looked at her, unsure where she was going with this.

"I was wondering if we could give you an alias. Perhaps we call you Isabel or Izzy Smith. I wouldn't want anyone to search you on the internet and find out you're really a lawyer and not an art dealer, It might raise more questions than I can answer right now."

"Of course. I should have already thought of that." I stood and began to follow her out the door.

But, one more time, she looked back to the computer screen, and somehow I could tell that she was pondering that one word—*obliterates*.

5

As I reached the front of the gallery, I felt the Chicago wind curling inside.

I wrapped my arms around myself instinctively but I noticed that Madeline did the opposite. She faced the door, arms at her sides, her body somehow moving outward, stretching to its limits as if opening itself to whatever those winds brought.

A woman had stepped inside. "Lina!" she called.

The woman wore a peach-orange coat that looked like soft cashmere and an ivory scarf that surrounded her face. She was one of those women, like my mom's friend Cassandra, whose age was impossible to tell—forty-five? Or a well-preserved sixty? She was lovely and elegant, her face smooth, so either seemed possible.

Madeline introduced her to me. "Jacqueline Stoddard," Madeline said. "This is my new gallery assistant, Isabel."

"Oh, a new assistant. Welcome." She shook my hand. "Lovely to meet you." She looked at Madeline. "Speaking of assistants, how is Syd?"

"Syd is doing well, thank you. I'll tell him you asked after him."

"Please do," Jacqueline said. "Listen, I stopped in

because I wanted to see if you have any of Roberto's work. I've got a client who is looking."

"Wait here and I'll see." Madeline gestured to me to follow her to the back room of the gallery again.

In the manner of a professor, Madeline walked to a high cabinet made with long, thin drawers and began to lecture. "These hold some of the canvases from our artists that haven't been framed," she said. "Jacqueline is looking for a Roberto Politico. Her gallery is on the other side of Michigan Avenue. Much more traditional, but occasionally we represent the same artists. She knows Roberto favors me, since I'm his Chicago gallery. She thinks that it will upset me that she might sell one of his."

"But it doesn't?" I asked, watching her slip on a pair of thin, white gloves and flip through some of the canvases.

"No, no of course not. Jacqueline is competitive with me, as many gallery owners are, because they think differently."

"What do you mean?"

"This is my passion, to show the world these beautiful things, to make people shift how they view the world. So it makes no difference to me who gets them out there. I simply hope for distribution."

We said nothing for a second. I watched her remove two canvases, one predominantly orange and one mustard-colored. They both bore tiny slashes in the paint to form a profile of a woman.

"Jacqueline called you Lina," I said. "Did I hear correctly?"

"Yes, she did." She put the canvases on a tall table. "I'm not sure where that came from. She started calling me Madelina, and then she just sort of shortened it to Lina." Madeline gave a casual shrug.

A moment later, we were back in the gallery's main space and Madeline placed the canvases on a glass table. She and Jacqueline discussed the merits of each painting, the subtleties, while I tried to absorb the conversation. There was clearly a dialogue, they said, between the two paintings, but Jacqueline's client was only interested in one, for a spot in a hallway that had certain measurements. Also, Jacqueline said, the artwork had to complement an eighteenth-century yellow Chinese vase. They launched into a discussion of prices. Seventy-eight thousand dollars, Madeline said. That was as low as she could go.

I blinked at the two women. *A seventy-eight thousand dollar painting, that's not even framed, that's going to be in a hallway next to a yellow vase?*

I had a lot to learn about the art world.

"Well, let me know about the paintings," Madeline was saying to Jacqueline. Then she turned to me. "And I am taking *you* out for a welcome drink tonight."

There was no question there, just a statement. Luckily, I had lots of time on my hands lately since I was sans boyfriend. "Love to," I said.

I expected her to invite Jacqueline, and from the vaguely anticipatory expression on Jacqueline's face, she might have been looking for the same.

But Madeline only repeated, "Let me know about the paintings," then walked Jacqueline to the door.

6

"I love this place we're going to," Madeline said when we were in the cab.

Now, as we walked in, I could see why. The interior was like the pearly pink inside of a shell, the walls curved, the lights trailing around and up and down in ways I've never seen light displayed before. I could see a bar at the back of the place. Like Madeline's gallery table, it looked as if it was made of clear glass. In front of the bar were acrylic stools with gray cushions. It was like a cave—but instead of being dark and foreboding, this cave was softly light-filled and soothing.

I looked at Madeline. "Where did you find this place?"

The small club was called Toi, which was a New Zealand Maori word, Madeline said, that referred to art, as well as the source of art. It was on a strange street, west of Halsted and one or two blocks north of Chicago Avenue. A few blocks away was Fulton Market, once the meatpacking district of the city. Now, Fulton Market contained fine restaurants and bars, shops, galleries and hip office buildings. But here, around Toi, the streets were dead, an odd collection of vacant lots, a random house or two and a few monolithic

brick buildings that looked as if they contained storage units. Apparently, even no-man's land in Chicago
could still offer up a little treasure like Toi. A happy
energy seeming to swirl around the building, despite
the lackluster architecture.

Ahead of us, an invisible cloud of laughter billowing out into the air.

Madeline stopped short. "Amaya?" She sounded
surprised.

"Hello, Madeline," the woman said, in a low but
trilling voice. She was Asian, her dark hair in a severe
cut—bangs straight across, the ends also bluntly cut at
her shoulders. Her black eyes bore a wary quality, as if
they were set farther back in her face in order to watch
the world closely, suspiciously.

Madeline pulled her fur collar tighter around her
neck. "I didn't think I'd see you until Friday." Madeline looked at me. "Amaya and I take a weaving class
together on Friday."

"Yes." Amaya sighed. "If I can get myself together
to get there. My little boy is sick right now, and I don't
know if he'll be better by then." Amaya was tinier than
Madeline, and she had a very slinky quality.

"What were you doing here?" Madeline asked.

"Jasper brought me. You know I bought another one
of his sculptures." She paused. "I'm sorry, I didn't purchase it from you. When he switched galleries…"

"No, of course." Madeline shook her head.

"I know you must be devastated."

"Not at all," Madeline said. "Jasper remains a dear
friend of mine."

"Well, as dear as someone can be when they've left
you," Amaya said. "I've got to relieve my sitter." She

swished past us, a small sea of black clothes and hair. "Goodbye, Madeline." Again that low, rolling voice.

A young blonde woman came to Madeline and greeted her warmly, hugging her. Madeline introduced us, and she shook hands with me. "Muriel," she said, and I had the brief thought that it was an old name for such a youthful and very beautiful woman. "I'm the manager here," she said. "As a friend of Madeline's, we welcome you. Anything we can bring you—anything at all—let me know." She spoke with a grace that belied her years.

I thanked her, and she walked Madeline and me farther into the club to a table near the back. When she reached it, Muriel whisked a reserved sign off with a flourish and gave a sort of head bow toward Madeline. I noticed how everyone in Madeline's life liked to contribute to the art of being her.

"Madeline," Muriel said, as we slipped into the satiny booth. "A number of people are here hoping you would come in tonight."

Madeline looked around, waved and smiled in a few directions.

"Everyone is going to want to say hello," Muriel said. "If you'll have them?"

"Please say hello to Jasper for me, but otherwise not just yet," Madeline said. "Isabel is my new assistant, and we have much to talk about."

"Of course, of course," Muriel said. "I'll send over some of your signature cocktails. Don't worry about anything." Off she walked.

"So that woman, Amaya," I said. "You're friends?"

"I wouldn't call it that. We met in the weaving class I mentioned. She bought a few pieces from me. But she seems to resent me for some reason." Madeline loosed her fur scarf and tossed her black shiny hair over her shoulder. "Or perhaps I resent her...." Madeline appeared open to both possibilities.

"Is she someone to think about regarding your—" I glanced around, knowing we were in the midst of Madeline's community "—your situation?"

She shook her head. "No, I can't imagine."

"What about Jasper, whom she mentioned?"

Madeline tossed the other side of her hair. She nodded across the room toward a group of men. "Jasper is a wonderful artist. In many ways, we had a somewhat typical artist/gallery relationship. I discovered him. Eventually, he felt he needed to grow farther than my wing span and I let him go. It's perfectly natural."

"And Jasper feels good about it?"

"Yes."

"Did Jasper or Amaya ever have any access to your gallery or house?"

"Never."

"Madeline, I have to ask. If someone stole the paintings from your gallery, it would take time to forge them and replace them. Wouldn't you notice that something was missing?"

"Well, I don't often purchase oil paintings—those take forever to truly dry. Also, I often have many works that are not yet stretched or framed stored in the back room of my gallery. If someone was able to remove them from my gallery, I would not necessarily notice right away. I have others in my house."

"Anyone have keys to your house?"

Madeline shook her head. "There's a doorman, so I've never given anyone extra keys."

"Mayburn mentioned that you've noticed doors open at your home."

"Yes. Sometimes it's my home studio, which I always close because of the chemicals. Sometimes it's a closet door that's open, one I rarely go into."

"Could it be the doormen?"

"I've asked and they said, 'Of course not.' I've asked my cleaning person, and she denies opening those doors, as well." She shrugged. "It's probably nothing."

I hoped so. But something made me doubt it.

The waitress delivered our drinks. It turned out that Madeline's signature cocktail was a lychee martini—a glass with a cloudy, whitish liquid and a cocktail stick speared with two round, gelatinous-looking fruit—the lychee.

I took a sip and moaned, "Shut the front door!"

Madeline looked confused, so I explained. "It's my way of saying 'shut the fuck up.' I'm trying desperately not to swear, but like my friend Maggie is fond of pointing out, I almost always end up saying the swearwords anyway."

Madeline laughed. "Have you ever tasted anything like this drink?"

I took another sip. "No! It's delicious." I put it on the table to stop myself from guzzling it.

Madeline and I started talking then, and the conversation flowed easily even though the topics we broached weren't always so easy. We talked about what a shock it had all been for her—finding out about the thefts, the forgeries, how she thought she might still be a bit in shock. She spoke about seeing the comments on her website.

Whenever there was a lull in the conversation, Madeline didn't seem to view it as something to fill. In fact, I'm not sure she knew what a "lull" was. Instead, she glanced around the club, serene, a small smile on her face, the sight clearly bringing her enjoyment. I made a few stabs at conversation during these times, but unless we stumbled onto something that made her eyes light up, Madeline had little taste for trivial conversation. Unlike most Chicagoans, she couldn't even be drawn into a discussion about the weather.

"It is cold," she acknowledged when I tried, then said nothing further.

In her serenity, I found calm, too; it made me look around and just…*notice.*

The next time I spoke, I chose my words carefully. "I'm really glad to have met you, Madeline."

She looked at me, her face breaking from enjoyment to joy. "You, too, Isabel. You, too." She reached across the table and squeezed my hand.

"It's funny," I said. "Because I've heard about you from Mayburn."

Madeline looked at me in sort of a curious way. "You call him by his last name."

"Yeah. Always have."

She gave a little laugh. "Mayburn. It seems such a tough name for him."

"Well," I said, shrugging, "Mayburn is a tough guy. As far as I know."

But Madeline didn't seem to share my assessment. "John is a sweetheart," was all she said.

I blinked a few times. "*Sweetheart* sounds like a brother/sister relationship."

She nodded. "That's what it became."

I couldn't help but raise my eyebrows. I knew that

Mayburn viewed Madeline as a great love of his life, second only to Lucy.

She seemed to read my look. "That's what it became…for me," she said, clarifying.

"Why is that?"

"In part because I'm an only child. I was adopted."

"When you were a baby?"

"Yes. My parents are blonds from Wisconsin." She smiled as she thought of them. "But my dad did a lot of work in Japan. That's where they adopted me from."

"Do you know your birth family?"

She shook her head. "They did give me a gift once." She smiled. "I'll tell you about it sometime."

"How long did you and Mayburn date?" I asked. "Years?"

"Six months," Madeline said.

"Is that it?" Mayburn had made it seem longer, or maybe it was the way he remembered it, the way he gave it import.

Suddenly it dawned on me that the people I considered of great importance in my life—Theo, Sam— might not think of me the same way.

Sam, for example, I hadn't seen or spoken to in months. For all I knew, he was once again with Alyssa, his ex-high school girlfriend. Maybe Sam felt, now, that I was a swerve, something he'd veered around before getting back to his first love.

And Theo—we'd dated about the same amount of time as Mayburn and Madeline. Right now, he'd told me, he simply couldn't be in a relationship. Theo, an only child, had been close with his parents. But recently, some disturbing events had Theo questioning not only himself but everyone around him. I understood such issues well. I understood that Theo needed to hide to lick his wounds. Who knew what—or who—was important to him at this moment.

"How did you and Mayburn decide he would work on your case?" I asked to pull my thoughts away.

"I told John what was happening—he's one of a handful of people I'll talk to when I'm deeply upset."

I wondered who the others were.

"And then John insisted he look into the matter," she said.

"Because he knows how important the gallery is to you."

She nodded.

"Talking about how he feels like a brother now, when I know he didn't feel the same, makes me sound so cavalier with my relationship with him."

"He was pretty hurt," I said, then immediately regretted it. Mayburn would kill me if he'd heard me say that. "Actually he was just sorta hurt," I said, reducing Mayburn's pain factor.

"Of course," she said, shaking her head back and forth. "He had bought a house he wanted us to live in."

"The one in Lincoln Square."

"Yes. And that's when I knew we had different ideas about what our lives would be. I'm not a Lincoln Square kind of person."

"I can see that." Historically, Lincoln Square was a predominantly German neighborhood. Much of that heritage was preserved in bars like the Chicago Brauhaus and Huettenbar. The streets surrounding Lincoln Avenue, the main thoroughfare, were populated mostly with wood-frame, single family houses. Wonderful cafes from other regions, as well as cute boutiques and bookshops, now flourished there, too. Still, the hood was more "livable city" than "urban city." Madeline Saga wasn't the type to live there.

"I was so shocked that he didn't understand the life he was planning would never be me," Madeline said. "That fact surprised me so much, hurt me so much, I just broke up with him. Just like that. And now I'm shamed by my cruelty."

I reached over the table. Now it was my turn to pat her hand. "Don't worry about it. He's wonderful. He's got a girlfriend, the kids, and obviously he still thinks well of you since he wanted to do this job for you."

She looked up at me, a considering expression on her face. "John had children?" she said, the words disclosing shock.

"No, no. He's dating someone who has kids. She's great. So don't worry about him."

"No," she said. "I suppose not."

She waved at a passing waiter who soon returned with another round of lychee martinis.

"Tell me about you, Isabel," Madeline said. "How do you know John?"

I told her my fiancé had experienced "some problems." The topic of Sam's disappearance more than a year ago seemed a little much for our first night out, so I only disclosed that I'd met Mayburn through that situation. "Now we're friends."

"He is an excellent friend."

I nodded.

"And where do you live, Isabel?"

"Old Town." I told her about the three-flat condo building I lived in. I was on the top floor, which was a drag because of the stairs but also a joy because of the private roof deck.

"And this…" She gestured around the bar. "Is this the type of place you would go to with friends?"

"I grew up in Chicago. In the city. So I have an affinity for dive bars."

"Dive bars!" she said, sounding delighted.

We talked about the city then, about how Chicago had changed so very much, had become, in some ways much more metropolitan, and yet it was still the same hard-working Midwest town it had always been.

Another round of lychee cocktails appeared.

Madeline beamed and thanked the waiter. "To Chicago." She lifted her glass in a toast.

I did the same. "To Chicago," I said, clinking her glass lightly, trying not to slosh the drink. The truth was, *I* was getting a little sloshed.

We both took a sip, then Madeline excused herself and left the table, heading toward the restroom. I sat and let myself just notice, as I'd watched Madeline do over the last hour or so.

I thought about Madeline. I was impressed with the way she was handling the forgery. I could tell it deeply distressed her, and yet despite that, she still allowed herself to enjoy her life when she could.

About five minutes passed, during which I contentedly sat. Then I began to look around the crowd. Madeline had said that many people from the art world—artists, managers, gallery owners, collectors, print makers, art writers—could be found there.

Another five minutes passed.

When the waitress came, I asked for a glass of water. I wanted to stay a little longer. I wasn't quite ready to stop basking in the light that was Madeline's attention when she shined it on you.

The water was delivered. More time passed. No Madeline. I looked at my phone—no texts or calls from her.

I got up and went to the restroom, but she wasn't there, either. I walked around the club, scanning the crowd. It was small and quickly evident that she wasn't to be found.

When I returned to our table, Muriel came up. "How was your night?"

"Delightful," I answered. "I love your place. I wouldn't have known about it if it wasn't for Madeline."

"Madeline," Muriel repeated with a smile. "Isn't she incredible?"

I nodded quickly. "She is."

"She paid the bill," Muriel said, "so stay and enjoy yourself as long as you want. Let us know if we can get anything for you." She smiled beatifically.

It was only then I realized Madeline was gone.

7

As I left the club, two doormen stood there, both huge, dressed in shearling coats and hats.

"Hi guys," I said. "Did you see a woman leave here recently?"

"Uh, yeah," one said, and I could tell he wanted to add, *duh*.

Muriel had said she didn't know why Madeline left, but that nothing had seemed odd. Madeline had told them to put everything on her tab, and that was that.

"She's a Japanese woman," I said to the bouncers.

Neither responded.

"She's really beautiful," I said.

"Lotta pretty women here," the other bouncer said.

I thanked them and left, stepping onto the sidewalk. Like a dark painting, the canvas outside was mostly black. Steel charcoal-gray beams slashed back and forth overhead, carrying lit boxes—the El train carting people east and west. Aside from the train, the neighborhood was desolate, very few cars.

Suddenly I wondered if Madeline was sick. Could that be why she had left so quickly? I walked up the block, looking in alleys. No sign of her.

I walked back, past the club and down a few blocks,

doing the same thing. I was thankful I didn't find her throwing up in an alley, but I was still worried.

I pulled my phone out of my purse. I texted, *Hi, it's Izzy. You okay?*

I paced the sidewalk again, hoping for a reply. An occasional car passed. It had snowed a little since we were inside, and the tires from each car shot a little spray of slush onto the street.

I tried calling her. Nothing.

I tried again. This time I left a message. *Hi Madeline. Sounds like you left. I just want to make sure you're okay. Can you call me?*

I couldn't shake what she had described—feeling like someone had been in her place.

One more round of pacing the sidewalk, then I decided it was time to go. I started searching for a cab but saw none.

I was making my way back to the club, to ask the doormen for help, when a sudden flurry of white and blue pulled to the curb. A Chicago police car.

The front door opened. A man stepped out. He wore a big gray jacket, bulky, not because he was fat but because he was wearing a bulletproof vest. You got used to the look in Chicago.

He turned to me. And I got a flash of a memory.

I opened my mouth. I could find only one word. "Vaughn."

8

Neither of them noticed anyone but each other that night, not Madeline or the redhead.

For nearly two hours they talked, a friendship seeming to grow on the spot. How easy it was for Madeline to connect with people when she wanted. It was always about what *she* wanted.

They drank the martinis Madeline loved, their camaraderie, their growing interest in each other obvious.

Then the redhead was alone. She was looking around, apparently for Madeline, who had been gone from the table for quite a while. It was almost laughable. At least someone else was being treated badly by Madeline Saga, being ignored and made to feel as if they were nothing.

So, really, it wasn't surprising that neither of the women had noticed someone watching them.

But the cop who had shown up? That had been a surprise. The redhead was walking up and down the street when the police car had arrived.

She and the cop talked, then the redhead got into the car. What had the woman done? And yet, the redhead hadn't been handcuffed. Was she being taken in for some kind of questioning? Could this be about what was going on with Madeline's art? What *was* going on here?

A short time ago, just inside the club, there had been amusement that someone else was being treated poorly by Madeline Saga. And yet now there was only fear, a sense of being out of control.

There was a measure of relief when the police car pulled away.

9

"This is my first time in the back of a cop car," I said.

Vaughn had offered me a ride home. Since there was a dearth of cabs, I agreed. But I had to ride in the back. "Protocol," he'd said.

From the front, I heard Vaughn scoff. "Seems like you would have seen a lot of that real estate back there."

"Excuse me?"

"Yeah," he said, "for all the trouble you find yourself in."

"Excuse me?" I repeated. "I do not find trouble." That was untrue, but I wasn't about to admit anything to Detective Damon Vaughn.

Detective Vaughn had made my life hell a couple of times—first when Sam had disappeared and second when he'd suspected me of killing one of my friends. In a stroke of brilliant luck (or maybe just the gods in my universe doling out some karma) I'd gotten the chance to cross-examine him at a trial recently. And let's just say it was the best cross of my career. We'd mended fences after that, even shared a couple of cocktails. But the fact remained that no one could irk me like Vaughn.

"Why do you always have to be so nasty?" I asked.

"I'm not. I'm just stating the truth. You get in a lot of trouble."

"Oh, fork you, I do not!" Again, I was shading the truth. Trouble did find me, but I didn't usually bring it upon myself. At least, to my mind.

"You could have gotten into some trouble at that bar," Vaughn pointed out. "That's why I showed up there."

"What do you mean?" I asked the back of Vaughn's head as he turned the car on Franklin Street. His hair was shot through with gray, but he was one of those guys who had a lot of hair, probably always would.

"The owner is a buddy of mine," Vaughn said. "He calls me when he's got issues but doesn't want to involve 911. He had an issue tonight."

"What kind of issue?"

"Suspected prostitution."

"Really? Yeah, I guess that's a good way for a bar owner to get closed down—having girls making money that way."

Vaughn stopped at a light, turned around. He had a rugged face and brown eyes. Those eyes were squinting at me. He shook his head. "*You're* the girl he thought was trying to make money that way."

"*What?*"

"He said that they had this girl walking up and down the street over and over, as if she was looking for someone. In general, that's pretty indicative. That's why they call it 'street-walking.'"

"My friend was gone," I said. "I was looking for her! She just disappeared without saying anything. She paid the bill, but I couldn't understand why she wouldn't have let me know she was leaving. I was afraid she was sick or something."

The light turned green and Vaughn shrugged, turned around and drove through it.

We remained quiet for a few blocks.

"Tell me what happened with your friend," I heard Vaughn say.

I felt a shiver of relief for the help. I told him about the night. As I spoke, I took out my phone. Still no texts or calls from Madeline. "So what do you think?" I asked, when I'd finished.

Another shrug from Vaughn. "What's she like?"

"Unique." I told him what I knew of Madeline Saga, what I'd learned and noticed about her since I met her.

"I wouldn't worry too much," he said.

"Really?"

"She probably got boozed up and took a header."

"What's a header?"

"When you realize you're wasted and have to put yourself to bed, and you just leave because you don't want people talking you out of it, and you're in no shape to say goodbyes. It's usually a guy thing."

"She wasn't wasted."

"When are you supposed to see her next?"

"Tomorrow."

"Call me if she's doesn't show."

Eventually Vaughn turned up North Avenue, heading east, then turned left on Sedgwick and another left at my street, Eugenie. He pulled over to the curb and put the car in park.

"Well," I said, "you certainly seem to know exactly where my house is." I noticed immediately that a fair amount of sarcasm had come out with my words. What was it about Damon Vaughn that got under my skin?

He turned around, his face a snarl of irritability. "Listen, McNeil, I was at your house recently for a couple of break-ins. Remember? And, wait, oh yeah, a *murder*."

He had a good point. My neighbor had been killed last year in my apartment, and Vaughn had soon been on the scene, taking care of it.

"So yeah, I remember where your place is," he said. "I'm not an idiot." He sounded not so much irritable now as he did hurt.

"I'm not saying you're an idiot. I'm sorry if it sounded like that."

Nothing from Vaughn.

I opened the door. "Hey, I'm grateful for the ride. Thanks."

He picked up his hand as if to wave goodbye, but he didn't turn around.

"Really," I said. "Thanks."

A pause, then, "No problem, McNeil."

And that, I supposed, was the best relationship Detective Damon Vaughn and I were going to have.

10

I woke up the next morning to the sound of my cell-phone. I hadn't turned it off in the hope that Madeline would call.

The display read, *Charlie. Cell.* My brother.

In days of yore, the sight of a call from my brother first thing in the morning would have induced fear. For years and years, he lived off a worker's comp settlement and nursed a back injury. He regularly slept until two in the afternoon, giving himself a solid three hours before he would open a bottle of red wine.

But in the last year, he'd landed a job in radio and then branched into other sound-production projects.

"How are you?" I answered.

"I'm fine." That wasn't a surprise. Charlie was always fine. He was one of those people—admittedly the only one I knew—who was always, generally, content.

"But it's Dad," Charlie said then. Another little shock.

Our father had returned to our lives, and to Chicago, only six months ago. So the word *dad* was a bit jarring. That word had been used when Charlie and I were kids, but once our dad disappeared, with no one else. We had grown up believing he had died, but in truth he had gone undercover to protect us. We'd always called our eventual stepfather, Spence, by his first name.

Another little recognition settled in. This was the first time, strangely, that my brother and I had talked, just the two of us, about my father directly. It was as if we were both feeling our way in the world of having a father again, neither wanting to disturb the other's development, both of us knowing, somewhere deep within, that we both had our own journeys.

"He's thinking about leaving," Charlie said.

"Leaving?"

"Moving. Out of Chicago."

"When did you hear this?"

"Last night. Met him for dinner."

Both Charlie and I had been trying to have regular visits with our father, trying to help incorporate his new life in Chicago into ours. Even our mom and Spence had done the same. But the fact was, Christopher McNeil was not a social animal. If anything, he was a loner. He'd left Chicago long ago to save his family and spent most of his life abroad.

"What did he say?" I asked.

"Not much. You know how he is."

"Yeah."

"I asked him a few more questions, but I didn't get too far."

I tried to let Charlie's news travel from my ears to my mind and from there to my heart and gut to see what I felt. But there were all sorts of blockages, too many feelings and wrong-way turns. For so long, I had kept my father compartmentalized. I didn't know what to feel about this news.

In the meantime, I needed to get to the gallery. I needed to find out where Madeline had disappeared to.

"I don't know what to think, Charlie. I'll have to call ya later."

When I walked in the gallery I was relieved to see that Madeline was there.

She stood at the back, talking to a man about a series of photographic prints hanging on the wall. Each showcased a mocked-up magazine cover, the model in each representing different ways women are viewed—from mother to whore and so many other things in between. I didn't think I understood the photographs, but I had been intrigued when Madeline showed them to me the day before.

I went into the back room and was slipping my arms out of my coat when I heard the ding of the door opening—probably the client leaving—and then the sound of high heels clicking gently toward me. Madeline.

When I turned to greet her, I expected an apology for her disappearing act.

"Last night…" she said. I nodded, interested in her explanation. "Didn't you say you wanted to meet someone?"

"Someone…?"

"A man. Someone to date."

I thought about it. "Yeah. I guess at some point in our discussion I did. I also said I thought I was fine being on my own, though."

"Well, anyway, I've got someone coming in for you," Madeline said, sounding pleased.

"What?"

"Don't worry about it." She gave me a sly wink.

I wasn't sure I was ready to meet a possible new

date, but I was still too distracted by the previous night to dwell on it with her.

"Okay, but Madeline," I said, hanging my coat on a rack, "what happened to you last night?"

She stood by the file cabinet, her hand on the drawer. She turned. "What do you mean?"

"You disappeared."

"What do you mean?" she repeated.

"You got up, I assumed just to go the bathroom since you didn't say goodbye, but instead—*bam!*—you were gone."

"Bam?" Madeline said, in a funny, slightly mocking tone.

"Well, that's how it felt, like suddenly you'd just disappeared." I crossed my arms over my chest. "Thanks for the drinks and everything, by the way. I don't want to seem ungrateful, but I was worried."

"Of course," she said. She opened a drawer, flipped through some files. "Isabel, I'm sorry. I do that sometimes."

"Do what?"

"I find I'm done with the night, and I leave. It's nothing to do with you. It's a bad habit of mine. And I apologize." Something struck me as slightly false about her words, but I couldn't put my finger on what. Madeline sighed. "I find goodbyes to be pedestrian. They don't add anything to life."

I wanted to ask her where she'd gone after she'd left the club—home?—but Madeline pulled out a file, then brought it to a table in the center of the room and opened it. Inside were photos of a sculpture of sorts, tall and oblong and made of white glass swirled with silver.

The photos made me remember something. "My

friend Maggie bought a sculpture last summer that was a little bit like this. At the Old Town Art Fair. Do you show there?"

I looked at Madeline and saw her lips, encased today in a pale pink gloss, suddenly purse. "No," she said. "I don't." The implication was clear—there was no chance she would show art at the Old Town Art Fair.

I thought about the fair, which happened in Chicago every June. The nucleus was at the intersection of North and Wells. The fair spread from there spanning blocks and blocks in every direction, holding stands showing art work, sculpture, sketches, prints and furniture.

"Those are local artists," Madeline said.

"You don't represent anyone from Chicago?"

"No, I do, it's just that, in general, those artists are amateurs. I represent a different level of art." She didn't sound haughty about it, just matter of fact.

"I didn't always," Madeline continued. "I began my career working with what's called outsider art."

"Outsider art," to my unknowledgeable ears sounded like art that was sold outside—like, say, at Old Town Art Fair.

But Madeline clarified the concept for me. An outside artist, she said, was one who had no classical education in traditional channels. Instead, what was prized about great outsider art was its naiveté, which led, somehow, to pure aesthetic genius.

She seemed in a reflective mood, so I stayed silent.

"I liked the discovery and the thrill of finding outsider art," she said, as she arranged the photos of the sculpture on the table. "I liked finding something no one else had realized was so wonderful. I opened a gallery in Bucktown showing original works. But eventually my tastes evolved and I got into secondary market work."

"What's that?"

"Put simply, it's buying dead artists' works from around the country and Europe."

The reason for getting into secondary art, she said, was not because she had some highbrow vision of what art should be. Rather, she became mesmerized by technique, by artists who had either studied their particular techniques for years or occasionally by current artists who had shown mastery of technique in a short time. From there, her tastes and her gallery had grown eclectically in all directions.

"I like to just wait and see what happens," she said.

I could see again what Mayburn meant when he told me Madeline lived for her gallery. Madeline Saga lit up when she talked about art. Her eyes were wide with wonder, her words faster than their usual calm cadence. "Some of the brilliance of these artists," she continued, "the *professional* brilliance—combined with their creativity...well, that, for me, is dazzling. I don't often see that in street art."

I thought I understood what she meant. I told Madeline about the sculpture that Maggie bought at the art fair. It was round and made with white plaster, on which the artist had placed broken white tiles, forming a mosaic pattern. It was a perfect accent for Maggie's sleek, light and modern South Loop apartment. Although maybe that would change, since Maggie was now living with Bernard, a Filipino professional musician, whose tastes tended toward a black-and-red Asian style.

"This sculpture my friend bought cost around a hundred and fifty dollars," I told Madeline. "So I suppose that's different than—" I looked down at the pictures "—a sculpture such as this one."

"Yes. But of course, there are so many facets of art appreciation." She lifted one of the photos to her face. "It isn't simply about price. The price is based on the techniques employed, as I mentioned, but also on the complexity the art carries in its message. Then there's also the question of whether it's derivative of another artist."

"Like art that was recently painted but looks like an Andy Warhol," I said, remembering something else I'd seen at an art fair.

"Exactly," Madeline said.

"Thank you for teaching me about this."

"It is my distinct pleasure." She paused and put a hand over mine that was on the table. Her hand felt so light, as if most of Madeline Saga was filled with air.

We heard the trill of a bell then, indicating someone had come in the front door.

"He's here," she said.

"Who's here?"

Madeline clapped. "Let's go."

11

Madeline led me into the gallery. I stalled for a second, standing next to the jeweled tree sculpture, taking in the man who'd just entered.

He was gorgeous. You could see that, even from the side. He appeared like any normal guy, wearing jeans and a brown velvety jacket and standing near the painting of the woman in two different times. But like Madeline, something was different in the air because of him. Something felt fun, electric. Or maybe it was Madeline's reaction to him.

"Isabel Smith," she said, "this is Jeremy Breslin."

Jeremy Breslin turned, took some steps toward me and shook my hand. I looked up at him, and into bright, navy blue eyes. Mesmerizing.

I started to pull my hand away, afraid that if I kept gazing into those eyes, I might say something silly. But he held on to my hand. He looked at me, very curiously.

He's looking at all of me. I don't know why I thought that, but that's what it felt like. Again, it reminded me of Madeline, the way she took in the whole of things.

Madeline explained that Jeremy operated a hedge fund, that he was originally from Boston and his wife's family had been clients of hers for years.

During this introduction, Jeremy kept holding my hand. When Madeline stopped, he seemed to realize it and let my hand go. It felt cold without his touch.

"My apologies for staring at you," he said. Then, as if for explanation, "My first girlfriend was a redhead."

"Ah," I said. "Well, you know the redhead rules."

He smiled. "What are the rules?"

"Let me ask you this, that first girlfriend of yours—would you say she was your first love?"

He nodded. "Yes."

"One of the rules says that if the first person you fell in love with was a redhead, or the first person you had…ah…you know, adult relations with was a redhead, then—" I shrugged "—you'll always have a thing for redheads."

He laughed. "You're right. I have a thing for redheads."

"Sounds like you're doomed."

"Happily," he said.

"So, Isabel," she said, "Jeremy is the one who—" She glanced around the gallery. No one else was there. "Jeremy," she said, turning back to us, "is the one who discovered…" She cleared her throat. "Some improprieties with the paintings."

"Oh, the…?" I said.

"Yes," Madeline continued, "Jeremy was the one who discovered the issue of forgery from some work he had bought from my gallery."

"How?" I asked him.

"I'm getting divorced, so we had to have our assets valued. My lawyer found an art appraiser to review what we'd collected."

"He determined you had fakes?"

"Yes. At first, he told us that something was bothering him about the pigment on the piece, something he didn't expect to see. He had it tested and found that the pigment hadn't been available—didn't even exist—when those pieces were done. It was very new. Therefore, they were forged."

"They? How many paintings were forged?"

"Two."

"And you bought both of those from..."

He nodded.

"Both from me," Madeline said, taking full responsibility. Madeline turned to Jeremy. "Isabel will be helping me at the gallery, so I wanted her to know everything."

"Of course," Jeremy said. "Having you work here will be wonderful." As he spoke, his eyes lighted on me again, and I felt some kind of current travel up my spine. I stopped myself from quivering visibly. I'm not really a quivering kind of girl, so the moment was odd.

Jeremy held my eyes a little longer. If he was upset about discovering that some precious artwork had been forged, he didn't show it.

"Izzy." He paused. "Is it okay if I call you Izzy?"

I nodded. "That's what most people call me."

"Even though 'Isabel' is much more beautiful," Madeline added, smiling.

Jeremy nodded. "Well." He paused. "Izzy, this may seem a little quick, but could I take you out sometime? Just for a drink?"

"Oh, I don't know..." My eyes shot to Madeline.

"You should!" Madeline said. "Jeremy has traveled everywhere, done so many things." She took a few steps and put a friendly hand on his arm. "He's a charming conversationalist. You can speak with him about anything. Absolutely anything."

It was those last two words, spoken firmly, that made me realize Madeline very much wanted me to go out with Jeremy. And even more importantly, to discuss the issue of the forged paintings with him.

I looked back at Jeremy Breslin.

"Tomorrow, perhaps?" he said.

"I'd love to."

12

Madeline Saga's oddly shaped gallery was well situated for frequent walks past the place, either on Michigan Avenue on one side or on the narrow pedestrian mall on the other. Both provided large windows to see the artwork inside, of course, but also to see Madeline.

These frequent, somewhat obsessive walks were an attempt to soothe ever-mounting emotions—toxic, hateful emotions—connected to Madeline Saga.

From inside the gallery, the glare of the glass made it hard to see pedestrians outside. And so it was simple to walk by, back and forth, to see what Madeline was doing. Everyone who had dealt with her knew how Madeline got when she was working at the gallery. But of course, Madeline didn't see the gallery as a job. It was her life.

And now Madeline could be seen through the Michigan Avenue windows, through the snow, growing lighter, while the skies grew yellow with sun. And, yes, there she was, introducing her assistant to Jeremy Breslin, of all people, the one who had discovered the fakes.

But how brazen, how bold, this introduction, as if Madeline felt no remorse.

Madeline didn't seem to notice people watching her—whether through her windows or in person. She didn't notice because they didn't matter to her, whether they were full of awe or hate or anything in between. Art mattered to her, her gallery.

But neither would be part of Madeline's life for long. They might be the end of her altogether.

13

I met my father for lunch. In addition to Charlie's news about his potential move, I wanted to ask him about the Madeline Saga case.

My father had developed this dining game of sorts; in every restaurant, he wanted to try something he'd never had before. I wasn't sure how he'd struck upon this, but I was happier than usual about it that day, since it gave the impression that he liked Chicago, that he would not be moving, and therefore I wouldn't have to decide how I felt about that.

This time, he'd picked the Bongo Room in Wicker Park. Currently my father was cutting into—I kid you not about this—Pumpkin Spice and Chocolate Chunk Cheesecake Flapjacks. And that wasn't all that was in the dish—there were graham crackers, too, and vanilla cream and all sorts of stuff.

I'd gotten a chicken and avocado salad that had melted provolone on it. I never thought I'd use the word *decadent* when referring to a salad, but that's what it tasted like.

"How is it?" I asked my dad after watching him take a few bites.

"I do not know." He took another bite, chewing it slowly. "Odd," he said.

Since no other information seemed forthcoming, and I wasn't quite ready to launch into the topic of his moving, I brought up Madeline Saga. "Mayburn said he had you do some general research," I said. "What did you find?"

"What I found was the defeating fact that art crimes usually aren't solved," he said. "So, Izzy, you're fighting an uphill battle with this one. Only around ten percent of stolen art is ever recovered. And the prosecution rates are even lower."

"You're kidding," I said. "Seems like it would be relatively simple to have security cameras these days and see everything that happens to a painting."

"Yes. If the art simply stayed on one wall. But removal is often needed for cleaning, for transporting to other galleries or museums, for an exhibition or relocation in the gallery itself."

"Madeline moved from Bucktown to Michigan Avenue last year."

"Well, then there are many danger points."

"Danger points?"

"In the moving process alone, there are many points where criminals can get in. There's the crating of art, there's leaving those crates standing until they can be shipped, there's loading of the crates into a truck, there's the driving part of the journey, there's the unloading. And then the art sits wherever it's been unloaded until it's unpacked. And then it sits there until it's installed."

"Wow." I felt overwhelmed at the realization. "So I should be tracking down and talking to everyone who was involved, even in the slightest, with the move of the gallery."

"You got it. I'd guess there were probably five to ten people involved. At a minimum."

He asked me what I did when I was at Madeline's gallery.

When there were no clients in the store, I told him, I tried to study what I could. Madeline had a binder for each artist she represented, almost like a catalogue, listing their bios, their previous shows and exhibitions, PR pieces and more. These files also contained manifests from each time a piece was shipped. I studied the information from the two forged works, hoping to find some sort of discrepancy or clue. As yet, I'd found nothing.

But I had begun to cobble together not only some understanding of art but also of the art world.

My father listened closely, taking occasional bites of his flapjacks. "You're learning," he said. "But it also sounds as if you've begun to nurse a healthy new appreciation."

"Exactly!" I said, thrilled to connect with my dad on something. "I not only know more, I appreciate more."

He nodded. "That's how your Aunt Elena learned about art, as well. Maybe you do have something from my family in your making." There was something so sad about the way he'd said those words—as if he was not only defeated but resigned to the fact that his kids were not like him, since he hadn't been around to raise them.

"Of course I have traits from the McNeils. We share the same name, after all." I smiled to show him I was making light of the situation. He had a hard time reading sarcasm or irony, I'd noticed.

He smiled. "That's good to hear."

I told him more then about the gallery itself—a sparkly and interesting space. The gallery was nearly triangular in shape, and two full walls were glass windows, facing different directions. As such, there were always odd angles of light, even when it was gray out.

When it was sunny, the light was filtered by the museum-quality film on the glass, so as not to fade the paintings. Many times, the sun seemed to create an orangey flash outside the gallery. Whenever I stepped closer to the glass, though, tried to look more intently, it had disappeared.

He asked me more questions about the gallery. We continued to eat. At some point our conversation lapsed.

"I heard from Theo," I said, apropos of nothing. "A postcard. He's in Thailand."

My father made a face. "That's one of the most patience-trying places in the entire world. Why is he there?"

"Mostly to escape. I think also to surf."

Another face. "Not much surfing there, except near Phuket."

When, I wondered, had my father spent enough time in Thailand, or reading about it, to know exactly where one could surf?

I thought of the postcard. "I think that's where he is," I said. "Phuket. He mentioned there was lots of diving and rock climbing. He's into that, too."

My father nodded.

"He asked if I was dating," I said. Why I was telling my father this, I had no idea. But it felt pretty okay.

"And what will you tell him?"

"The truth. I haven't been really ready to date anyone." I paused to see how this further emotional disclosure felt. And again—pretty okay. I thought of Jeremy. "But I feel like I could be ready to do that again."

My father nodded. Said nothing. So I changed the topic to the one I now felt prepared for. "I hear you might be moving."

He looked at me, from one eye to another, as if he were trying to look inside them, to read my reaction to the concept.

When I opened my mouth, I found out how I felt about it. "I don't want you to leave."

Was that a smile on my father's face? His facial expressions changed little from one to another, but I thought I saw his eyes crinkle a little under his coppery glasses.

"Is it possible you'll stick around Chicago for a while?" I asked.

"It's possible." He smiled again. I could tell that time.

"I don't want you to go," I said.

"Thank you, Izzy."

"Hey, maybe you should start dating, too," I said.

He groaned.

"No, really. When is the last time you dated?"

"Suffice to say, a long time."

It was my turn to raise my eyebrows. "A long time, as in years?"

"Yes, a long, long while."

"Well, that's it, then. You don't need to move. You need to date a little, see if you're ready. Just like I need to do."

He laughed, gave a small shrug. "Well, then, Izzy,

I suppose, for once, we're in the same place," my father said.

And I really liked the sound of that.

14

When Jeremy texted about the location of our date, he suggested Girl and the Goat, an intriguingly named restaurant that was one of the hottest in town.

Isn't that place hard to get into? I texted back.

I know a few people there. I'll take care of it.

Now, in the cab heading to the restaurant, I started experiencing a jittery kind of nervousness, realizing that I was, essentially—since I'd met the guy for all of ten minutes—headed to a blind date. I rearranged the lavender silk scarf under my hairline and tightened the belt on my long, hound's-tooth-patterned coat.

The restaurant was on Randolph, just west of Halsted, and black-framed windows showed happily dining customers. Inside, most of the walls were brick, the floors dark hardwood, the ceilings beamed. A fantastical painting hung on a side wall featuring—interestingly enough—a girl and a goat. It dawned on me that I might not have noticed the painting before I started working in Madeline's gallery. Or I might have noticed, but that would have been the extent of it. Being in the gallery made me want to look closer at anything having to do with art.

I didn't see Jeremy, so I took a few steps toward the

painting—a huge, square canvas painted in bold reds, greens and golds. The primary focus was a little girl with big eyes and a pink dress running after a galloping goat with equally large eyes.

I felt a hand on my shoulder. "What do you think of the painting?"

I turned, smiled. Jeremy was still gorgeous, dressed now in gray jeans and a black corduroy jacket.

I managed to tear my eyes off him to look back at the painting. "I think it's a little crazy, and I think it's great."

When I looked back at him again, he was grinning, showing white teeth. "That's *exactly* what I think. Bizarre, but excellent."

"So then the question is, which came first, the painting or the name of the restaurant?" I'd noticed that Madeline often spoke about the genesis of a painting, the history behind it.

Jeremy looked at the painting. "I don't want to know. I like it so much I don't need to hear more."

Just then the manager greeted Jeremy with some happy thumps on the back. "Haven't seen you for a while, bud," he said.

The waitress, too, greeted him warmly as we were seated. "What are we drinking?" she said.

Jeremy looked at me for an answer. Out of habit, I almost asked for a Blue Moon, but that's what Sam and I used to drink together. And I was moving past that, wanting to try something new. "Red wine?"

"Perfect." Jeremy and the waitress discussed and decided on a bottle of pinot noir.

"How do you like it?" Jeremy said when it was delivered and opened.

I took a sip. "I like that it's a little cinnamon-y, and it's not tart at the end."

"Yeah, I don't like an acidic finish, either." Jeremy swirled his wine and sniffed it, then took a sip. "Did you catch that other flavor in there?"

I took another taste and tried to pay attention to what remained in my mouth. "It's something familiar, but I don't know what it is."

"Is it chocolate?"

I took another sip. "Yes!" I noticed it now. "Chocolate and berries."

"Exactly."

We were seated at a rough-hewn wood table, a flickering candle between us.

I mentioned what he'd said before. "You don't like knowing the genesis of a work of art?" I asked, gesturing to the goat painting.

He looked at it. "Usually I do. But it was my Fex who got me into art, and she said—"

"Sorry, I have to stop you," I said. "Did you say 'Fex'? Like sex with an *f*?"

"Hmm, that's interesting when you put it that way...." Jeremy looked up, as if considering something. "I hadn't thought about that before. But yeah. I'm talking about my soon-to-be ex-wife. She's my Future Ex. So I call her the Fex."

I wasn't sure if the nickname was intended as an insult or not. But as our conversation pleasantly meandered, he mentioned his Fex a few times and it always seemed with respect.

The restaurant featured small plates and I happily let Jeremy order some of his favorites—fried peppers and parmesan, fennel rice cakes with butternut squash, chickpea fritters.

He was so easy to talk with. Our discussion led us through our childhoods and all the important facts—the colleges we'd attended, the reasons we were in Chicago, our jobs. I glossed over the details of my "job" at the gallery, and instead focused on asking Jeremy questions. He was from Boston, met his wife in college, and she was the reason they'd started their family in the Chicago area.

"Okay, let me ask you this," he said at one point, leaning toward me, the flickering candle highlighting his cheekbones, the strong jaw. "What's your favorite place? Like if you could go anywhere tomorrow and stay for a few weeks, where would you go?"

I thought about it. "I was in Rome last summer and I didn't have the time to really see everything." I halted, deciding that a first date wasn't the time to introduce the topic of the father I once thought was dead and how I'd gone to Italy to find him. "So that's where I'd go."

"I love Italy," Jeremy said.

"Where would you head off to?"

"I've traveled a lot. When I want to get out of town, I actually just go to Door County. The Fex and I have had a house there for years."

"Who gets the house in the divorce? Or is that too touchy a question?"

"No, not at all. We're sharing it. We both love it so much, and the kids do, too. We're going to split time."

"That sounds civilized," I said. "Good for you. How old are your children?"

"They're nine and six," he said.

More plates were delivered then—scallops, ravioli

and mussels. Our conversation kept rolling, and it felt then as if we were on a minivacation, someplace warm, in the middle of a cold winter.

When the waitress delivered the dessert menu, Jeremy excused himself to the bathroom.

"Great guy, isn't he?" the waitress asked congenially. She had long, curly hair like mine, but hers was dark and pulled back in a wide orange headband.

"Yeah, he seems cool."

"He is," she said. "And he tips good. Everyone around here loves him."

"I just met him recently."

"Ah, so you've managed to avoid the divorce? Nice luck."

I frowned. "It sounds like it's going well. Their breakup."

She raised her eyebrows, shook her head. She looked over her shoulder than back at me. "I've heard it's *nasty.*"

I wasn't sure what to say. I had never been a waiter but it didn't seem as if she should be gossiping about a good client. Or maybe she was doing so because she had a crush on Jeremy and was trying to wave me off?

Jeremy returned then. He and the waitress chatted about a bartender they both knew who had recently moved. The waitress left.

And I remained slightly jarred.

But any suspicions that arose during my chat with the waitress didn't stop me from returning his kiss. His kiss, in the car, in front of my condo building.

15

Jeremy put his warm hands lightly on my cheeks and drew me to him, kissed me once, pausing to look at me before putting his surprisingly soft lips back on mine.

I can't say how long this went on. I'd been transported. When we finally broke apart, I was nearly breathless.

He looked a bit shaken himself. "Well," he said, "that was…"

"…good," I said.

"Great," he said.

"I'll up you again," I said. "That was amazing."

"That kiss—" he leaned closer to me "—was fan-fucking-tastic." He gave me the most adorable smile. "Do you mind if I swear?"

I squeezed my eyes shut, giddy. Although I was, as I'd told Madeline, trying to quit swearing, the truth was, I loved swearing. But in a classic double-standard, I often found it crass when other people did. However, Jeremy sounded *so* good. Crass from that gorgeous face and that gorgeous mouth was just fine.

I opened my eyes. "No, I don't mind."

That started another round of kissing. Things were getting a little heated. Eventually, it dawned on me that now would be the time when I could ask him up to my condo. *If* I was going to ask him to come up.

But…what was that odd feeling? It was awkwardness, I realized. My place was where I'd spent a lot of time with Sam. The place where Theo had lived with me rather recently. And the fact was, my place was sacred to me. The fact that it had been broken into last year only made it more so.

Reluctantly, I moved back from the gentle pull of Jeremy's lips. "I should go. I have an early morning tomorrow."

"It's Saturday tomorrow."

"I know but I still need to get to work…" I let my words die away. I was about to say that I needed to do some work at the law firm, since I'd spent time at the gallery this week. But then I remembered Jeremy didn't know Izzy McNeil, the lawyer. He only knew Izzy Smith, the art assistant.

I wondered how that made me seem to Jeremy. What did my position in the art world do to shape Jeremy's impression of me? Did that concept make me seem creative and artistic and maybe a little wild? Would he like me more if he knew I was a lawyer? Would that make me seem smarter? What about a criminal defense lawyer? He began kissing me again, and my questions quickly fell to the wayside.

After a minute, he stopped. "Okay," he said. "I'll let you go." He leaned his forehead on mine. "But only if you agree to go out with me again."

"Sold," I said.

I kissed him once more and got out of the car.

16

Every Friday night, Madeline met with other Japanese women. They were the only Japanese people she knew. Like she'd told Izzy, she had been adopted by Americans when she was an infant. Her desire to know more about women from Japan—and therefore herself—was how she'd found herself involved in this Japanese dyeing and weaving class.

Solace. That's what she sought there, from people who were inherently like her. And after what she'd received just before she got here, she desperately needed solace.

You will never be forgiven for what you did.

She could probably call her family for support, but she simply wouldn't turn to them for something like this. She didn't dislike her adoptive parents. She had always respected them, appreciated them most years (except for in high school, when she'd hated them in the requisite teenage way that she still felt guilty about). And yet she'd always felt detached from them, from the corn and cow farms in Wisconsin, from others in their town (although everyone had been kind and still were, when she went home, infrequently, to visit). Mostly, her parents visited her so they could take in Chicago, so they could show relief that she'd ended up here, somewhat close to them, and not in New York.

New York. Madeline had fled there when she was eighteen, deliriously happy to have been accepted to a city college. In Manhattan, she'd found herself immersed in the melting pot of everything that was the city. She'd stumbled into the art world by mistake, then dove into that world with fierce determination and ambition. She did well. But not as well as she wanted. It was so very tough to make it in the New York art scene.

That was when she got her inheritance—from a trust fund in Japan. Or at least "trust fund" was what she understood. Her parents had hired an attorney, who learned that the gift had been made by one of her birth parents or a family member, and that they wanted to remain anonymous.

Her adoptive parents were great about it. They had asked if she wanted help managing the trust—it was a lot of money. But they also wanted to know how it made her feel, this gesture coming from Japan, from her biological family. They worried that she would be emotionally wounded somehow.

But the inheritance had beguiled her with the opposite effect—she felt comforted; she felt taken care of. She had never really felt Japanese, but the gift helped tremendously.

Of course, there had been many legal hurdles to go through. Her attorneys had explained this was not uncommon with an inheritance that size. But after everything was settled, even with monstrous legal bills, she had more money than she would ever need.

Enough so that, soon after, when she heard from a friend that Chicago was a different kind of art city and in some ways much friendlier and more open-hearted, she knew it was time to leave New York. To spread her wings, with the lift that was now beneath her, both financially and emotionally.

And now, decades later, here she was with these other Japanese women from Chicago, all of them leaning in over another kind of stewing pot. A real one—a vat full of what would soon be indigo. The vat sometimes reminded Madeline of a witches' cauldron, steam billowing from the top.

"It's only supposed to take half an hour," one woman said. It was Amaya, the woman she'd seen outside the club with Isabel.

Amaya had joined the group at the same time as Madeline. She even bought two sculptures from Madeline after she learned of the gallery. But Amaya tended toward pessimism, and although Madeline wasn't particularly superstitious, the weaving process was so organic, so filled with spirit that she irrationally feared that Amaya's bad attitude could sour the process.

Weaving was Madeline's one consistent connection to her Japanese heritage. Evenings such as these, the process of dyeing and weaving, were how she escaped. And after the email, she needed escape.

This was the moment in the dyeing process that she liked the most—when the contents of the pot turned into something different entirely and then from their depths something floated to the surface and then...

"It'll come," Madeline said to Amaya. It *has* to come, she thought.

"Maybe not," Amaya said. She spoke in a soft, singsong voice and looked right at Madeline. The words sounded like a taunt.

Madeline glared at her. As she'd told Isabel, she and Amaya seemed to have struck up some kind of unspoken dislike for one another.

After last week's group, Madeline had looked up the name *Amaya,* and found that it meant "night rain," which seemed just about right. Amaya's personality tended toward dark and inky.

"There it is!" one of the woman said excitedly, pointing.

They all peered closer as a copper-green film rose to the surface, slowly, as if it were stalking them.

The thought of that—stalking—made Madeline shiver. Her art, for one, was being stalked. Somehow, someway—she couldn't get her head around it—those art works were being stolen from her and replaced with forgeries. She'd *sold* forged art. The thought of that caused intense shame, in addition to many other emotions. And now that email…

"Are you all right, Madeline?" one of the women asked.

She opened her eyes, realizing that she'd closed them against the shame, the fear, the vague but piercing feeling of betrayal.

What she saw jarred her. She had accidentally leaned too close to the pot and the green scum seemed to loom into her entire field of vision, as if it were lurching toward her.

She pulled herself back and fell onto a wooden chair behind her.

The women turned to her with questions of concern. All except Amaya, Madeline noticed, who stayed peering into the vat. Madeline assured the others she was fine, reminded them that they had the indigo to tend to. After a few more questions, they turned back to the vat.

But Madeline could not seem to find her breath, felt her heart pattering fast, as if she were in a corner, panting.

"Stop." She said the word under her breath to whoever was doing this to her. And then, although she'd never begged anyone for anything in her life, not once, she sent a beseeching prayer in her mind to the person, the thing that felt like a force. *Please stop doing this to me.*

17

When I woke Saturday morning, I immediately thought of Jeremy and smiled. Then I peeked out my bedroom curtains and saw snow falling on the city. At the sight, I got a quickening—an excited feeling like the one a child gets when they realize the universe is shaking up their snow globe and the day is uncharted territory.

Since I didn't have to dress for the gallery, had no clients to see on a Saturday and no court to attend to, I happily threw on jeans and pushed my feet into fur-lined, brown suede boots with gold tassels. I topped the outfit with a brown cashmere sweater, tied my red hair in a scarf and was off to Bristol & Associates to catch up on things I'd missed that week.

I expected to find the place empty, but when I arrived, Maggie was there. She wasn't as cheerful and focused as she usually was on weekday mornings. I could tell because I stood in her doorway for at least ten seconds before she realized I was there, and even then she had to blink a few times as if to clear her brain.

"Oh," she said. "Hi..." Her voice died away, a confused look on her face, as if she'd forgotten my name.

"Izzy McNeil?" I said. "Your best friend?"

She shook her head. "Sorry."

I laughed. "Pregnancy brain?" That was what Maggie had been attributing everything to lately—losing a file on the way to court, arriving in court unable to remember what kind of continuance we wanted, picking up the phone to call a state's attorney she'd known for years and forgetting his phone number.

I couldn't hold the question in any longer. "Verdict?" I asked hesitantly. I'd waited for Maggie for six hours, hoping for a verdict on behalf of the Cortadero family before the judge excused the jury for the night.

The question about what verdict had been rendered was always a difficult question to ask. Even the most revered trial lawyers received guilty verdicts and the toughest defense lawyers lost what were assumed to be slam-dunk cases.

"NG," Maggie said. *Not guilty.*

I let out a whoop and stepped to her desk, giving her a high-five. "Congrats!"

Maggie and I grinned at each other. My phone rang then. *Madeline Saga,* the display read.

I answered.

"Izzy."

"Hey, Madeline. How are you?"

"Well…" Silence. "Izzy, where are you?"

"I'm at the law office, sitting here with my pregnant friend."

"Oh, that sounds lovely." Madeline's voice sounded delicate somehow. "Izzy, is there any way you could come in to the gallery? I'd like to show you something." A pause. "Rather I…I need to show you something."

I realized Madeline's voice not only sounded delicate, but fearful.

"I'll be there in a half hour."

Outside the snow was slowing. Plows and trucks criss-crossed the city and spewed salt in fast streams that looked like smoke, but not much else was moving. I had to walk four blocks before I scored a cab.

As I took the taxi to the gallery, I opened the window, despite the cold. Somehow, over the past few days or so—since I'd met Madeline, I guess—I'd become more aware of the sounds of Chicago. When we were out the other night, Madeline had said something about using all her senses as a gallery owner and an art collector. And later, she had said that anything could be art—most art simply showed a different way of looking at life. The ideas were fascinating and questions had been growing in my mind since then. *Could sounds be art? Could scents—something you had to smell to experience?*

For the last few days, I had paid attention to sounds. I found such an exercise eerie, in a way, because once I tuned in it struck me that those sounds had been there all my life, just waiting for me to turn up the volume.

Now, through the cab window, I listened to the distant chug of the El, the screech of a snowplow's brakes, a siren in the distance, a lonely sound that waxed and waned. All these things made me realize how many lives—each one its own form of artwork—existed in the city.

By the time I reached the gallery, the snow had stopped and the sun was shining, making Michigan Avenue look like a star in daylight.

The fluffy white snow reflecting the light would soon turn slushy gray. But not now. People were rousing themselves from homes and businesses, stepping out to check the now-friendly weather. A buoyancy played in the air. It was Saturday, it was sunny, it had snowed and it had stopped—the perfect recipe for Chicago city-wide happiness.

I wondered what Madeline wanted me to see.

18

I found Madeline in her office, which was tucked in a corner at the back of the building. I'd never really been in there before, and I looked around. It was tiny but fanciful. On one wall, blue curtains were pulled back to show a painting of a window overlooking the Caribbean sea, with islands in the distance.

On the opposite wall was a lone portrait that depicted a woman who looked a lot like Madeline—distinctive pink lips, long, shiny black hair.

A tufted purple chair sat in front of Madeline's black lacquer desk. Madeline nodded at it.

As I sat, she pushed a latch and lifted up a panel that was built into the desktop. I craned my neck and saw that behind the panel was a tablet computer. *Very James Bond,* I thought.

It occurred to me that the panel hiding the technology was also very Madeline Saga—a woman who rejoiced in life and art and love and sex but, I assumed, had other parts that she kept hidden. It seemed obvious that Madeline Saga held layers of complexity—like so many pieces of her artwork.

After touching a few things on her tablet, Madeline swiveled the panel around until it faced me, then she slid it forward, nearer to me. I saw that the screen had been opened to an email.

The email had been sent from an address that was a random jumble of numbers and letters. The subject line was empty. I read the body of the email.

You will never be forgiven for what you did. For your falsity and selfishness, you should be cut and stretched like a canvas.

"Whoa," I said.

I read it again. *You should be cut and stretched like a canvas.* "Whoa," I repeated. The words were cold, clinical...scary.

I looked up at Madeline, who looked very scared herself. "Any idea who sent it?"

She shook her head.

"Do you think it's the same person who left the comments on your website?"

"I don't know."

"The part about 'falsity.' Do you think they're referring to the forgeries?"

"I don't know! This—cut and stretched like a canvas? Why would someone say that?" She turned the panel around, reread the words herself.

"Let's go see Mayburn," I said.

"I can't right now." She explained about two appointments at the gallery that day that couldn't be canceled. The first was with an interior designer and his high-maintenance clients, who'd been in about ten times already to visit a sculpture. This, she hoped, was the day they would make a purchase. The other appointment was with a journalist from an art magazine. She'd already rescheduled the interview twice.

Madeline put her head in her hands. I felt helpless.

Before I could say anything, she raised her head and looked at her watch. "The designer should be here shortly. I need to pull myself together."

"Do you want me to get you a coffee?" I offered.

She shook her head.

"Something to eat?"

Again, she shook her head.

"Vodka?"

She laughed. "Now you're talking."

I smiled at her. "I'm sorry you're going through this."

"I am, as well." A sigh. "But I'm glad you're here to go through it with me."

I felt something different between us enter the room. I wasn't sure what it was. "Me, too," I said.

I tried to think of what I could do for Madeline in the short-term, before her appointment arrived. I decided that getting her talking about art would be best. It would put her in the right frame of mind for her appointments.

I looked up at the portrait on the otherwise white wall. "Were you the subject for that?"

She smiled. "No. It's actually from one of my favorite Japanese artists. He created it in the fifties, a woodblock print."

It appeared as if the woman in the portrait was looking out a window, but instead of the sea, like the other painting, the outside was full of flowers. Lush red flowers with yellow centers.

"I always thought that if my world looked like that, I would look outside all the time, too," Madeline said.

We heard the bell of the front door.

"Can I stay in here?" I asked. "I'd like to use your

computer to study the email some more. Do some research."

Madeline Saga didn't say "yes" or "sure" or anything like that. Instead, her eyes closed for a longer second, then opened and focused on mine. A calm expression graced her face. She said one word. "Please." And then two more. "Thank you."

19

I read the email again. And then again. Who could have written it? If "falsity" was referring to the forged paintings, then the author had to be someone who knew about the forgeries. According to Madeline, Jeremy was the only person—other than Mayburn and I—who knew. Madeline was working to determine if she'd sold fakes other than Jeremy's, but she didn't know anything yet.

But the thought of Jeremy writing the email didn't sit right with me. We'd been out only once, granted, but the words didn't seem like what I knew of him.

I read them again. *You should be cut and stretched like a canvas.*

The person was clearly threatening violence against Madeline. And yet Madeline, though rattled, was now dazzling the designer and the couple who had just come in. From the gallery, I could hear Madeline's laughter trilling as she described a sculpture. I could hear the joy in her voice. "Of course," she said. "You may see something entirely different than the artist did. That's art. That's good."

I heard her voice change as she showed a different piece. Because she saw everything as unique, her enthusiasm for one thing often sounded very different than her excitement for another.

"Isn't it remarkable?" I could hear her saying. "And you know, he usually does nudes."

The designer gasped. "That's right!"

"They're stunning," Madeline said.

"Stunning," the designer echoed.

"But he's moving on to other mediums," Madeline said.

I peered back at the email. *Cut and stretched like a canvas...cut and stretched like a canvas...cut and stretched like a canvas.*

I called Mayburn and updated him, then sent him the email.

"I'll analyze the wording," he said.

"For what?"

"The cadence of the words, the use of certain vocabulary, patterns, repetitions."

He would, he said, test his data against the comments that had been posted on the website. We hoped his research would show that the same person wrote both, and we'd have enough evidence to figure out who it was.

"How is she?" Mayburn had asked near the end of our call.

"I don't know for sure." I thought about it. "I could tell the email freaked her out, but she's out in the gallery right now with clients, and she sounds fine."

I thought I heard Mayburn sigh. "Yeah, that's how she is. And that's good. Because if she still has the ability to care about art, that means she's okay."

We both fell silent then, both thinking of that email—*cut and stretched*—and hoping Mayburn's words would turn out to be the truth.

20

When Madeline was done with her clients, I updated her on my talk with Mayburn and what my father had told me about danger points. She nodded as I spoke, agreeing with everything. I asked her about her move from Bucktown to Michigan Avenue. "The artwork that was forged, did Jeremy buy those after the move?"

Madeline, behind her black lacquer desk, nodded. She told me how Jeremy and his wife (*the Fex,* I thought involuntarily) had looked at the pieces when she was in Bucktown, but purchased both a few months after the move.

We both fell silent, trying to work out what, if anything that could mean.

"Speaking of Jeremy," Madeline said. "How was your date?"

"Great," I said. I thought about that kiss. *"Great."*

"What did the two of you do?"

"Dinner at Girl and the Goat."

"Nice. And then?"

"And then he drove me home. And…" If Maggie or Q had been sitting in front of me, I would have launched into details. I would have described the ex-quisite kiss. But this was Madeline—not quite a yet friend, but more than just a professional colleague. "He asked me out again," I said.

"Excellent."

I remembered how Madeline had seemed eager for me to go out with Jeremy. "You mentioned his wife. Do you know her well?"

She nodded. "She and Jeremy became quite the collectors. Very knowledgeable. Very intuitive about art."

Something occurred to me. "Jeremy said it was his lawyer who hired the appraiser, leading to the determination of forgeries. Did they apprise his wife or her attorneys of this yet?"

"I don't believe so. He told me he would wait until I…figured this out."

"What is she like? Personally?"

Madeline cocked her head to the side. "It's hard for me to say. She's not someone I would choose to spend time with. I find her a little hard to access, like she's got some kind of resin that coats all parts of her."

"That's surprising. Jeremy seems so warm."

"Well, some people really seem to enjoy her. And maybe Jeremy is one of the people she opens up with."

"What have you heard about their divorce?"

"Amicable," Saga said.

"The waitress at the restaurant told me she'd heard otherwise."

Madeline's black eyebrows arched. "Really? Interesting. Waitstaff do hear a lot of things while they're working."

"I know."

We fell into a contemplative pause.

"What about Jeremy?" I asked.

"What about him?"

"Could he have written you the email?"

"Of course not!"

"Don't protest too fast," I said. "Trust me, I like Jeremy, and I don't have a gut instinct that it was him, but he is the one with the fakes. Maybe he's *not* as amiable about it as he seems. Maybe he's pissed off."

Madeline paused to consider this. She shook her head. "It was his wife who adored those works more than him. And if you think about it, he's probably excited in a strange way—if those paintings aren't worth as much, that reduces his net worth for purposes of the divorce."

"And, therefore, reduces the amount of money he has to pay his wife."

Madeline's lips pursed. "I see what you mean."

I thought about it. "He's been the one who made their money?" I asked.

Madeline nodded. "But she's the true collector in the family. Like I said, she loved those pieces."

"Just another reason to fake them to get back at her."

Madeline said nothing.

"So maybe she wrote the email."

"I really don't think Jeremy told her yet about the forgeries yet. He promised me he wouldn't tell anyone until we could get a handle on this."

A handle on this. Thinking about that gave me a cold feeling. We had a lot of suppositions flying around, but we weren't close to having any concrete knowledge.

"Assuming it's not him, will you see Jeremy again?" Madeline asked.

"Yes. Maybe I'll hear more about the divorce then. But in the meantime, we need to make a list of everyone that was involved in any way with your move from Bucktown to Michigan Avenue."

I still had Madeline's tablet in front of me, so I created a document and began to make a list—*movers, packers, armored car drivers*. We talked some more and added the commercial real estate people who had found the gallery for her, and as a result had access to the space.

"How would they enter the gallery usually?" I asked.

"Through the back."

"The video feed Mayburn has—does that show who comes and goes back there?"

"Not necessarily, unfortunately. The previous owners installed it, mostly to show cars that were blocking access to the delivery door. It shows most of the alley, but if you walk down the alley close to the wall, you won't be seen. It doesn't show who's at the door."

"Okay. Who else to put on this list?"

Madeline explained that she'd hired a specialist, a woman whose sole job was moving art.

"Her name?"

"Margie Scott. She was highly recommended."

I typed the name in the document, along with the phone number Madeline gave me.

"And who recommended Margie Scott?" I asked. I was starting to warm to our task. Making this list reminded me of taking depositions, something I'd gotten good at in my days of civil litigation.

"Jacqueline Stoddard," Madeline said. "The gallery owner I introduced you to."

"What's Jacqueline's number?"

Madeline gave it to me.

"And the name of her gallery?"

"Stoddard Gallery."

I typed that in, too. "Now, that day you introduced me to Jacqueline, didn't she mention something about a former assistant of yours?"

"Yes, Sydney Tallon."

"And Sydney is a man," I said.

"Oh, yes." A small—and sexy?—smile.

"Was he involved with the move?"

A brisk nod. "Very."

I gave Madeline a raised-eyebrow look.

"Syd is *not* stealing from me," Madeline said. "I know that. I know that deeply inside me."

"I don't mean to sound skeptical, but that's what we hear from the Chicago police department all the time. They believe, in their gut, that they have the right suspect, so they don't consider anything that might either exonerate the suspect or point the finger at someone else. It's a widely studied phenomenon. It's tunnel vision."

Madeline looked at me curiously, openly. And that made me like her even more, the attitude that kept her constantly attuned to new information in her galaxy.

She nodded. "Okay. I'll consider that. But I just *know* Syd. I *know* he wouldn't do that. He wouldn't steal my artwork. He couldn't be responsible for the forgeries. He wouldn't try to bring me down like that."

"Would he have the expertise to copy the pieces?" I asked, my voice determinedly casual.

"Yes. He's highly educated in the art world and is an interesting artist himself."

"Okay." I tried not to sound a little triumphant. "And you said he had access to the galleries. Do you mean he still has keys?"

Her lack of reply said it all.

Madeline paused. She seemed to be weighing the import of this. And I held my breath, because while there certainly were a lot of "danger points" in the transporting of Madeline's artwork, who had more time and accessibility than an assistant?

"I should tell you something else about Syd," Madeline said. "We dated. We were lovers." She pulled out her cellphone and showed me a photo of a man with dark skin, haunting dark eyes and cut cheekbones beneath shiny black hair. He looked like an Arabian prince.

"When did you date? Before or after the move to Michigan Avenue?"

"Before and during. He was a fantastic assistant. He researched acquisitions and kept records. He wrote catalogues and organized exhibitions. He helped me budget. He gave presentations to groups and schools to raise awareness about openings and eventually the new gallery."

"How long were you together?"

"Three years."

That sounded pretty long for Madeline Saga.

"It felt like such a partnership," Madeline said. "And then it became a real one. We fell in love." She let out a long breath. "It was wonderful." She gazed up then as if she could see, above her, the pages of the story of her and Syd.

I thought of Mayburn telling me that Madeline lived only for art and love. "That must have been amazing for you."

"It was the perfect romantic situation for me. Except for one thing. I knew he desperately wanted to have children, and I did not. I've never wanted kids."

"I haven't, either."

She looked at me, surprise in her expression. "Really?"

"Really. What's that look?"

She blinked, appraised me. "You're different than I thought you would be."

"How did you think I would be?"

"More...typical. A typical Chicago girl."

"There's no typical Chicago girl. We're all unique."

She laughed. "Maybe." She sighed. "But kids were very important to Syd, and I simply couldn't be the person to provide that. So we ended things."

"And you broke up after you moved?"

"No, we'd broken up during the planning of the move. But he stayed on to help me complete it."

"Who did the breaking up?" I asked.

"I did," she answered.

I said nothing. I didn't have to.

Madeline shook her head. "It's not what you think. He wasn't mad."

"What was he?"

"Sad. Our breakup killed him in a way. But he would never want to hurt me."

I must have made a disbelieving face, because Madeline spoke with a defensive tone. "If you met him, if you saw us together, you'd understand. He wouldn't do that."

"So maybe I should meet him," I said.

"I agree."

"When?" I said.

She reached for her phone, typed something in.

Seconds later her phone dinged and she read a message. "Tonight," she said.

21

We landed at a secret club that night.

"What is this place?" I asked Madeline as we disembarked from a cab at a bizarre location near the soon-to-be closed Belmont Police Station. The building hunched under two highway overpasses. There was no sign on the front door, and the glass blocks in front of the establishment had been painted black.

"We try not to give it a name," Madeline said.

"We?"

"A group of my friends have owned it for years and included all of us in the planning of it. Sometimes we change the place a little, sometimes a lot. The patrons tend to be art types."

"Like a joint piece of art," I said.

She gave me an appreciative smile. "Yes. But we have found that when we put labels on the place—when we say it's a champagne bar or an art bar or a dance club or a salon or…" She shrugged. "Or anything. Well, then it's not as good as when it's organic."

"Ah, so, it's an organic bar. It's green."

My sarcasm didn't seem to affect Madeline. "Come in, friend," she said to me.

And at her words, I felt welcomed.

Inside, the place was draped in velvety fabric—the walls, the banquettes, the front of the bar, the chairs.

The manager greeted Madeline with a hug. As at Toi, a reserved sign was flicked off a table for us to take a seat.

"Sydney Tallon will be joining us," Madeline told the manager.

In the meantime, Madeline and I launched into an easy discussion. Once again, I found Madeline fascinating to talk to. It wasn't that she spoke a great deal or that she told funny stories, it was more to do with how she listened. I hadn't exactly noticed it when we were out last week, but it occurred to me that I might never have felt that *listened to* before. Madeline leaned in a little when I spoke; she cocked an ear toward me as if unwilling to miss even a syllable. The way she'd listened made you feel at the center of a comforting bubble. That bubble expanded when she contributed something. Usually it was a small phrase. *Life is made of many things to desire, but we still have to choose only one at a time.* Or *I like how you said that.* Or she might murmur, *Hmm, yes, interesting, interesting.*

I excused myself to go the bathroom at one point. "You'll be here when I get back, right?" I said to her.

She laughed. "Yes."

The bathroom was bizarre, as if the whole room were made of black patent leather. When I came out of the stall and went to wash my hands, the unending look of patent leather made difficult to know where to step. And where the hell did the floor stop and the counter and sink begin?

Another stall opened. "Isn't that counter the most impossible thing?"

I turned, surprised. "Oh, hi. You're—"

"Jaqueline Stoddard," the woman said. She wore the same peach-orange cashmere coat and a scarf around her neck. She reached out her hand. "And you're Isabel."

"Yes." I shook it. "Please, call me Izzy."

"Well, Izzy, let me show you how this works." She pointed at my clutch purse. "May I?"

I handed it to her. She reached out, then down at an angle. "It works best if you just walk at it." She took a few steps, stopped when her hand hit something, then placed the clutch down. And right then, it was apparent exactly where the counter was, leading up the sink.

"It's an optical illusion," Jacqueline said. "Neat. But frankly, a pain in the behind."

I laughed, thanked her.

When we reached the table, someone else was with Madeline. Syd.

Madeline had told me in the cab on the way over that Syd's family was from Pakistan. As I'd noticed in the photo of him, he resembled a prince from a faraway land. His sleek hair was long, black and in a ponytail. He was a very handsome man.

He stood and greeted Jacqueline warmly. When she left, he turned his gaze to mine. It was a powerful one.

Jacqueline and Madeline talked in some kind of art shorthand about a phone call they needed to have tomorrow, then Jacqueline excused herself.

"Syd, didn't I tell you Isabel was gorgeous?" Madeline said as we sat.

"You did, Maddy," Syd said. "And you were right."

"I think it's the hair," Madeline said. "I've often wished I could be a redhead."

"You're kidding," I said.

"It's true."

"Maddy," Syd said again, laughing. "Your hair is gorgeous."

"Well, so is yours." She looked at me. "Sometimes Syd and I used to wear our hair the same."

"What do you mean?" I asked.

Madeline pulled up some pictures on her phone. In them, Syd and Madeline both wore their long black hair the same length, in the same style. I couldn't tell if I found the image disturbing or beautiful.

As I gave Madeline her phone back, I felt Syd looking at me again, but not in the way Jeremy had. It made me feel a little uncomfortable, as if I were being studied as a specimen of...what? I didn't know. And I didn't really enjoy the feeling.

Madeline caught it, too. But when she spoke, her voice was filled only with interest. "What are you thinking, Syd?"

"Have you ever had your portrait painted?" he asked me.

"No."

"Who would you want to paint her?" Madeline asked.

Syd looked at Madeline, a huge smile covering his face. "Axel Tredstone," he said.

Madeline blinked, then again. She looked at me, looked me up and down. "Oh, my God," she said. "Oh, my God."

"What?" I asked. "What are you talking about?"

"Axel Tredstone paints women."

"Okay..."

"No, like he really paints them," Syd said.

"Right, I get it," I said. "He paints portraits."

"No," Madeline said, and somehow in that one word her voice was even more intrigued. And definitely sultry. "He puts the paint on your body. Covers you in paint."

"She'd be perfect," Syd said. "At least I think so. She's so his type."

"I agree," Madeline said.

"What's his type?" I was almost afraid to ask. What if his type was "vacuous gingers"?

"Intriguing women. Women he finds mysterious. He clearly sees something in each of the women he paints, sees something in their personalities, their souls."

"He started out painting traditionally," Syd said. "As he became popular, his fame led him to a lot of women."

"He's a lothario," Madeline said. Appreciatively.

They talked more about Tredstone, explaining his artistic evolution. As they spoke, Syd stopped studying me. Instead, he gazed at Madeline as if mesmerized. He glanced at her constantly, even when I spoke, as if wanting to register all her reactions. He smiled appreciatively, almost wistfully, when she said something funny.

"In painting portraits of these women, and often bedding them," Madeline continued, "eventually he felt like he had a new understanding of women. So his art changed. His work became more abstract, bold and linear in parts, soft and gentle in others."

Now Syd's gaze was locked on Madeline. And instead of studying her, as he had me, his look held awe.

"Tredstone has said that the women are wonderful," Syd said, speaking up. Still, his gaze was on Madeline's face. "But certain women, he says…certain women have something else entirely. Something so complex that they don't even see it."

"He began painting on their bodies," Madeline said, seemingly unaware of, or perhaps simply accustomed to the adoration Syd appeared to be sending her way. "And after he paints the women," Madeline said, "he photographs them."

"He's been wanting to do Maddy for over a decade," Syd said. Now he didn't sound exactly adoring. He sounded jealous.

"Why wouldn't you do it?" I asked Madeline.

"Axel and I have been friends and business partners since I was young and just starting out. We know each other on a very deep level."

I glanced at Syd. His eyes were slightly hooded now.

"And I love that relationship," Madeline continued. "I don't want to change it because it's already so multilayered and beautiful."

At that, Syd looked down.

There was a pause that, to me, felt awkward. "Why would you think *I* would be right as a subject for this kind of thing?" I asked.

They both looked at me now, almost as if they were seeing something that they knew I never would.

"What?" I asked.

Syd smiled, shrugged. "Your asking that question is what would make Axel consider painting you."

"Absolutely," Madeline said. "I'm calling him this week."

Syd's attention, less intense now, shifted back to me. "You look uncomfortable."

"No. Well, maybe a little. I've…" I faltered, about

to say, *I've never been involved in the arts before,* but that would lead Syd to wonder why in the hell Madeline had hired someone with no experience.

"I can't quite imagine standing naked in front of someone who is a stranger to me and letting him cover me in paint."

"Maybe you should be a part of different kind of installation first," Syd said. "Something…easier."

"I could get her into Pyramus," Madeline said.

"Perfect," Syd said. "You always know the perfect thing to do, Maddy. Who would you put her with?"

Madeline shrugged.

Syd looked back at me. "Pyramus is a huge installation that's taking over a whole gallery."

"The *whole* thing," Madeline said.

"It's essentially a pyramid with a treehouse kind of space inside. This structure will be built into the gallery."

"And two people at a time," Madeline said, her voice slowing slightly, as it did when she told an interesting story, "will climb up the pyramid and into the treehouse and spend an hour together."

"Doing what?"

"The time the people spend together could be the genesis for anything. Would you do it?"

I felt a little overwhelmed by the idea. But I might as well be a good sport, and I might learn more about the morphing concept of "art." Meanwhile, sitting in an adult tree fort for an hour seemed an easier route than being painted naked.

"Sure," I said.

"Actually," Madeline said, "I think I might be able

to get you in tomorrow. And I think I know who I'd put you with."

"Who?" Syd and I said at the same time.

Madeline jutted her chin at Syd. "You."

When we left, I still didn't understand exactly what I was getting into the next day.

But I did understand two things. One, Syd Fallon was still very—*very*—much in love with Madeline Saga. And two, I'd have him to myself for an hour.

22

It was enraging, literally enraging. Who was this woman? This woman with the long, orange hair who had grabbed Madeline's attention like never before? Their connection at the club had been obvious, when they were drinking lychee martinis and paying no attention to anyone around them. And now Madeline was introducing her to people in the art world, her many devotees. Or were they her friends? It was hard to tell with Madeline, who cared so little about anyone else.

So was this woman simply a new favorite pet? Or was she more?

It was that thought—the thought of Madeline developing a relationship with someone, when she'd denied so many others—that made the rage overwhelming.

23

That night, I couldn't sleep. I was, I realized, sexually riled up. I had been in a relationship for so long—first with Sam, then Theo—that I'd forgotten the desperation that can accompany those moods. The throb that won't quiet, the one that grows with the thought that you might not be able to fulfill it. Unless on your own. Which wasn't a bad option. Not at all. But still, when things have gotten past a certain point....

I threw back the covers and switched my bedside light on. I couldn't help but turn and look at the other side of the bed—smooth sheets and blankets, when they used to be twisted with heat, with a man.

I shook my head to shake away the image. I tugged on some comfortable socks, pajama bottoms and a robe and made my way to my home office. Bristol & Associates had recently bought me a slim, white notebook that was synced with their network so I could work from home. But I wouldn't be able to focus on work. I woke the computer, pulled up a search engine.

Now, what to do? What to do to get my mind back into my mind and away from my body? But the question only registered at the end—the word *body*—and then

I thought of the artist that Syd and Madeline wanted me to work with.

I typed in *Axel Tredstone.* Immediately the screen proliferated into a sea of images, most of women, stunning in ways that embodied power and sex.

I found the work Syd and Madeline had spoken of— where the women's bodies were painted so that they looked clothed, as if in a bodysuit that detailed what you might see inside the women, their emotions, as if you could even peer through their skin, into their layers.

One showed a woman in shades of peaches and pinks. Clouds swirled up and down her arms. Her breasts had been painted as if she wore a bandeau top with a string around her neck, but if you looked closer the string was actually a rope.

Another showed a woman with a mass of contradictory colors in her torso but her legs had been painted blue with fins, and she reclined on her side, her feet hidden. She looked like a contemporary mermaid.

I clicked through some of the other images. I found Tredstone's bio and a series of articles about him.

Axel Tredstone was born in Munich, Germany. He came to the U.S. when he was 18 to attend the School of the Arts Institute. There he met former students Jim Nutt and Art Green, who took him under their artistic wing. However, instead of focusing on Chicago Imagism, the world that Nutt and Green inhabited, Tredstone's development as an artist led him on a different path, one that turned an adoring yet analytical eye on women.

He started with portraiture. Later, he used a technique in which different parts of the subject were removed and shuffled, so that the end result was a painting that had been cut and reassembled, like puzzle pieces that didn't exactly fit together. Or did they?

I stopped there and read the last paragraph again, focusing on the word *cut,* then seeing it in the email Madeline had received. Was Tredstone someone to explore as a suspect?

The piece concluded that Tredstone became unsatisfied with his new, reassembled portraiture. It still did not capture the mystery of women. The article went on to explain how Tredstone's technique evolved to painting directly on the women's bodies, using his intuitive abilities to capture what he saw, felt, heard, smelled for each subject.

I sat back and wondered what Axel Tredstone would see in me.

24

The next morning, I was back at the computer, settling quickly into work, emailing Maggie to update her on certain cases. When that was finished, I opened the email Madeline had received yesterday and that I'd forwarded to myself. I read it again. *You will never be forgiven for what you did.*

After meeting Sydney last night, I wondered if the writer could be him. It seemed apparent that he still craved Madeline Saga. Madeline had said that their breakup had almost killed him. Was that true? Could Madeline's rejection have devastated him so much that he wanted to destroy her in some way? Or maybe he knew that stealing her artwork would kill *her* and her business.

I made a few notes about Syd on a white notepad, some other questions I wanted answered.

Next, I thought over some of the other information Madeline had given me about the move from the Bucktown gallery to the new one.

I did an online search for "Margie Scott," "art specialist" and "moving."

She was easy to find. Ms. Scott, I learned, was the owner of a company called Chicago Fine Arts Courier. I read the information on the company's website. *Packing and transporting fine art, from painting and sculptures to rare antiquities, requires attention to detail beyond measure. Ordinary moving companies do not possess the necessary expertise. Chicago Fine Arts Courier employs specialists to delicately pack your works of art, using temperature-controlled vehicles and other state-of-the-art moving equipment and security to ensure your art is secure, every step of the way.*

Every step of the way. I thought about how many— *many*—steps my father had listed that were involved in the art-moving process. That would give someone from Chicago Fine Arts Courier a lot of opportunity.

I clicked on the site's link for the owner. Margie Scott, it said, had a degree in art history, was a licensed architect and also an artist with a successful following in her own right. In fact, it was when a relocation of some of Scott's architectural art pieces went awry that she decided to form her company.

I sat back from the computer and thought about that. Margie Scott was an artist and knew, from her own experience, how and where the process of moving art could go wrong.

I pulled up the document I'd created with Madeline and bolded Scott's name. Then I thought of something else I could do about the email. Or rather, I thought of *someone*. Vaughn.

I dialed his number. Voice mail. It was a Sunday, but Vaughn had said something the other night about having to work weekends. I listened to his message, then left my phone number.

He called back within a few minutes.

"So what do you do?" I said, trying to joke around.

"Do you sit in your office and wait for someone to leave a message and then check it?"

"Hell, yeah," he said, sounding cranky. "You wouldn't believe the kind of shit calls we get over here."

This wasn't how I wanted things to go. "Hey, I was just calling to say thanks for that ride home. I know you were irritated with me, but I really mean it—I'm grateful."

He was quiet for a second. "Well, thanks," he said. "It's part of my job, you know?"

"Yeah? Well, I was actually calling because I was wondering about another part of your job."

He made a reluctant grunt for me to continue.

"I know from cross-examining you," I said, "that you're a *very* accomplished detective, who has solved all sorts of crimes."

"Cut the crap, McNeil."

"No, really," I said. "You've worked a lot of different cases, including stalking, right?"

"You mean cyber-stalking or the old-fashioned kind?"

I thought about that. "A little of both. I need another favor."

The phone was silent for a moment. "Is it about the friend who disappeared from the bar?" he asked.

"It is. She was around the next day. I guess you were right—she took a header or whatever you called it. But now she's gotten this threatening email." I briefly explained the circumstances, not mentioning any names or the art world.

"You want me to take a look at it?" Vaughn asked. "Forward it. I can look at it now on the phone. If it's short."

Vaughn gave me his email address, his personal one, and that felt oddly intimate.

I forwarded the email to him. I listened to his soft breathing as he took a minute to read it.

"My guess is, it's a woman," he said.

"How do you know?"

"The whole 'cut and stretched' thing. It's passive."

"What do you mean?"

"If a guy had written this, he would have said, '*I* want to stretch you, and *I* am going to cut you. When men are feeling violent toward someone, particularly a woman, they decide what *they* would do. But this person is saying someone, maybe someone else, *should* cut her. They don't talk about doing the action themselves. So I think it's a woman."

"Any other reasons you think this might be authored by a woman?"

"No. That's all I got."

"That's not much," I said. I immediately regretted it. Vaughn always took things from me so personally it seemed.

But not that time. "Sorry," he said.

"What do you think I should do from here?" I told him that I was waiting on data analysis of the email without mentioning Mayburn. I let him think this was all for a case I was working on at the law firm.

"You've done good. So far," Vaughn said. He mentioned a few other avenues to try.

I told him I'd call him if we needed him. And I hung up, feeling bleak at the thought that I was pretty sure we would be calling Vaughn again, soon.

25

I'd promised my mom and Spence that I would come over to their house for a "late Sunday lunch," which was Spence's way of labeling an occasion that would invite the opening of wine.

As I was walking up North Avenue toward the lake, I called Mayburn. I asked about his analysis of the email, and he told me that he was "ninety percent sure" that the *"cut and stretched"* email had been written by the same person as the comments under the Dudlin painting on Madeline's website.

I told him what Vaughn had said about suspecting the author of the email was a woman.

"Could be." A pause. "But since when do you ask Vaughn for help?"

I passed by Wells Street, trying not to slip on some of the snow-turned-black-ice. "Do I sense professional jealousy there?"

"No." Mayburn sounded irritated. "What you sense is that I don't like the guy because he was a *douche* to you. Remember that?"

"Yeah," I said, letting my own irritation show. "Yeah, I remember." And with that reminder of the

Vaughn of old, some really nasty anger flooded in. *Damn, thought I got rid of that.*

"Hey, Lucy's been telling me to say hi and that we need to get together," Mayburn said.

"I agree. Tell her 'hi' back." I took a breath. "And really, I haven't forgotten about the jackassery Vaughn has sown before. But I do think he can contribute to this case."

"Fine. Cool. Look," Mayburn said, "on that front, my own analysis shows a probability that it's a woman who wrote those emails. But that's not conclusive. Still, we should ask Madeline about this, about any women she knows who she thinks could have done that."

"But it could be a man?" I asked, thinking of Syd and Jeremy.

"Absolutely."

Mayburn also reported that the email address, from what he could tell, was registered under a bogus name and fake identifying information. Millions of people used the site anonymously, he said. And the company's privacy policy was notoriously strict.

I called Madeline on her cellphone and told her what we'd learned from Mayburn and Vaughn. I took a right onto State Street and headed toward my mother's place.

"A woman?" Madeline said, surprise in her voice.

"That was just Vaughn's opinion." I explained Vaughn's reasoning, and also told her about the odds, according to Mayburn, that it could be a woman.

"Mayburn said his analytics aren't definitive. No one's are," I said. "But I need you to think of any women in your life who might do something like write those comments and the email."

"No," she said quickly. "There's no one like that.

Absolutely not. I mean, I don't have lots of girlfriends, but I adore the ones I have. I'm not one of those women who says she can't stand other women."

"I'm not, either."

We ran through a list of any women who had worked at Madeline's gallery, or any outside contractors who might have spent enough time there to know the ins and outs.

I reached the iron fence outside my mom's elegant graystone at the corner of Goethe Street.

I told Madeline I was going out with Jeremy that night, and that I would see her tomorrow. But the conversation weighed on me as I neared my mom's house. I hoped very much, for Madeline's sake, that she was right; that whoever was threatening her, whoever had forged her artwork, was not someone she considered a friend.

26

It felt good to be in my mother's kitchen, tucked behind the bay window table, a soft lap blanket on my legs, sipping red wine and chatting with her.

My brother, Charlie, a frequent guest and drop-in at the house, loped into the kitchen. "Hey."

"Hey," I said in return. I noticed that his hair was looking redder as he got older, as if he was in the autumn of his life.

"Mom, is Cassandra coming over?" Charlie looked at my mother with a bit of a smirk. Without waiting for an answer, Charlie turned to me, "Did Mom tell you she's setting Dad up with Cassandra?"

I blinked at my brother. Then I blinked at my mom. "Wait. Did I just hear right? You're…" I let my question fade, and then got my focus back. "You're setting up your ex-husband with your best friend?" I heard my own incredulousness.

My mother cast a stern look at Charlie, then back at me. "Is that strange? I mean, I can't get a handle on the appropriateness of this situation. You know, I'm usually fairly adept at etiquette…."

Charlie and I nodded in agreement. My mother was nothing if not the pillar of etiquette. And not in a haughty kind of way, but rather a she-was-made-like-that kind of way.

"The fact is…" My mother looked around, apparently trying to determine the location of her current spouse. "Sometimes I really don't know how to act when it comes to your father." She looked at her watch. "Cassandra had said she may stop by after some shopping." My mom looked at the two of us. "I feel okay about this set-up, but it occurs to me she might be a bit uneasy when it comes to you two."

We heard the sound of the garage door closing and my mother's husband, Spence, hustled through the back door into the kitchen, shedding a coat. He was dressed in his usual uniform of a blue jacket and pressed khaki pants.

Spence hated to miss any McNeil family gatherings. "Hello, hello," he said, crossing the room to kiss my mother on the head. "What can I get you? What can I get you?" He looked around.

"We have drinks already, darling," my mother said.

"Ah, some cheese and olives, then?" He took off his jacket and began rolling up his sleeves as he moved toward the refrigerator.

"Ask Spence about it," Charlie said, leaning on the counter, looking toward Spence. "Do you think it's strange that Mom is setting Dad up with Cassandra?"

Spence straightened from a bent position at the fridge. "Not at all! It's a marvelous idea! Your father is entitled to love, just like anyone else."

It sounded like a bold line from a play and Spence had nearly delivered it that way, too.

My mother looked at him, her expression adoring. "I agree," she said.

My mother stood to help Spence as we heard a voice calling from the foyer, "Hello? Vicky? The door was open..."

"Cass! We're in the kitchen!"

I loved to see my mother act so casual.

Cassandra Milton strode into the kitchen carrying a big shopping bag. She looked salon fresh and ten years younger than her actual age. "I got those bowls I told you about," she was saying.

She stopped short when she saw Charlie and me in the kitchen, then regained her composure. "Charlie. Nice to see you awake and dressed for the day." She chuckled. Charlie's former laziness was a running joke to many of my mother and Spence's friends. Charlie laughed, as well, taking everything in stride, as usual.

"And you, Izzy," Cassandra turned to me. "I saw you the other day through the window at Madeline Saga's gallery. I knocked on the glass to get your attention, but you didn't seem to hear me."

"You know Madeline?"

"Oh, gosh, I've known her for years. Stan and I first bought a painting from her when she was in her old gallery space." Cassandra's husband, Stanford, had died six years ago. "We've been friendly since then. I see her sometimes at gallery events or restaurants. I occasionally still drop in to see what new works she's gotten. I just adore her joy about art. But I have to be careful when I'm there. Her excitement is contagious, and half the time I go away with something I hadn't intended to own at all." She laughed at her own impetuousness.

Cassandra turned to my mother and began regaling her with a tale about the bowls in her shopping bag. Charlie smiled at me and left the room.

I remained sitting where I was, struck with the thought that Madeline's love for art and her gallery put her in contact with so very many people. The net we used catch our thief, I realized, might have to get wider.

27

It had felt satisfying at first, typing in truthful words, letting frustrations out to the world—frustrations about Madeline. Hitting the send key with a satisfied thump of a forefinger, a surge of redemption.

After years of hating the disjointed and unappreciated feelings that Madeline caused, the reason for those feelings had emerged. And it was this—Madeline Saga's devotion to her art, her understanding of artists, was at such a level that no one else seemed to be able to achieve it, or even in many cases, to be aware that such a state existed.

And so sending the comments and the emails—at first, it was gratifying. But when the understanding came in—that Madeline's level couldn't be achieved, that was when the true anger began.

And that was when the worry started, the understanding that soon the words—words typed into a computer and sent over the internet—would no longer be strong enough to convey the hatred.

You should be cut and stretched like a canvas. There had been pride in the phrasing of that, in the creativity still possessed.

That pride wasn't going to satisfy for long. But effort would be made. And hopefully, by letting the hatred float to the surface and allow it some air, maybe it would become easier to carry. Maybe it would become easier to bear.

28

Jeremy had arranged to meet me at Madeline's gallery for our date. I was ready at least an hour early, so I spent a lot of time in the front part of the gallery, acting busy, but really just vacantly looking at the art, trying to figure out when I'd last gone on a real date, much less a second date.

My former fiancé and I had met at a party, and we'd started right from then, as if we'd been waiting for each other. And Theo? Well, we met at a bar, and we started that very night in a different way. The point? No traditional dates with either of them.

So I was slightly nervous, slightly giddy with excitement, when the front door chimed softly and in walked a woman.

She blinked at me. "You're not Madeline."

I laughed. "I've been trying, but I've got about five inches on her. You're Amaya, right? I'm Izzy, Madeline's assistant. I met you the other night at Toi."

The woman didn't laugh in return.

I walked toward her, hand outstretched.

She nodded vaguely, gave my hand a limp shake.

Madeline came into the front room. I heard her stop, say, "Oh, Amaya," then the click of her heels toward us.

The two women almost hugged, but their bodies didn't touch except for vague pats on the back.

"I wanted to see what was new," Amaya said, gesturing with a tiny hand around the gallery.

"Please," Madeline said, nodding. "One of us will be with you in just a minute."

She drew me toward the back room. "Do you think you could show her around? I have some cataloguing to work on, and honestly—" she glanced toward Amaya "—she's a bit much for me sometimes."

"Sure," I said, excited to use the knowledge I'd acquired that didn't have to do with shipping or packing the art.

And as I spoke with Amaya, I found I knew more than I thought, had retained more. I was easily able to talk to her for the fifteen or so minutes she spent in the gallery. At first, she didn't seem to be shopping for anything in particular, but I got her talking about the ice sculpture.

I tried to draw her into more personal discussion, but she had little interest. And yet, I was interested in her reaction. It struck me that, if she knew I was a lawyer, she might have a different response to me than when she thought I was a twentysomething art assistant. She frequently glanced at the back as if for a glimpse of Madeline.

When Amaya left and I went to the back room, I found Madeline musing over a sculpture, setting it on a pedestal and turning it around to view it in different lights. No catalogue activity in sight.

"She's gone?" Madeline asked.

"Yes. Why didn't you want to work with her?" I asked, thinking it was a bit rude.

"We just don't like each other."

"Well, she's interested in the ice sculpture."

Madeline turned. "Really?" She raised her eyebrows. "It fits, I suppose. She has an icy personality."

She turned back, apparently lost in thought.

Then the front door dinged again.

My date had arrived.

"What do you think of it?" Jeremy gestured with his wineglass at a large painting of a woman.

In it, the woman was on her knees, her buttocks in the air and, larger in scale than everything else on the canvas. The woman was looking behind herself, as if waiting.

"Wow," I said. *Nice, Iz. Way to use that art lingo you've been learning.* "It's sexual." *And there ya go again.*

"Do you like that?" Jeremy asked.

We were at a party at the Museum of Contemporary Art. It was part happy hour, part art opening, part concert.

"Do I like the painting or do I like that it's sexual?" I said, not taking my eyes off it.

"Either," he said.

"In general, yes, I like that."

A pause. Then, "Wait, which one do you like?"

I laughed and walked to the next piece, a block of blue sketched on a black canvas.

Jeremy stood next to me at the blue painting. The crowd began to bump us from all sides—people pushing into different installation rooms, guests glutting the common space and the bar.

"Want to go outside?" Jeremy said.

"It's the middle of winter."

"It's pretty warm today." It was true. January in Chicago, and yet our recent snow was starting to melt as the temperature rose. "Plus, they have the deck tented and there are heaters." Jeremy gestured at the back door of the museum, and I saw a few people out there.

"Let's do it," I said. The truth was, I wanted to be alone, or at least more alone, with Jeremy Breslin for two reasons. First, I wanted to find out more about his divorce—was it amicable or otherwise? The more I thought about it, the more I wondered—did he need the money enough, or hate his wife enough, to steal and forge their art?

Second, I really, really wanted to kiss him again.

Outside, Jeremy gallantly took off his brown velvet jacket and draped it over my shoulders. I liked that he hadn't asked if I wanted it. As a Chicago girl, I'd been taught that I could withstand anything, weatherwise, so I tended to ignore offers of help when it came to temperature.

I wore a purple dress—tight and sexy—also in velvet, and I felt even more sexy when the silky lining of Jeremy's jacket hit my shoulders and my arms, already warmed by him.

"So…" he said.

"So…" We were each holding something to drink. We walked to the railing of the balcony, still under the warmth of the heat lamp.

"How long have you been coming to this museum?" I asked. I didn't want to admit it, but this was only my second time.

"Since they started. The Fex is on the board."

"Is she here tonight?"

"I doubt it. It's not her scene anymore."

"What's her scene?" I asked.

"Getting as much of my money as she can."

Now we were talking. "I thought you guys were having a good divorce," I said. "Splitting the second house and all that."

"I'm trying. I'm really trying." Jeremy wore a blue button-down, striped delicately with white, and it fell slightly open at the neck as he leaned on the railing. I could see his skin was lightly tanned—a Christmas vacation in Mexico? "You know, in Illinois, when you divorce, you split anything you've acquired together."

I did know that, but I stayed silent.

"We've been married since just out of college, so what we split is pretty much everything." He looked down, staring deeply into his vodka drink. "It's like we're dividing our whole world."

Now I didn't know what to say because of the emotion I sensed there.

"I have this one friend," Jeremy continued, "and he says that having a happy divorce—or as happy as one can be—is the biggest accomplishment of his entire life. He has a really successful company, he played college basketball, he's on a bunch of boards in the city—and yet the thing he takes the most pride in, he says, is the amicability of their split. The kids are happy, he's happy and so is his ex."

"Sounds good." I took a sip of my red wine.

"Right?" A sigh from Jeremy. "I swear I'm trying to do the same thing, but lately she just won't have it. It seems like she keeps trying to piss me off."

"Why?"

"Great question. I guess it's money. But I can't believe she'd treat me like this over money. I've paid for everything—for her life and mine and our kids' for nearly twenty years, and now, suddenly, she wants it all." He took another sip. "Or at least that's what it feels like."

I felt bad for him then, and I put my lawyer hat on without actually telling him I *was a* lawyer. "Just out of curiosity—because I have a friend who is an attorney—what family lawyer did you go with?"

It wasn't a lie, I reminded myself when I didn't feel so good about not being completely honest with Jeremy. The truth was I had a *lot* of friends who were attorneys.

Jeremy told me the name of the divorce lawyer I'd heard had a reputation for being one of the best—he would try to settle, and he would try to be nice, but he could also come out of the cage swinging if you needed him to.

But then he mentioned the name of his ex's attorney. I tried not to wince. That lawyer had a reputation for being one of the biggest jackasses around. I didn't know if I should tell him that, given the lawyer, their wrangling would likely continue, despite his best efforts.

"Hey, let's move on to a lighter topic," Jeremy said then, smiling. "I hear Madeline wants to get Axel Tredstone to paint you." He raised his eyebrows in a slightly lascivious and yet charming way.

If it weren't so dark out, he would have seen me blush. "Yeah," I said. "Like *really* paint me."

"I think you should do it. How many members of the public will ever get a chance to be the subject of a famous artist?"

"Uh, let's see. I'm going to guess about three percent."

"Maybe. If they're lucky. I'm going to say it's less than that. Plus, let's face it…" He got closer to me, and he smelled like something you rarely smelled in the city's winters—warm sun. "You being painted nude?" Jeremy said. "I don't think I have to tell you that that sounds really, really hot."

But now that I had my lawyer hat on, I couldn't get it off. It dawned on me—if I did this, could I be disbarred for being photographed nude? What if I didn't appear nude? The point of the photos was to paint the persona, making each subject look clothed. And maybe I could get Axel to paint my face so no one would recognize me?

I imagined myself, maybe ten years in the future, deciding to go back to a big law firm. "Yes," I would say while being interviewed again at Baltimore & Brown. "You heard correctly. I was, in fact, the subject of a work of art." I then imagined the partner, while interviewing me, pulling the photo up on his computer and promptly dismissing me.

On the other hand…some of the criminal defense clients that Maggie had…the ones that I was now partially representing, and would be mostly representing as soon as she had that baby… What would their reaction be to a technically naked photo? I laughed out loud. We would get more business than we could handle.

"Why are you laughing?" Jeremy asked. "You are hot. You have to know that."

I shook my head. I couldn't tell him about my law gig. "I'm just thinking of something else. Look, I'll think about this Axel Tredstone thing. I mean, who knows if he'd want to work with me?"

He was yet closer. "Trust me. As an art aficionado

and a personal fan of Tredstone's? He would want to work with you."

With a quick intake of breath, we had one of those moments, one where he was close enough to smell me now, too, and we both wanted to kiss, no more fleeting wonders or doubts. The only question would be who would lean first. It wouldn't be me. It was never me. I don't know why, but while I could be very impatient in other areas of my life, I could be forever patient with those first few kisses of a relationship. The wanting and wondering made the air thick.

He didn't lean. He held the moment.

And so I kept talking. "In the meantime, they got me into some installation tomorrow called Pyramus."

"Who's *they?*" he asked.

"Madeline and Syd."

"Ah, Syd." Jeremy turned the slightest bit away from me then, the moment broken.

"Why do you say his name like that?" I asked. "Like he's trouble?"

"Oh, I wouldn't say anything like that. He seems like a cool dude. It just sounded like Madeline had a hard time getting rid of him."

"Really?"

"Yeah, if I remember right, he got kind of stalker-ish."

I felt my eyebrows lift. "In what way—stalker-ish?"

"Writing her fucked-up emails." Jeremy made a dismissive gesture with his highball glass and took another sip.

Writing her fucked-up emails? Wasn't that something Madeline should have mentioned to me? Why hadn't she told me that Syd could be like that? Could he have sent the recent email she received?

"So anyway," Jeremy said. "The installation? Pyramus? That's excellent. So many people want to be a part of that, but they can't get in. Of course, Madeline could."

"But what am I'm getting into? You climb into some space and then…?"

"No idea. But I'd roll with it." He looked happy then, like he was excited for me to have been fortunate enough to fall into an adventure.

I liked the sound of an adventure.

I took another sip of wine. "So, back to *your* art," I said, raising another part of the topic I'd been waiting to approach. "Does your ex know yet about the forgeries?"

"I tried to hide it for Madeline's sake," Jeremy said, "but she was waiting for the asset allocation. I had to tell her they were worth nothing."

Or did you want to tell her that? I wondered. *Had you stumbled on the perfect crime—saving the art work for yourself and having it faked so you wouldn't have to pay the Fex anything for it?*

"What was the reaction?" I asked.

"Displeasure?" Jeremy said, clearly understating.

"So, the Fex was not happy." Immediately I covered my mouth with my hand. "I'm sorry. What's her name?"

Jeremy laughed. "Corrine."

"How about you?" I said, leaning a little closer. "How do you feel about owning forged paintings?"

He turned to me. "I'm feeling like I really enjoy my circle of friends right now. Even if it means having to reveal that I am the owner of fake artwork." He stepped closer to me. I could breathe his scent again. "Can I just show you how much I'm enjoying this?" he asked.

I nodded. And he kissed me.

29

The papers the next morning, all blazed with the same story. "Blizzard to Rip the Windy City!" one headline read. "Snowmaggeden!" said another.

I rolled my eyes. Sure, Chicago had some tough winters, but really, the old snow was half gone. Plus, the news media tended to exaggerate when it came to the white stuff, and most of the time nothing much happened. "Snowwhere Near Expectations." That would be a better headline, I thought. Or "Snowvereaction."

Plus, it was bright and sunny out. I decided to walk to the gallery.

I don't particularly remember the walk because the whole time—and I mean the *whole* time—I thought about Jeremy. Kissing him on the back deck of the Museum of Contemporary Art. Kissing him in his car. Letting him walk me to my building. And kissing him on the steps. And then moving just inside the front door of the building and kissing there.

Eventually, I told him I had to go to bed. I had to meet Madeline at the gallery in the morning, so I could be part of the art installation. I needed, I said inanely, my "art beauty sleep."

"You're already stunningly beautiful," he said, and

he said it with such conviction that the next kiss nearly flattened me, nearly made me swoon, nearly made me drag him up to my condo. But still something stopped me. Was it the memories of Sam and Theo? I considered that for a second, but the answer was no, not really. I just wasn't ready.

I pushed his chest gently away. "Absence makes the heart grow fonder, right?"

"Uh…" He cleared his throat. "I don't think I could get much 'fonder' right now." He took a deep breath.

We both laughed. And then I'd gone upstairs and gone to bed. Alone. But fine with that.

Now, walking to the gallery, I replayed it over and over and over in my head, treasuring the deliciousness of it.

But just as I walked down Wells Street, my phone started ringing in my bag, breaking into my mental reenactment of the way Jeremy had—gently—bit my bottom lip, and held it there for a moment when we were kissing on the stairs.

It was Madeline. "Are you almost here?"

I looked at my watch. "Probably fifteen minutes."

"Okay," she said, her voice tiny.

"What's up?"

"I got a letter." Nothing else.

"In the mail?" I prompted.

"No, it was on the floor of the gallery. I found it today. Right inside the front door, but off to the side."

"So someone pushed it under the door while you were gone?"

"Or maybe yesterday, and I didn't notice it when I left."

"Was it written by the same person who wrote the email or the comments?"

"I don't know."

I switched my cellphone to my other hand and crossed the street. "Any chance Syd sent it?"

"No. Why would you say that?"

"Jeremy mentioned something about him sending you what he called 'fucked-up emails.'"

Madeline *tsked*. "Syd was simply telling me how much he loved me and missed me." A pause. "In truth, they were love letters." She exhaled hard. "But this one isn't."

The concern in Madeline's voice was enough to make me hail a cab. Within five minutes, I was sitting on the tufted chair in front of her black desk, reading the letter. It had been typed in a font that looked like Times New Roman. The text was centered in the middle of a white piece of paper and was italicized.

Madeline, I saw you here. I saw you there, the letter started. It almost sounded like a children's poem.

Then it continued. *I saw you at the bar at the Ambassador East, the pharmacy on State and Division, the opening at Andrew Rafasz gallery,* and on it went.

After a list of about fifteen places or gatherings was a space that set off the last locations on the list— *dining at Henri on Michigan Avenue. By yourself. And you didn't even notice me. As usual.*

The letter ended, *But I always see you.*

30

Madeline and I walked down Franklin, headed for a gallery a block or so away—the gallery that held the Pyramus installation. The truth was, I couldn't be completely sure that I even knew what the word *installation* meant in this situation. And right now, my mind was on the letter that Madeline had found only two hours ago.

"Are you sure you want to do this today?" I asked her, belting my coat tighter against the wind that had gone from friendly to decidedly cranky. "I mean, I know it's a huge deal in the art world, and it's amazing you got Syd and me in today, but don't you think we should wait, since you just got that letter?"

Madeline stopped, midstreet. She wore a cashmere coat of the lightest blue. She looked like a cloud on the street. "Isabel, we've done everything we can with the letter for now. Right?"

"Well, we've scanned it, but haven't handled it. We sent it to Mayburn and Vaughn. We read it about eight hundred times."

"And it's not Syd."

Madeline had said many times already that she

didn't think Syd wrote the letter or the email. *He's not like that.*

But I wasn't entirely convinced. So I wasn't unhappy that I was going to have Syd to myself. I just wanted to make sure Madeline would be all right.

She smiled. "Act like we haven't received that letter."

"But we did receive the letter, and that changes things. Someone needs to stay with you."

She said nothing, but looked a little scared.

"Because, Madeline." I stepped a little closer to her. "That letter makes it clear that someone has been following you." I'm not sure why, but we hadn't spoken this truth out loud yet.

"I know."

"Maybe we should call Mayburn to come over."

She shook her head. "John is doing enough by having you work with me. You've been an immense comfort." She put her hand on my arm. "Izzy," she said. It was the first time she'd called me that. "I think that life is a piece of art. And the more you let it unfold as it wants to, as it does, the more beautiful it is." She took a breath. "So let's just allow this to be."

Madeline linked her arm through mine, and led me down Franklin toward the art gallery. Toward the Pyramus.

31

As I climbed the white steps of the pyramid, heading toward the square hole at the top, my heart rate increased.

I took deep, deep breaths, hoping I didn't get one of the flop sweat attacks that occasionally hit me. After last night's date, my sexual tension at that moment was, let's just say, healthy. That was all I needed—to be stuck in a pyramid with a hot guy while I sweated my ass off.

The installation truly was a pyramid shape, and as promised, it took up nearly the entire gallery. I'd been to the gallery once before, when a friend of Sam's had been a DJ for a party. It was large and normally held a number of collections by both local and international artists. But now there was nothing inside except this white pyramid that looked as if it was constructed out of papier mâché.

We'd been greeted by the gallery owner, who said Syd had not yet arrived, and that we could simply sit down next to "the book." The book was like something out of *Alice in Wonderland.* It was huge—maybe three feet long and two feet wide. The cover was made by hand of what looked like a tight silk weave, all black except for the white letters in the center, at the bottom—*THE PYRAMUS*.

"Go ahead," Madeline said, nodding at the book for me to open it.

I lifted it from the glass coffee table in front of us. It was lighter than I had expected. I hesitated before opening the cover. I don't know what I expected—flying monkeys?—but inside was a huge ivory linen page that held the same two words—THE PYRAMUS—this time in black. The next pages were blank, except for where people had written their names and the date. Some of the pairs had written a phrase or two. One read *Strange, Sublime, Superb and all other Superior S words.*

Another was more matter-of-fact. *We didn't know each other before. We still don't now. But we get each other. Thanks, man!*

Syd arrived. Like Madeline, he carried with him an energy that was palpable once he was within a few feet from you. And the longing, awestruck energy he directed at Madeline was even easier to feel, to see.

Seeing that gave me a serious pang. I had been adored once. No, more than once. Sam had adored me, I was suddenly certain, as had Theo, and I adored them. I missed that feeling.

Now I was climbing a pyramid.

It was such a strange thought, one I'd never expected to have—*I'm climbing a pyramid*—that I lost myself for a moment, turning it over in my mind.

Then I looked up and quickly came back to the present when I saw Syd climbing the steps on the other side of the pyramid. He glanced at me and our eyes met, then our gazes darted down. It felt strange—as if I was about to do something illicit with this man. When we both reached the top, we looked into a square hole. Inside the hole, attached to the top and leading down, was a ladder. Farther inside, at the bottom, was a wood-clad room and a couple of chairs.

Syd looked at me. His black hair had partly fallen from the headband he wore.

A quick thought went through my mind—*how many men look good in a headband?* Syd was the only one I knew. He rocked it. A shiny hank of hair hung near his eyes.

"Let me go first," he said.

I appreciated his chivalrousness.

He swung his legs over, then climbed down the ladder, gesturing for me to do the same once he'd reached the bottom.

Right then, I could only think that I was glad I'd worn black jeans rather than a dress. My legs trembled a little as I descended the ladder, my body seeming to fear…what? The unknown—both from the perspective of the art and also from Syd. Could this be dangerous? I didn't know. Syd stood below me, arms up in case I fell. We were in it together, I supposed. Whatever *it* was.

Finally my feet felt the floor. I looked around. It was almost like being in a treehouse—a well-made treehouse with two modern designer chairs made of curved wood and a coffee table. That was it, nothing else in the room. There were no instructions. There didn't seem to be any cameras or recording devices. Syd and I were, it seemed, alone. As Madeline said before we'd started the climb, "It's just you two, nothing else."

I looked at Syd. "This is kind of strange," I said.

He smiled. "This is just like the kind of thing Madeline loves to see artists create," he said. "Something eye-opening, meant to be aesthetically pleasing but also to allow people to enter a space or a plane they didn't know existed."

His words sounded kind of cool, kind of weird and eerie at the same time.

"So, what plane are we in?" I asked.

He shrugged. "Madeline just likes to make people aware of how many ways there are to look at the world."

He seemed to be able to work Madeline into nearly any topic. I thought of what Jeremy had said about Syd being "stalker-ish."

I looked down at the chairs. "Shall we sit?"

We did. Syd put his arms on the chair, crossed his legs and he looked at me—patiently—as if he'd seen something, and now was waiting for me to do the same or perhaps to see something all on my own.

But I wasn't struck by anything in particular. "Let's ask each other questions," I suggested, thinking of no particular casual conversational opener. "Or something like that."

"Yeah," Syd said. "Free association. Look at me."

I took in his appearance once more.

"What do I look like to you?" Syd asked. "Don't think it, just say it."

"An Arabian therapist," I said. Then I blinked. "What did I just say? Arabian therapist?"

We both laughed. It felt as if the words had come from someone else, but Syd did have the *feel* of a therapist—open, understanding, nonjudgmental, mysterious.

"Have you been to therapy?" Syd asked.

"Not individual therapy," I answered, not sure as I said it whether the distinction mattered. Sam and I had taken a stab at couples' counseling. "But I really should, after the year I've had."

For some reason, this struck both of us as funny, and we laughed.

"Wait, we have to get back to where we started," I said. "Free association questions. And I'll give it back to you." I paused for a beat. "Look at me. Now, answer the question—what do I look like to you?"

"The way God should look." Syd also looked surprised at his own words. "Wow, sorry. That's bizarre, sorry."

"That *is* bizarre. But I think that's the point of this," I said, waving my hand around the room, warming to the concept. "And I'm liking the sound of this bizarreness. Continue, please."

Syd smiled. "I think you're incredibly sexy and… something else…I don't even know what. But I didn't think I could feel a sexual appreciation like this for anyone but Madeline. I'm kind of relieved."

Madeline and Syd had broken up around the time she moved to her new gallery last year. And in all that time, he hadn't found anyone else attractive? "Nothing has been sexy to you except Madeline?" I asked.

"That's about right. Since I met her. It's fucked up."

He said nothing.

I said nothing. Finally, I asked, "So what exactly did you mean when you said I look like God should look?"

He breathed out hard. "What did I mean?" he said, somewhat quietly as if asking himself. "I'm not traditionally religious, but if I did have to put an appearance to God, it would be magical and fiery."

"And that's how you see me?"

He nodded.

"Okay," I said, immensely flattered. "I will pretty much love you forever." If he had any sense that I was working on Madeline's thefts and he was trying to distract me, he was doing a good job.

Syd laughed.

"Do you believe in God?" I asked then. I had never asked that question of anyone, and I was surprised by the boldness of it.

"Well…" He looked like he was thinking some more. The moment stretched, and I started to feel a little uncomfortable.

"Maybe that's an unfair question," I said, "because everyone's idea of God is different."

"Do *you* think I believe in God?" Syd asked.

"Yes."

"Why do you say that so definitively?"

"You seemed like someone who sees the world as amazing, and usually those people believe in God as the world."

"Well put," Syd said. "And you? Do *you* believe in God?"

No easy answer came. My parents had taken us to church when I was young, but I couldn't even remember what denomination the church was. I was envious, sometimes, of people who seemed so clear about their faith. People like Maggie, who went to church nearly every Sunday, and so did her family and they all knew exactly what they meant when they spoke of God.

"I'm fascinated by the concept of saints," I said. "My friend Maggie's family is always murmuring requests to one saint or another. Like St. Christopher. Apparently, he can make sure you travel safe. And there's another one who can help you find lost things."

"My family is from Pakistan, and they're tradition-ally Muslim. We *really* like our saints."

"You're kidding."

"Oh, no. People visit the saints' tombs—they believe that by being close to the tomb they can share in some of the saint's spirit." He stared at me. "I used to think Madeline was a saint or a goddess of sorts."

"Used to?" I asked.

"She's human," Syd said. "I know that now."

"Because you've seen her failings?"

He shook his head. "Because my longing for her is waning. Finally."

I wasn't sure what to say to that. Because I didn't think I believed it.

I asked him about Pakistan, and he explained he'd only been there once. I asked him how that culture had influenced his art and his life. He felt fortunate to be Pakistani, he said, but also to be an American. "Seeing my family's heritage from a distance—I think that's a gift."

He talked about how Madeline was the first person who allowed him to see his outsider status like that. Before her, he hadn't felt entirely Pakistani or entirely American, and as a result, he always saw that as a bad thing. Until Madeline. She was an outsider, too. Even more so, since she didn't know her birth family.

Syd looked in the distance, a wistful gaze. "I want so badly to take Madeline there. To Pakistan."

Every road, every conversation, it seemed, led back to Madeline Saga.

We had been talking for a while when we heard a faint knock, then another, this time louder—two raps.

"Has it been an hour?" I asked Syd. The gallery

owner had told us that when the hour was over, he would knock on the pyramid to let us know.

"No."

Another knock. "That's the signal."

"No," Syd said again, sure and definitive. Then silence. Suddenly the room felt too quiet—tomblike.

"Our hour is not up," Syd said.

"Uh, what do you mean?"

More silence.

"Seriously," I said, starting to feel seriously itchy.

"Seriously," Syd intoned back. "The hour is not up, until…"

"Until?"

"Until you answer the question."

"What question?" It was hot in there, too.

"The question," he repeated.

It felt as if the hidden room was sealing itself, becoming airless. I listened for another knock, but there was nothing.

"Do you believe in God?" Syd asked.

"Is that the question?"

"That's the question."

Did he really want an answer?

He said nothing more.

"Yes," I said simply. "If I can say that the universe is God, then yes."

I turned and grasped for the ladder. As I climbed it, I realized that my own questions hadn't been answered. I believed Syd was obsessed with Madeline still, but had he been stalking Madeline? Had he forged the paintings? Did he write that letter?

But I couldn't stop myself from climbing up those stairs, out of the Pyramus, as quickly as possible.

32

Syd, Madeline and I all went back to the gallery. I was confused about why Madeline had invited him, but as we talked and walked, it was clear she still didn't believe the letter was from him. And I think it was that letter that made her want Syd around as protection.

I felt more at ease now that we were out of the Pyramus. Thankfully, I was losing what we'd experienced in there. The hour hadn't been physically taxing, but it had been intense. And spiritually? I didn't often use that word, but yes, it had been spiritually intense, too.

When we got back to the Wrigley Building, we said hello to the security guard, who pointed to a small crate that had been delivered for Madeline. "Madeline," I said. "Would this be a good time for you to show me how you unpack deliveries?"

"Of course," she said.

"And Syd probably knows about the process, too, right?"

"Yes," Madeline said. "Probably more than me."

Syd smiled in awknowledgement.

Interesting.

In the back room, Madeline and Syd began unpacking the crate, both giving me instructions about how to pry open the top, how to ensure that nothing inside was touched.

Madeline pulled off the top of the crate and opened the packing slip.

"Who is it from?" Syd asked.

"It doesn't say." Madeline shrugged.

"Maybe it's that Rothkov," Syd said. It sounded like they had shared such conversations many times before, and clearly they still spoke about the art Madeline currently represented.

Madeline's gloved hands finally found something inside and she lifted it out.

"What in the hell?" I heard myself saying. I clamped my mouth shut. Clearly, I hadn't developed my art tastes very much because to my eye, what she was holding was gruesome. And I'm not a girl who says *gruesome* very easily.

It was a wooden pedestal, painted black, with something plastic above it. The plastic had been molded to look like a block of flesh, and in the top was a knife. The knife's blade was sunk deeply into the block, a ring of blood around the handle.

Madeline put it down, the curiosity on her face turning to something verging on horrified. I looked at Syd. His black eyebrows were furrowed, his face suspicious. He stood and walked toward her, looking over Madeline's shoulder. None of us said anything. Instead, we all looked at the depiction of a block of flesh with a knife deep in it. The wood handle of the knife gleamed with gloss, the "blood" below it looking coarse in comparison.

Syd reached into the crate and looked around. "There's no other information." He glanced at Madeline, concerned. He picked up the packing slip. "I'll call the shipper." Taking out his cellphone, he walked to the far side of the room when the call was answered.

I went to Madeline's side, trying to let go of my judgments and associations about that piece of art. If Madeline had taught me anything, it was to let go of my usual reactions to things. *Acknowledge it,* she had said once, asking what I thought of a certain sculpture she'd received. *Feel what you feel, then put that down and step around it. Let yourself be a blank slate. You are part of the art, the way you look at it, the way you take it in. View each moment as fresh, each sight as a treat to your other senses, as well.*

But I couldn't help it, because the more I made myself lean in, the more my senses reeled. I looked at Madeline, who was gazing at it, slightly openmouthed, as if trying to make sense of it.

Syd came back to the table. "No info," he said. "The person filled out a sheet to ship it from a storefront delivery place, but they tried the numbers listed and they're both bullshit. They think the name is, too."

"Like the email," Madeline said in a toneless voice.

"What's the name of the shipper?" I asked.

"They wrote a company name, Abunai Enterprises." He spelled it for us.

I typed it into the search engine on my phone. "It's Japanese for warning or look out."

"Really?" Madeline said vaguely. "I don't speak much of the language."

Something dawned on me. "Does Amaya?" I asked. She was the only Japanese person I'd met through Madeline.

"I believe so." Madeline said nothing else, just examined the piece.

"It's wood," she said, nodding at the base. "And plastic, I think, and the knife appears to be real."

"Could it be a nod to Conner?" Syd asked.

"Connor who?" I said.

"Joshua Connor. He was a sculptor who often used things like knives and scissors."

"Are they always that…that violent?" I asked, nodding at the piece. I thought of the email Madeline had received. *For your falsity and selfishness, you should be cut and stretched like a canvas.* Was the knife a reference to that?

"No," Madeline said. "In fact, they are quite peaceful images."

"It's probably a stunt," Syd said. "New artist and all that." I studied Syd to see if he was acting, pretending not to know what this thing was. I couldn't tell.

"What do you mean, a stunt?" I asked him.

"Well, a lot of artists try to gain the attention of a gallery by doing something flamboyant or aggressive. Sometimes anonymously. And then, later, they'll pop up and tell you it's them. They're trying to say something by sending just the art itself."

"I don't think that's it," Madeline said.

"Then what is it?" Syd asked.

"*Who* is it?" To me, that was the truly scary thing. We still didn't know.

Madeline sighed, stepped away and pulled her phone out of her pocket. She seemed to want to distract herself, but a moment later she froze.

Then she spun around. "I got another email."

I didn't have to ask which one. "What does it say?"

Madeline said nothing, just read it one more time, then stepped forward and held out her phone for Syd and me.

The email said, *I hope you, somehow, feel the pain, the agony, of being dismissed so many times.*

33

"Enough is enough," Mayburn said, when I'd finished telling him about the anonymous sculpture Madeline had received. "It's time to smoke this dude out."

"Or this woman," I said.

"Right."

We were at Lucy's house, a mansion in Lincoln Park that took up three lots on Bissell Street. The house was L-shaped, with everything facing a large courtyard. That courtyard was mostly bare of bushes and grass now, but a number of pine trees held white lights, making the courtyard a glittering yet relaxing site.

We sat together in Lucy's living room. Mayburn was waiting for Lucy to get home so he could watch the kids while she went to an evening yoga class. I'd insisted we meet asap so I could explain the latest.

"So, how do we smoke someone out?" I asked Mayburn. "Like a sting operation?"

"Yeah."

"Ooh, exciting." I held myself back from clapping. Not only was I excited to take part in such a thing, but I really wanted to figure out this situation for Madeline, sooner rather than later. It was taking too much from her, adding too much stress. And the whole thing was getting freaking scary.

Mayburn leaned back in the armchair where he sat and looked out the windows at the courtyard. "Clearly she has someone following her, and now threatening her. But before we can stop that, we need to know *who's* doing this."

"And why," I added.

"Right," Mayburn said. "So, Madeline is still into the clubs and parties and the art openings, I assume?"

"Yeah."

"Any events coming up this week that you know about?"

"There's an opening at some gallery and a party after at a club."

"What club?"

I thought about it. "It's on Hubbard. That place with the two floors at the top."

"Near Dearborn?" Mayburn asked. I nodded. "That's perfect."

"Perfect for what?"

"You need to let Madeline move around, but stay close to her and find out who is watching her."

"How am I going to stay close to her and find the person at the same time? Especially if they've been watching Madeline at the gallery lately? I'm pretty easy to spot."

"Good point." He furrowed his brow, thinking.

We heard the garage door open, and Lucy and her two kids came inside. "John!" Noah and Belle yelled, running at Mayburn and launching themselves onto his lap.

I watched with a smile as Mayburn hugged Belle and then tickled Noah, both of them crawling all over him.

I stood and hugged Lucy. "Hi, Iz!" she said. "I've missed you."

"You, too."

We stood and looked at Mayburn, still playing with the kids. "They love him, huh?" I asked.

"Love," she said.

"Hey, one second, one second," Mayburn was saying to the kids. "I've got to say hi to your mom." He looked up at Lucy and me, like he was about to extricate himself from the kids and stand. But then he froze for a second.

"I got it," he said.

"What?" Lucy and I asked at the same time.

Mayburn directed his gaze at me. "You know the problem we were just discussing?"

I nodded.

"Have you ever wanted to be a blonde?" He didn't wait for an answer. "Now is the time."

34

"So, how's the dating going?" I asked my dad.

We were sitting at breakfast place called Toast in Lincoln Park. Across the table, my father wrapped his hands around a white coffee cup and blinked under his copper glasses. I had never seen him do that before, the quick blinking.

I was about to retract my question when he broke into a smile. Then he quickly dropped it, as if the expression had embarrassed him.

"What?" I said.

He seemed to not be able to help it—he laughed, then dropped the laugh just as quickly. But he answered. "It's just so remarkable."

"You met someone?" I hoped he didn't hear the surprise in my voice.

"No, I mean, I've been out with a few people," he said. "But they seem to expect me to…" He looked around as if searching for the word. "Well, they seem to want me to…emote."

"What do you mean?"

"You know, they want you to talk, to share yourself." He said the word *share* as if it were something exotic.

"And you don't like to share." It was not a question.

He shrugged grandly, and I could see that he'd retained some of the gestures he'd acquired from his Italian mother and from living in Italy. Italians are masters of the grand shrug, one that can be used as a response to anything.

"Look, when your mom and I were young, nobody really *shared*—" he made air quotes "—as they call it. And then I was out of the country."

"Yeah, you were out of this life," I said. Sometimes when I was talking to my dad, I snapped at him out of the blue, as if some comment had formed at the outer reaches of my memory and came out of my mouth before the rest of my brain could process it.

"Sorry," I said.

"No problem." My father looked at his coffee cup, nonchalant, then continued, as if eager to talk. "The thing is, when I left the country, when I was…as you said, out of this life, I kept a low profile. I never 'shared' with anyone. I never talked to anyone."

"Except for Elena," I said, referring to my dad's sister.

He gave a single nod. "Yes, with the exception of Elena. But I never did know everything about her, did I? She never fully shared with me."

Our waitress put our meals in front of us—oatmeal for me. I looked at my father's plate, which held something called a pesto scramble. "So, you know," he continued, "I have an entire protocol in my head for determining whether or not something is classified. On a number of different levels." He shook his head now, as if not wanting to bore me with the details. Meanwhile, I stared at him, rapt. Every once in a while, he let me behind the curtain of Christopher McNeil, and as Madeline had once said about art, it dazzled me.

"The thing is…about the sharing…" His words died away and he stared at the ceiling as if searching for his words there.

"They want you to share, and when you don't, they get annoyed at you?"

"No." He looked at me with a big smile. "They all seem to think, in one version or another, that I'm slow to love. And maybe I am."

"*Maybe* you are?" I said, intentionally letting the sarcasm leak in this time.

"Okay, I'm agreeing with you." Another Italian shrug. "But they *like* it."

I laughed at the surprise in his voice. He talked some more, then we ate for a while in companionable silence, a new thing for us.

"Did Mayburn tell you his idea about me as a blonde?" I asked.

My dad nodded. "I think it's worth a shot."

"I wonder if people will buy me as a blonde."

"Only if you like it," he answered quickly. "You can't just sell it. You have to be it. And *you* have to like it."

"Why is that?"

"Because if you enjoy it, then you'll have credibility."

I wondered how much my father knew about being someone else. I couldn't help but return to the topic of his dating, and a question I wanted to ask. "Is Cassandra, Mom's friend, one of those people who thinks, and likes, that you're slow to love?"

A couple beats went by. "She is, in fact."

"You felt okay having Mom set you up with her?"

He put down his fork. Paused. "I did, in fact."

"Huh," I said. The wonders never ceased with my parents. "You know, Dad, anyone would be lucky to go out with you."

He had been picking at his scramble, lifting up pieces of vegetables and inspecting them. He put his fork down and looked at me. "Thank you."

"Sure."

Stirring brown sugar into my oatmeal, I noticed he'd stopped talking, hadn't continued with his food. I looked up at him. I wanted to ask him if he was still considering leaving Chicago, but I didn't want to press him too much.

"Thank you, Isabel," he said again. "Very much."

And that was all I needed to hear for now.

35

A few days later, I got out of a cab on Hubbard Street, right behind another cab that happened to hold Madeline Saga. I handed my cabbie a bunch of money, told him to keep the change and then said I'd be sitting in the cab for a minute or two. I had to watch Madeline closely, and I didn't want to get into the club before her.

I had thought about bringing Jeremy, someone I could talk to. But I had the distinct feeling that I would want to kiss him.

I liked kissing him. I couldn't imagine doing anything else with him because I hadn't ruled him out as the source of the forgeries. But the kissing was great. I also needed to keep an eye on Madeline. Plus, Jeremy had told me that he was seeing the Fex tonight to discuss custodial arrangements and 'more financial bullshit.' Things, if they had been amicable, didn't seem to be so any more.

Madeline must have been paying with a credit card in her cab or getting change, because it took her a moment to get out. We'd already been to the gallery opening, where I stood far apart from Madeline, watched her work the room. There was no one obviously following her.

I glanced out the cab window at the brick building painted black. The club took up the top two floors. Through the snow that was starting to come down, I saw red lights flashing from those floors. When I opened the car door, I heard the music pulsing from within.

I saw Madeline get out of her cab, wearing a blue fur over a black dress. She was stopped by a guy I'd seen at the opening. They began talking.

"Can I hang here just another minute?" I asked the cab driver. He nodded, apparently pleased with my tip.

I watched Madeline and the guy talk. He didn't seem threatening. If I remembered correctly from meeting him at the opening, he was an interior designer. A man came up to them and the designer introduced Madeline. The three of them stood under the outdoor heat lamps and seemed in no hurry to get inside, so I sat back in the cab seat. And I couldn't help it—I played with my hair. My new blond hair.

I'd refused to cut and dye my hair the way Mayburn had wanted me to. *Are you insane?* Lucy had said when she'd overheard. *Izzy McNeil does not color that red hair!*

So I'd gone to a stylist recommended by my mom, who'd custom-fitted me with a wig that was white-blond, chin length and wispy.

In order to complete my transformation as someone who was...well, someone who was simply not me, I'd bought a dress I probably would never have worn before—a thin, yellow sweater dress with a peek-a-boo cut-out over the chest. I wore it with camel patent-leather boots. It was all very seventies mod, and they seemed like blonde clothes.

Madeline's eyes had gone big when she spotted me at the gallery opening. I saw her smiling as she turned away. And the time or two I caught her glancing at me, she was beaming. I think she saw me as a changing art installation.

It had been hard to keep an eye on Madeline, though, because my new blond self kept getting hit on by men who would never had noticed me before—Euro types, hipsters in skinny jeans. I had no idea what kind of slogan they were reading from me as a blonde—*Easy but not cheap?*—but in the hour we were at the opening, one of the guys had offered to buy me a featured sculpture—a graphite hand that was part silver, part black with colored finger nails. I hadn't liked the sculpture very much (and I knew that it would freak me out if it lived in my house) so it was easy to say no. When I got a look at a price list, I almost choked on my champagne. Thirteen thousand dollars.

"Hey, ya using this cab?" It was a bouncer from the club, opening my taxi door farther and gesturing for me to get out.

"Yes, I am using it. I'll just be a minute."

Madeline was accepting a business card from the second guy, and again, they didn't seem in a hurry to move.

The bouncer pulled the cab door open more. "Let's go, lady."

"'Let's go, lady?'" I repeated, my blond hair making me feel a little frostier than usual. "I have paid this gentleman—" I held my hand toward the cab driver "—to wait for one moment."

The driver smiled and nodded.

"One." The bouncer held up his index finger. "There.

Your one moment is up. I got customers I have to put in this cab if you're not using it."

"*I'm* about to be one of your customers," the blonde said.

"That remains to be seen."

I huffed. Or the blonde did. One of us was really pissed off.

I started arguing with the bouncer, using legal terminology to explain the concept of sales transactions as they pertained to my paid use of the cab. I was no dumb blonde.

But then I looked away from him. And Madeline wasn't there.

"It's all yours," I said, stepping out of the cab.

I hurried toward the club door. No sign of Madeline. The club had to be reached by elevators, and yet no one was at the elevator bay. Clearly, she had already gone upstairs.

Another bouncer inside studied my ID intently. "This is you?"

"Of course," I said, somewhat distractedly, hoping to nonchalantly draw him away from the fact that the person in the ID had deep orange-red hair. "Hey, I have a question for you," I said. "What floor is the entrance to the club? Three, right?"

"Or four," the bouncer said. "Doesn't matter. There's entrances on both."

"Damn." *How was I supposed to tail Madeline if I didn't know where she was?*

"Damn what?" the bouncer said.

"What?"

"What are you saying 'damn' for?"

"What is this, church?" Geez, the blonde was sassy. "I'll talk how I want."

The bouncer frowned. Waited. Then finally, slowly, he handed me my ID.

"Thanks." I snatched it from him and half jogged to the elevator, wanting to see if I could read the display that indicated the floor where the elevator had stopped.

Right then, though, the elevator dinged and the door opened. I dodged inside.

"Hey, there's a fifteen dollar cover!" I heard the bouncer say.

"I'll get you on the way down!" the blonde yelled, right as the elevator doors closed.

36

I got off at the third floor, and thankfully I saw Madeline immediately, still with the two guys she had been speaking with outside. The designer held her blue fur coat over his arm, looking gallant.

I ordered a club soda with lime and made my way around the place, all the while keeping an eye on Madeline. The place was dark, sexily lit with candelabras, filled with little conversation nooks and crannies.

After the second round about the premises, a bartender signaled at me. I went up to the bar.

He pushed a martini glass across the bar. "Your friend said to give you this."

I sipped it. "A lychee martini?"

The bartender nodded. I turned and found Madeline with my eyes. She was sitting at a high-top table now, with the original two guys plus three others. She glanced at me and winked. Then she nodded at the dance floor in front of her, as if to say, *Think about getting out there.*

I made mental notes about each of the guys she spoke with, utilizing the way I'd seen witnesses and suspects described in the police records that had become a part of my legal world. *Male, light brown com-*

plexion, eyes brown, short hair. And *Male, Caucasian, eyes blue, hair gray* and so on.

The lychee martini slid down nicely, and Madeline was sitting tight, so I could scan the crowd for anyone who was watching her, as well. No one stuck out.

I took a few steps back and ordered another martini from the bartender. When he delivered it, I took it to the edge of the dance floor on my side of the room, looking around, checking out the DJ, dissecting the group of girls now behind Madeline. *Female, dark complexion, eyes green, hair—braids.* But no one I saw seemed to be super aware of anything but their own fun at that moment.

The second martini went down smoothly, perhaps too much so. The blonde started to sway her hips to the music. This soon drew a few guys my way. They were all very cute, all seemed very nice, but if I paid attention to them, I wouldn't be able to do the same for Madeline.

To get a little privacy, I stepped onto the dance floor, made my way about ten feet forward, past a few people. I was far enough from Madeline to observe her and those around her.

I swayed my hips some more, but I must have looked mechanical because Madeline glanced my way, frowned and made a show of taking a deep breath in, then letting it out, then nodding her head my way. *Try it. Relax. Enjoy.*

So I did. I closed my eyes, and I breathed. Then I did it again. And again.

The music pulsed around me; it pushed and pulled me, that's what it felt like, suddenly. I let my head fall back, but I kept my eyes closed, and inside my lids

I saw red lights that spun, sparklike, over the room, breaking up before they hit anyone on the dance floor. Before anyone could feel them. Except for maybe me.

I liked this blond thing. I liked how my hair was like white light, wispy. Without my heavy, long curls, I felt free to take in more, something I'd been doing since I'd met Madeline—more emotion, more desire, more everything.

I sensed a shift in the crowd, sensed I had been given more room. I heard Madeline's message again—*relax*—and so I kept trying. I let my arms fall out from my sides, let them arc as I spun more.

"That's enough." The harsh words jarred me, the voice even more so.

I stopped, felt the wisps of light hair hit my face and then settle on my neck.

His eyes bore a disappointed—or was it disgusted?—tinge. I felt a wave of shame, but then pushed it away. I would not be shamed by this man. Oh, no.

As if to steal some power from her, I gazed across the room.

But Madeline was gone.

"Let me guess," Detective Vaughn said. "You had a friend who was here, and now she's gone. Again."

"She is here." I looked around. Didn't see her. "I was watching her, because we're pretty sure someone is following her, and…"

I was relieved, despite myself, when I glanced at him again and saw that the potential disgust disappeared from his features. But then Vaughn frowned. Deeply. More disgust? Or just confused disappointment? Both?

"Did you pay to get in here?" he asked. Vaughn crossed his arms.

"I came with my friend," I said.

"There's still a charge."

"What are you, a bouncer now?"

Vaughn uncurled his arms. He wore his gray coat and jeans rather than his usual khakis, along with black snow boots.

"Turn around," Vaughn said. "Hands behind your back."

"Excuse me?" My tone was indignant.

He repeated his words. "Turn around. Hands behind your back."

I still couldn't read the expression on his face. He was frowning, that much was clear.

"Fine," he said. "I'll do you favor and cuff you in the front."

I felt something cool against a wrist. I looked down, saw something silver, heard someone say in my mind say, *Handcuffs? Really? A little much, don't you think?*

But no sarcastic or other actual voice came out of my mouth. And so I was wordless as Vaughn and I both stared at my hands, as he finished one motion—*click*—then another. *Click, click.* Our eyes met. He looked surprised or maybe regretful. I almost thought he was going to apologize to me, but then he led me out.

37

The police?

Yes, an officer apparently, because the man was flashing a badge. Then flashing handcuffs.

Was it cracking apart—this life. (This *was* a life, wasn't it?)

Had revenge gone too far? Were the police in on it?

But no, he was handcuffing the redhead. He was taking her outside.

And that's when a wonderful realization hit—Madeline was alone.

38

It had been snowing—thick, fast snow—when Vaughn and I had first gotten in the car. Now, as we headed down Western Avenue, outside was a blur of white, the snow pelting the windows of the car.

"I *have* to find Madeline," I said.

He ignored me.

"Vaughn, seriously. Someone has been following her. As a cop, you should be helping me."

Still nothing.

"Give me back my cellphone," I said.

"Can't. Protocol."

"Don't be a jackass."

He glared in the rearview mirror. "Say that again and I'll book you for something else."

I was about to ask what in the hell he was doing, when sirens screamed and a snowplow barreled through the street, making way for two ambulances.

The night was veering away from me, the situation hard to process. Although I'd been questioned by the cops before, although Vaughn had had me in the back of his car recently, I'd never actually imagined myself being arrested. Not ever.

And what of Madeline?

The blonde wanted to give him a piece of her mind, but more sirens, more plows barreling and then a fire truck.

What is happening?

I bit my lip. Stayed quiet for a few minutes.

"Goddamn it!" Vaughn said, smacking his dashboard.

"What are *you* all worked up about?" I said.

"Shit," Vaughn said.

"What?"

"Shit."

I looked outside, saw drifts of snow collecting along the street.

"I don't know if we're going to make it," Vaughn said, almost as if he were talking to himself.

Vaughn turned onto a side street to avoid hitting cars that were starting to get stuck in drifts. "Shit," he said again.

The side street was narrow and covered with more drifts.

"It's a one way," my blonde said, unable to help herself. "You're going the wrong way."

Vaughn said nothing, and somehow I could feel his stress pouring through the hole in the safety glass between the front and back seats. There was no point in trying to get him to help me find Madeline until he calmed down.

"So," I said, trying a nicer tone. "Are we supposed to get a lot of this stuff?" Outside the window, snow pounded harder. It began to be difficult to make out the homes on the sides of the road.

Vaughn lifted his chin, moving his face toward his

rearview mirror, so I could see his irritated expression. "You fucking kidding me? There's a blizzard coming."

"Right. Snowmageddon. Well, if there's a blizzard coming, why are you out picking me up from a night-club for… What was it again that you're charging me with?" I said this somewhat nonchalantly, but frankly I was scared suddenly.

"Why am I picking you up?" Vaughn said with scorn. "Because you're getting in trouble. Because you have to turn this ship around."

"Turn this ship around?" I repeated incredulously. "What does that even mean? And more importantly, why are you captain? Or first mate?" And the blonde was back.

"Did you pay to get in that place?" he asked.

"I came with my friend," I said. "The one who's missing."

"There was still a charge."

"Are you seriously arresting me for not paying a fifteen dollar cover?"

Nothing from Vaughn.

"Why do you even care?"

Still no comment.

"Well?" I said, leaning toward the safety glass and angling my mouth toward the talking piece. "Well?"

I was about to demand that he stop the car and let me out. I was about to argue that he had no cause to arrest me (although I could probably make an argument for the other side of that, as well). I was about to tell him again that I *had* to find Madeline. But then the car stopped.

I looked through the front windshield. It was hard to see with all the snow, but I could feel what happened. The car had stopped. We were stuck.

39

Minutes—very slow minutes—passed. Minutes that consisted of Vaughn swearing, hurling himself out of the squad car and into the storm, and scooping at the tires with a tiny shovel that looked a lot like a kid's toy, which he had unearthed from the glove box.

Vaughn stomped around the squad car and rocked it back and forth. He had had enough decency to take the handcuffs from my wrists, and so now I sat inside, worrying about Madeline, watching Vaughn. Every time he glanced at me, he scowled more.

He got back inside muttering, "Fuck, fuck. *Fuck*."

"For a police officer in the city of Chicago," the blonde said, "you are remarkably ill-equipped to handle this situation."

He said nothing, which just ratcheted up the blonde's desire to tweak him. "Seriously," I said. "That shovel? Or whatever you call it? Was that issued by the department?"

"My partner always handled the weather."

"That big guy?" I thought of the first time I met Vaughn—in my law office, after Sam disappeared—and how his partner then was a tall man with hands as big as catcher's mitts.

"Yeah."

"So where is he?"

"Budget cuts."

"And yet, with all the budget cuts, you're spending your crime-fighting time on this? Really?"

Apparently, Vaughn was done talking about that. He rubbed his hands in front of the heater, then left the car again.

I peered through the window, through the snow, as Vaughn made his way around the car, trying to dig out the wheels of the car with his gloved hands now.

He got back in.

"I want my phone call," I said to him.

He turned around, scowling. "What are you talking about?"

"I want my phone call."

"You'll get your phone call when you get to the station."

"But clearly you can't *get* me to the station." I held out my hand. "So I want my cellphone back."

He took my phone out of his jacket and handed it to me.

40

Madeline got into bed, shivering. *Where was Izzy?*

At first, it had seemed fun. The opening, the club, seeing Izzy as an exquisite, sexy blond. She could tell Izzy was serious, on the job. But it seemed apparent after a few hours, by the time they reached the club, that no one was following her. And so Madeline began to send Izzy signals to go ahead and enjoy, breathe into it. Eventually, Izzy had danced, and watching her turn into someone else on that dance floor was a delight.

But when she looked back again, Izzy wasn't there. Initially, she'd chuckled. Maybe Izzy was playfully getting her revenge, getting back at her for the time Madeline herself had disappeared from the club. But that was crazy. Izzy wasn't like that.

And that's when she saw across the room—a guy about forty leading Izzy out of the room. In handcuffs.

She'd run outside, just in time to see him put her in a car.

She stood there shivering, not knowing what to do. Her purse and her coat were inside. After a few minutes there was no sign of Izzy's return, making her feel increasingly vulnerable, alone. She called her, but got no answer. She went into the bar, retrieved her things quickly.

Back outside, she saw the snow coming down harder. She decided to go home while she still could.

She found a cab, and thankfully, made it to her apartment. When she reached her bed, she was exhausted. From all of it—from the forgeries and the emails and the comments and the letter and the knife sculpture. She had never been a worrier. She realized now she had never before had anything to truly worry about.

She shivered in bed, the exhaustion building until she finally fell sleep. Her dreams were strange— so strange that she tried to wake herself up, but she couldn't.

In one dream, she was like the painting in her gallery—one woman, but two different versions. Then, the dream shifted and instead of seeing the two Madelines side by side, as in the painting, Madeline instead saw the doorway of her bedroom open, saw a version of herself standing there. She stared. Her alter ego stared back, and the delusional dream moment lasted an eternity.

At first, their gazes felt comforting. But then the dream took on the quality of a nightmare. The self in the doorway was angry, her stare a sneer, and suddenly Madeline Saga was terrified.

It was then that she heard the sound, and it pierced the vision.

What? What was that?

Her cellphone. Grateful to wake, she gulped in air and grabbed it from her nightstand like a lifeline.

41

I heard a scrambling sound. Then a fierce whisper. "Hello?" Madeline said.

"It's Izzy."

Silence.

"Madeline, it's me. Izzy," I said louder.

"Izzy. Oh, God." Her voice was an even lower whisper now, but then she coughed. "I apologize, Isabel. I was…I was dreaming."

"Oh, I'm sorry to wake you up. You left the club okay?"

"When that cop led you out," Madeline said, her voice stronger now. "When I watched that police car pull away, it was awful."

I glared at Vaughn who was glaring out the window at the snow.

"You've become important to me, Izzy," she continued. I noticed that she'd called me "Izzy" twice now. "I've come to rely on you a great deal," she said, "but I don't think I realized it until I watched that police car."

"Thank you. I—"

"Shit," she said. It was the first time I'd heard her swear. "My cell battery is about to die, but—"

The call disconnected. I felt, suddenly, as if she had been about to say something important. *But what?*

I stared at the phone. I hit redial. It went right to voice mail.

"All right, you've had your call," Vaughn said, turning his torso around.

"I need another." I dialed Madeline's number. No answer. Just voice mail. I hit Redial again and again until Vaughn turned and snatched the cellphone from my hand.

"Hey!" I said.

But Vaughn ignored me and climbed out of the car. And once again started digging futilely at the snow.

42

Dear God, that had been close. So close. So close.
Too close?
No. No, never.

The feeling left over from seeing her tonight was more powerful than any before. There was only one thing to do that would douse this feeling. Go to the closet. Extract easel, canvas, palette. Then finally, pull out the Darger. Madeline's favorite Darger. She'd owned it for years, she'd told an interviewer for an art magazine. She'd always set the price astronomically high because she loved it so much.

But apparently, Madeline hadn't found the right place for it at the Michigan Avenue gallery, or maybe she couldn't bear to sell it, and so it had been languishing. Which meant there was more time with this one. More care could be taken with the reproduction; it could be made into a seduction rather than a race. But soon it would be ready to be returned to Madeline while the real one stayed.

Place the original Darger, depicting a group of pre-adolescent sisters, on another easel.

With every copied stroke, the enjoyment increased,

the reminder that creation was occurring and that creation would also take away something from Madeline, something she loved. Just as she deserved.

43

After refusing to let me call Mayburn, Vaughn got out of the squad car for another long stretch of time, waiting, he said, for "Garcia" to arrive.

Meanwhile, my mind ran around and around, but more and more often returned to Madeline. In particular, I kept snagging on the inheritance she'd recently told me about.

She'd told me that the inheritance had allowed her to open her first gallery in Chicago. Although she didn't say it, I got the feeling that the money could have opened a number of galleries in Chicago. Which suddenly made me wonder—shouldn't she just acknowledge the forgery situation, offer to have the rest of the art tested to ensure authenticity and then get on with it? It seemed suspicious, suddenly. But that was my lawyer side talking, not a budding art fan, and certainly not Madeline, who loved art and the gallery above all else, and wouldn't risk her reputation in that world by admitting to the forgery.

My bladder began asking to be relieved of the lychee martinis. I pounded on the window. Vaughn was standing in the slashing snow, staring at the back of the squad car like he might be able to figure something out. I tried pounding on the back window, but found it was actually an internal layer of safety glass.

"Mother hen in a basket!"

Nope. The fake swear words wouldn't cut it.

"Mother fucker!"

I turned back around and tried to calm myself.

What to do? I wondered. *When I had nothing to work with but my own mind.*

I'd been spending time at the gallery, listening to Madeline. One thing she she'd said was that art is anything that makes you shift your thinking from one plane to another, even if it's the smallest shift.

And so I wondered, *Could I shift my thinking? What would that feel like?* Immediately the answer came to me. *It would be easiest if we could get rid of this anger.* This was true. My irritation about Vaughn, which was the usual emotion I felt when he was around, was ramping up, boiling to make a cauldron of anger. And I really didn't like it. Anger had never done much good for me.

What's the opposite of anger? I thought. *Laughter?* But how could any of this—being stuck on a *really* uncomfortable plastic seat in the back of a squad car, having been arrested for I didn't know what, trapped in a blizzard, with *Vaughn*—be viewed as funny?

I decided to give Vaughn and his pointless attempt at snow management a musical soundtrack. I tried a screeching heavy metal song. Oops, that was the anger again.

I channeled Monty Python and hummed "Always Look on the Bright Side of Life." Nope. Couldn't go that far.

Then I thought of a Charlie Chaplin-like French

number I'd heard in a boutique last week. And it stuck.
I kept humming.

The song had so much whimsy that as I watched
Vaughn, as he paced back and forth along the car, peering at one tire after the other, my mood began to shift.

By the time Vaughn slid back into the front seat,
clapping his gloved hands for warmth, I was smiling.
Genuinely.

He turned around and looked at me. "Why are you
such a whack-job lately?"

My good humor evaporated. "Whack-job?" I repeated with indignation. "Why would you say that?"

"Are you fucking kidding?" He turned around farther to face me. "You're in the back of a goddamned
police car, McNeil."

"I have been wrongfully accused! And inanely so,
I might add."

"Jesus, don't start…" He turned around.

I shifted on the hard plastic seat, trying to cross my
legs and gain some semblance of dignity.

"Honestly," he said, looking at me in the rearview
mirror. "What's going on with you? First, you're walking in a shitty neighborhood in the middle of the night,
acting like a pro. Then a short time later, you piss off
some bouncers and refuse to pay for admission."

"And let me guess? You're friends with the owner
of that bar, too?"

"Same owner. He owns about twelve bars in the
city."

I shrugged. Sighed again.

"Honestly," he said. "I want to know. What's going
on in your life lately?"

This was asked without scorn, with what sounded like actual curiosity. But still.

"I don't have time for chit-chat. I need to get out of here."

He gestured outside. "Not anytime soon."

His voice was even-keel. *Sounds like a shift of mental plane.*

"All right. Fine. What can I say? It's just been a little stressful dealing with my friend's situation. I'm about to take more responsibility at the law firm. And I'm dealing with a breakup."

I made myself stop then. No matter how he was acting, Vaughn wasn't the kind of guy to whom you made emotional confessions, and he already knew all this stuff.

But he surprised me. "Yeah." He held my gaze in the mirror. "I know how it is."

"So anyway," I said. "What were you saying about my whack-job status?"

He grunted. "Okay, fine, maybe that's not a nice way of saying it."

"And what would be the nice way?"

He paused, appeared to be thinking about it. "You seem a little lost when I've seen you lately."

"Both times have been late at night," I said, annoyed.

"Yeah, I know. It just seems like someone should be taking care of you."

His statement landed with a thud in the middle of the squad car.

I debating saying, *Thanks. In a weird way.* Or retort with an *I'm taking care of myself just fine, thanks,* but my circumstances seemed to rebut that.

"I'd like another phone call," I said to Vaughn, as if I hadn't asked before. "To someone different."

He shook his head, as if he just didn't know what to do with me.

Finally, he turned. "You know, you make it really hard."

"Really hard to what?"

"To help you."

"Help me? Is that what you're doing? I am trying to help a friend. A friend who might really need me right now, and you have me trapped in a squad car for a lousy fifteen dollar cover. How in the hell are you *helping* me?"

His mouth was a tense line, lips clamped together.

"Honestly," the blonde said, unable to help herself. "How are you helping me?"

"I'm trying to show you that you have to get your shit together."

"Excuse me?"

"Look, forget it. I shouldn't have even tried. I am a drama-free zone right now."

"You're a 'drama-free' zone?"

Now he faced me again. "Yeah. You don't see that? You don't *get* that?"

"No, I *don't* get it. All *you* do is bring drama to my life. To me, you're the Goodyear Blimp of drama."

Vaughn's face turned snarly. He opened his mouth to say something awful, I was sure, something biting. I steeled myself for his lambasting.

But Vaughn closed his mouth and something gurgled from his throat. A chuckle. Then it became a laugh. "Seriously?" he said, incredulous, still laughing. "The Goodyear Blimp of drama?"

I thought about it. "Did I take it too far?"

"Just a bit."

I cracked up. "It seemed like a good metaphor. You're so dramatic. You just hijack a situation and you hover over everything."

His laughter stopped. "That's how you see me?"

"Yeah, of course. I—" But my words trailed off. I suppose I hadn't seen Vaughn as so terrible *all* the time.

He turned around. The silence grew cold. I tried to think of something to shift the plane again

"Hey, look, you're a decent cop at heart, right? I know that."

Nothing. Why was it I wanted him to feel better?

"And you love your work, right?" I said. "That's great. You're one of those people who loves his job and that's why you're good at it, and…"

He turned around. The cold in his eyes stopped me. "I do not love my job. My divorce is too expensive to quit, and I got a kid starting college."

"A kid. *You?*"

"Yeah, me." His voice was aggravated. "Why do you have to say it like that?"

"I just don't see you as a father."

A heavy pause. I thought he might growl.

"Although I'm sure you're quite capable," I added. More weighty silence.

"Probably a very good father," I said. And I was surprised to find it feeling like I was speaking the truth. Vaughn might not be a walk in the park for me to deal with, but I suppose it would feel good to have someone like him have your back, to support you and discipline you and encourage you.

He took his cellphone out of his pocket and tried

a few numbers. "Garcia," he said. "Fucking finally. Where you been?" He paused maybe two seconds. "Yeah, I don't give a shit about that. I'm stuck." He glanced at me. "And I have an arrestee present."

The drama blimp appeared on the horizon.

"Good," Vaughn said. A beat went by. "Sooner!" he barked into the phone. He gave our address. "See you in fifteen."

He opened his glove compartment and began removing a messy array of department forms and going through them.

"Is that it?" I said. "We're done talking?"

"Yeah," Vaughn said. "Oh, yeah."

44

After her phone died, she thought she saw ghosts again. No, that wasn't exactly true. She felt them. So, in her dark apartment, the winds howling against her pre-war windows, Madeline Saga pulled on winter clothes and boots.

She put on a hat and a heavy coat. She hurried out into the snowy night, the wind even more furious and lashing outside, the snow falling heavier and faster.

She trudged through the knee-high snow. No one had yet shoveled the sidewalks in her Gold Coast neighborhood. But her destination wasn't far—just on the opposite side of LaSalle Street. If she could get there.

She looked behind her. But of course, no one was out on this night—not even the diehards who loved a good blizzard. And yet she felt as if someone were there. She knew, from the letter she'd gotten, that she was being followed. And then that dream. But when she looked, there was no one there. No one at all. It made her feel crazy.

Now the edges of paranoia cut deep, causing real heart palpitations, causing her stomach to want to reject anything inside it. Causing her to feel the ghosts.

It occurred to her then that she supposed she should

have expected this type of haunted feeling at some point in her life. Being adopted, after all, probably should have caused more soul-searching. She must have, she realized, demons. Ones she couldn't see or feel.

A loud horn sounded and Madeline stopped, gasping, her hand on her heart.

A snowplow hauled past her, driver leaning on the horn, almost hitting her. She couldn't believe she hadn't heard it coming.

Madeline panted. She looked behind her. The snow was even thicker. She could see even less.

She saw no one. But she could feel them.

She put her hands in her pockets to find her phone. She would call Izzy back. She would at least text her to report where she was.

But she'd forgotten her phone in her haste to get out of the house. And it was dead anyway.

Get away from the ghosts.

Madeline only wanted comfort from this disquieting evening, from the dreams. And after she had hung up with Izzy, she had craved more human comfort.

She crossed the street fast, arms wrapped over her chest, protecting her heart against…what? She didn't know.

When he opened his door, he wore white flannel pajama bottoms, a black T-shirt. His hair was tousled. He rubbed his eyes, then seemed to wake up. "Are you okay?"

She shook her head "no."

He stepped forward, encircling her with his arms and she squeezed him around the middle.

Having Izzy in her life had helped Madeline—being

near someone whom she liked very much, someone who knew what was happening.

But he would not only sympathize, he would understand the dilemma at every level.

So she told him everything, and when she got to the end of her tale—that someone was apparently following her, and she and Izzy had been trying to "smoke out" the person (as Mayburn had put it) but then she'd lost Izzy in the crowd, and she'd had the strangest dreams, and she felt jumbled and jarred. That she felt like ghosts were following her.

"You feel broken," he said.

She nodded. He knew.

She cried. And he held her.

45

When I woke, I wiped what felt like grit from my eyes and looked into the front seat. Vaughn was awake, chewing gum, his eyes flicking around.

He'd let me out of the car to pee in the snow, making me feel like a golden retriever in my blond wig. Once that was accomplished and Vaughn was cranking the heat, I'd found it surprisingly easy to sleep.

I glanced outside now and with the streetlights' glow, I could see that while I had napped, Vaughn had made additional attempts to clear some snow with the pathetic scraper/shovel instrument. The snow was slowing.

"Car still dead?" I asked. It had died half an hour or so ago, and it was beginning to get cold.

He shook his head tersely. "Fuckin' CPD cars—when these pieces of shit decide to go, they go."

We looked out the window. "How long have we been in here?" I asked.

"Couple hours."

I looked for more signs of irritation on his face, maybe even rage, but he looked...well, he looked rather chill. I suppose I shouldn't have been surprised. He was trained to be calm no matter what. It was just that whenever I was around, Vaughn always seemed short-tempered.

He put a headphone earpiece in his ear. He listened.

"What's going on?" I asked, when he'd taken it out.

"It's a shit storm. No. It's a *snow* shit storm. Lake Shore Drive is frozen over."

"Shut up."

"It is."

"No, it's not. There's no way."

He turned and glared. "The Drive is frozen. There are hundreds of cars frozen on Lake Shore Drive. And I can't be there. I can't help. I can't assist. I cannot report for duty."

Both of us sat in silence. Something occurred to me.

I opened my mouth, then closed it. I wondered whether raising the point that was poised in my mind would be right. One never knew with Vaughn.

Why the hell not raise it? The blonde was, apparently, back. "That's kind of a good thing, right?" I said to Vaughn.

He said nothing, didn't reply.

Might as well go all the way. "Because you don't like your job. And right now, you *can't* do your job. It's kind of a windfall if you think about it."

Vaughn looked at me. Both I and the blonde leaned back a little, unsure how this would go over.

"I know." He smiled. "Chew gum. That's what I've been thinking about. I've been just going over it all." He chewed his gum harder, faster.

"Can I have a piece of that gum?"

"Yeah, sure." He tossed one back at me. "It's what I do when I'm thinking. I like to pace, but obviously..." He waved a hand at the window.

"Anyway," he said, chewing, chewing. "I've been going over and over it all."

"Like what?"

And right then, Vaughn started talking.

Previously, I'd barely heard the guy utter more than a sentence or two at a time, even on the witness stand, but now he was talking—about how he usually spent his time at work, how he'd started in the business, what he liked and didn't. There were a lot more didn'ts. At the top of the list was the grunt work, which he said was what comprised most of his job.

"Ninety percent of the leads you get are dead ends," he told me. "And you wait for-fucking-ever to talk to someone, which is why I got this thing." He gestured at the dashboard, which was tricked out with an iPod dock and a state-of-the-art GPS. He'd used his own money, he said and he brought them in and out of the car every day. The new superintendent was apparently considering disallowing detectives to do that. Which was another thing that pissed him off.

As he said this, he shifted and I saw him gesture toward the gun in his holster.

"Do you like carrying a gun?" I asked.

He looked at me, sort of surprised. "Yeah. Ya gotta. At least it scares some people."

"Some?"

"You're not gonna scare the friggin' gangbangers. They've seen more shit than you and I could even imagine."

"So how do you handle them?"

Another shrug. "With respect. Everybody deserves that, no matter who you think they are or what you you think you did."

"Really?" I couldn't help but let some sarcasm seep out into that word.

"What?" he said.

"You didn't give me much respect when you came to question me that first time."

"You're not a friggin' gangbanger."

"But you just said, *everyone* and—"

"Forget it." He turned and he sighed, and that sigh contained all the heaviness in the world, all the frustrations with his job and the sadness I assumed he suffered from his divorce. "What I should have done with my life," he said, staring forward, "is be a lawyer. With all the experience I have, I might as well be an attorney right now."

"How do you figure?"

"I'm just saying. I get subpoenaed by lawyers like you, and I'm good."

"I was able—"

"Yeah, yeah," he said, cutting me off. "When you cross-examined me at trial, you got me to admit a few things. Whatever. But I know what's admissible, what isn't. If we're on the same side, you tell me something you want to get into evidence, and I'll find a way."

"You should go to law school."

"Nah."

"Why not?"

"Like I told you. I have an expensive divorce and a kid to put through college."

I thought about it. "You would be a good lawyer."

He didn't turn, but I felt a stillness, then heard a different tone enter his voice, one that was lighter, curious. "Really?"

"Yes, really."

"Thanks."

We heard a rap on the window. They were all steamed. Vaughn rolled his down. "Garcia!"

I felt a little sinking in my chest. I had, I realized, been enjoying talking with Vaughn.

But then the sinking went faster, held something heavier. Because I remembered what was happening— really happening—outside the reverse-snow-globe confines of the car.

I was supposed to be watching over Madeline. And yet I was being taken to Belmont Police Station.

46

The next morning, I immediately remembered Vaughn and the blizzard, and knew that I did not want to open my eyes. I reached down and felt for my clothing. My fingers touched the yellow sweater-dress. Yep, I was wearing the same clothes I'd gone out in. Not good.

I took a few deep breaths, not eager to start a day with a new low point—jail. I felt, at that moment, as if I were two different Izzys—the one who represented people who had been to jail, and now, the one who had firsthand knowledge of being arrested.

The fear was growing, and I really don't like fear. So I decided to get it over with.

I opened my eyes.

Vaughn.

I growled, closed my eyes, summoned my courage and opened them again.

And this time they opened wider and I saw Vaughn…in my condo? He was slumped in my favorite yellow-and-white chair, sleeping.

I stared at him. I remembered Vaughn arresting me, the blizzard, then Garcia and the snowplow that came to get us, and then…

It all came back with a rushing-river surge of relief.

Officer Garcia, a short, friendly guy, had talked to Vaughn, assessed the situation and told us they had bigger problems. Vaughn, he said, should get me home and get his ass "back to the station."

I was shocked to hear anyone talk to Vaughn like that. I didn't think he would take it. But either he was feeling kinder or he was realizing the storm was even more massive than he'd thought. After his car was jumped, we slowly drove home.

It was a strange time to be in Chicago, to drive through the city led by one of the few vehicles that moved. The blizzard had driven everyone inside. The convenience stores appeared depleted. Most of the bars and restaurants bore closed signs. Cars were stranded mid-street by the snow. The sidewalks were empty. And over it all, now that the snow had stopped, the moon shone for the first time in weeks—a full moon.

The snowplow guys told Detective Vaughn they would wait for him and lead him to the station, but he insisted that he would see me to my door and get himself to the station. The men looked a little concerned, looking at me as if to say, *You okay with this?*

I nodded. I knew that Vaughn didn't have any nefarious intent toward me. I now knew he just wanted to get out of work, like a third-grader wants to get out of school.

When he'd walked me up, I opened the door and turned. I actually started to thank him, like we were on some kind of forked-up date. When the truth was, he'd *arrested* me.

He saw that all in my face. He must have, because his words rushed in, one after another. "I'm really sorry, Izzy. I mean, technically, what you did, running past those bouncers without paying, is against the law. I had a right to arrest you."

"Uh-huh. And is that what you would usually do when your buddy, the bar owner, tells you about a problem like that? Do you usually arrest them without even speaking to them? Or does the bouncer just throw them out?"

A sheepish silence.

"Well, then." I turned and opened the door farther, then stepped inside and turned around, my body blocking the entrance.

"I really am sorry," he said. "I don't know why I do this...why I keep doing this to *you*." He shook his head glumly. "I don't know what's wrong with me."

I felt bad for him. He appeared sincerely confounded and also severely depressed. And on an impulse, I invited him in for a cup of tea.

We sat on the couch for about five minutes before I fell asleep again. I hadn't wanted to go to my bedroom and leave him out there alone. And, somehow, it didn't seem a bad thing to have Vaughn there, to have some protection from the fear for Madeline that had been growing, making me feel some of that old fear myself. I had been followed before. More than once. I knew *exactly* how it felt. And I was starting to feel it again. Whether it was sympathy pain for Madeline or actual instinct for myself, I didn't know.

Madeline! I sat up on the couch and grabbed my home phone. I took it into my bedroom, which was massively bright with new sun bouncing off all that snow. I called Madeline. Just as it had the night before, her phone went right to voice mail.

Minutes later, I was standing at my kitchen counter. I stared at Vaughn, his long legs stretched out and crossed, boots stacked one on top of the other. His face had slumped to his shoulder as he slept.

My cellphone, on the table in front of Vaughn, rang and he leaped to his feet.

I mean that literally—he went from slumped and sleeping, directly to standing and staring.

He seemed to assess the situation in one quick second. Then his body relaxed. He lifted the cellphone and handed it to me.

It was a 312 number I didn't recognize. "Hello?"

"Hi, it's Madeline."

"Where are you?"

"Not too far from your place, I think." She gave me an address on Goethe.

"Yeah, that's about four blocks from me."

"Can I come see you?"

"How are you going to get here? Isn't everything still snowed in? Are you okay?"

"I'm definitely okay. And they're getting it plowed now," Madeline said. And then she giggled. It was a delightful, unexpected sound. "I've got a ride, so to speak, so I can definitely get there."

"Then, sure."

"Great. I need to tell you something."

47

"You told Syd?" I demanded after Vaughn had left, Madeline had arrived and we had rehashed last night's craziness.

I had told her about getting arrested by Vaughn. Then she had told me about taking a cab home, her weird dreams, her walk to Syd's, feeling haunted by ghosts and how she'd spent the night with Syd. And how she'd told him everything—about the paintings being stolen, about someone betraying her and invading her gallery and about the paintings being forged. How she'd sold those paintings and how she, and her gallery, were barely hanging on by a string—a string that was someone else's to cut.

She was talking on and on, quickly.

"Let's go back to when we spoke on the phone," I said. "You were there one minute, and then you suddenly had to go."

Madeline nodded.

"I called you back over and over, and you never answered," I said.

"My battery went dead, and then I just wanted out of my house so badly that I forgot the phone. By the time I realized it, I was too far to go back."

She told me about how comforting it had been to tell Syd about the forgeries and have him understand. She told me how Syd had gotten her over to my house that morning. "He found a guy with a sled, and he paid him one hundred dollars to buy it, and he pulled me here. Can you believe that?"

"Hell, yes, I believe it. He's still in love with you."

This didn't seem to concern her. She readjusted her position on one of the counter stools. Compared to how gritty and exhausted I felt, Madeline looked refreshed, relieved.

"You really told Syd?" I asked.

"He's one of my best friends."

"Mayburn and I asked you not to mention this to anyone until we could start eliminating people."

"And you haven't eliminated Syd?" Madeline asked.

"Let me stop and ask you a question. Did you tell him I was working on the case, helping you to figure out who had done this?"

A pause. Then she nodded.

"So if it *was* him, the one who'd done all this, then you just tipped him off. Not only about yourself and the investigation, but about me."

She took a quick but deep breath. "I hadn't thought of it like that." Another breath as if adjusting. She nodded. "But Izzy, I know it will be okay. Because I believe in him."

"Well, I don't." I paused. "I can't yet," I said, revising. Something struck me. "Is that why you put us in the Pyramus together? So he could convince me that he wasn't part of the forgeries?"

"Are you saying that you discussed the forgeries in the pyramid?"

"No!" I said. "Of course not."

She studied my face. Was she trying to tell if I was being honest?

"I didn't," I insisted.

"Then, of course, I didn't pair you with Syd for any particular reason other than I think he is fascinating and wonderful, and I think the same of you."

I smiled. A little. "Thanks."

But it seemed to me that something had crawled between Madeline and me. Some kind of mistrust.

She was such an aware person, so creative, and at the same time, matter-of-fact. She called it like she saw it. And yet she was talking about her nights being filled with ghosts and dreams and ghosts inside of dreams. It was all sounding a little…well, iffy.

As if sensing my hesitation, Madeline changed the topic. "Oh, and I spoke with Axel Tredstone, sent him some pictures of you. And he wants to talk with you. If he likes you, he'll paint you the same day."

"Really?"

"Of course. You would be exquisite." Madeline turned and smiled my way. "Didn't you like creating yourself as a blonde last night?"

I put my hand to my head. Sometime last night, I'd pulled off my wig, which had grown heavy and itchy.

But I had to admit—I had liked being a blonde very much. I couldn't imagine going there on a regular basis, but I'd enjoyed last night (*before* getting arrested)—the feel of weightlessness, as if losing a version of myself, just for a little while.

"Do you think I'll get that same experience with Tredstone?" I asked Madeline.

"Oh, no. Better. Much better. You would be his canvas, his clean slate." She looked at her watch. "Izzy, will you come to the gallery with me today?"

"I am not going on a sled with Syd," I said.

Madeline laughed. "Syd's gone. He had plans to meet a friend."

I turned around and looked out the window over the kitchen sink. "Actually, I'm seeing cabs." And people shoveling and salting and a few kids in the playground tackling each other into the snow.

I turned back around to Madeline. "I thought you might leave the gallery closed, what with the storm."

"Oh, absolutely not," she said. "This is an incredible opportunity for us."

I noticed that I liked the way she said *us*.

"The hotels are all full to capacity," she continued, "because no one could get out by car or plane, and now it's Friday, so some people are staying. We should have a fair amount of traffic."

"Well, then all right." I took a breath. "I'm exhausted after spending the night on the plastic seat of a squad car, but I need to go over the shipping documents again." I growled. "Vaughn," I muttered. "What a jackwhistle."

Madeline raised one black eyebrow at the word.

"You know what?" I said. "Let's just call it like it is. He's a *jackass*. A real jackass."

She blinked. "And you are referring to…?"

"Vaughn again. The detective. Sorry, I was sort of talking to myself."

"Yes," she said, and a vaguely amused tone had entered her voice. "That's what I thought."

"You thought that I was talking to myself."

"No. I meant that I thought you were speaking of

the detective," she said with a small smile. She stood. "Shall we?"

I looked down at my dress. It showed no signs of wear. "Madeline," I said, standing, too. "I need you to keep in mind a few things about Syd. More than a few things, actually. Number one—he has keys to your gallery. Your new gallery, where your paintings may have been stolen from you. Unless you got the keys back from him last night?"

She shook her head, no, she hadn't gotten them back. I searched her face for signs of annoyance, found none.

"Number two," I continued, "Syd's name is *all over* those shipping manifests from when you moved art from your old gallery. He had access to pretty much every danger point—the removal of the art from the walls, the packing, the sitting, the shipping…."

Madeline held up a tiny hand. It struck me for a moment that her nails were perfectly painted—a blue-lavender color—as if she'd just had a manicure moments before. "Enough," Madeline said, stopping my near rant about Syd.

She looked at me with that Saga energy—*Go with me,* it said.

I picked up my coat from the hook on the back of the front door. "All right, then let's go," I said, hoping I wouldn't have to say, *I told you so.*

48

Madeline was right. People were in and out of the gallery all day. The sun was so bright against the mounds of new snow that we were constantly squinting and moving paintings around. Often I noticed that orange-ish flash outside, one I'd noticed when I first started working.

We moved a sculpture that Madeline was concerned would not fare well with any sunlight into the back room. After we'd carried it together and put it next to the file cabinet, the ding of the front door sounded.

"I'll get it," I said to Madeline. Over the past few weeks, I'd been trying, whenever possible, to do the things a real gallery assistant would do. And now that Madeline had just tipped off one of our biggest suspects, I needed to understand the art world even more.

Stepping through the front door was a woman—petite, with lustrous, brown hair to her shoulders, wearing fabulous boots and a long ivory coat. In short, she was gorgeous.

She stopped walking when she saw me.

"Ah," she said. "You must be Izzy Smith."

I crossed the room, and I held out my hand. "Yes. Welcome to the Madeline Saga Gallery."

She looked at my hand, then looked at me. She made no move to shake it. "I'm Corrine."

"Hi, nice to meet you."

Still she didn't shake my hand. "That's all you have to say?" Her tone was incredulous, her words a little louder. Like Madeline, she was a small woman with a big presence.

"Um…" *What was going on here?* I dropped my hand.

"Are you kidding?" she said. A hand went to her hip, her pretty face twisted into a snarl.

"Can we show you anything or are you just browsing?" I applauded my ability to dredge up a gallery-ish sounding question until I could get Madeline out here to see if she knew this woman.

But apparently, she was going to tell me. "Do you know who I *am?*"

"Umm…"

"I am Corrine *Breslin,*" she said, enunciating her last name.

And then I got it.

The Fex was in the house.

"It's nice to meet you," I said. "Have you been here before?" I thought it best to feign ignorance until I figured out the right way to handle this. "Any art work in particular that you're looking for?"

"I've already purchased a lot—a *lot*—of artwork from here."

"Oh. Great. Well." I clapped my hands together inanely. I'd had little experience in the world of married men and their exes, and I decided, right then, that I did not enjoy it. The energy that flowed from Corrine to me felt like seething fury, so I suppose *flowed*

was much too gentle a word. It was palpable. And a
tad scary.

I was grateful to hear the delicate *tap, tap, tap* of
Madeline's heels on the floor.

"Ah, Madeline!" Corrine said. "I'm glad to see you."
Corrine took a few steps closer so that she, Madeline
and I now formed a triangle in the middle of an already triangular gallery. "Madeline," she continued,
"I'm glad to see you, the woman who introduced my
husband—and he is *still* my husband—to *this*." She
waved at me dismissively.

"Didn't you initiate the divorce?" Madeline said.

So, I thought, *I guess there'll be no idle chit-chat.*

"Yes," Corinne said. "Technically, I did. But that
doesn't matter."

The two stared at each other. Madeline's gaze was
curious, and yet at the same time very calm and strong,
as if she could stay that way forever. Corrine, meanwhile, was squinting with anger.

Madeline stepped forward then and put a hand on
the Fex's arm. It seemed to be a comforting gesture, yet
I wouldn't have expected Corinne to take it. She took
a deep breath, though, and visibly calmed down. She
nodded at Madeline. Madeline had something about
her that was hypnotic to people, it seemed.

Madeline's phone vibrated. She reached in the
pocket of her black skirt, pulling it out. She looked
at the display, then quickly answered. "Axel, how are
you?"

She looked at me and held my eyes. Which made
Corinne look at me curiously.

"Tomorrow?" Madeline said. "Oh, that's right. I forgot you're going to the L.A. Art Show on Sunday." She listened, nodded. "Let me call you right back."

Madeline slipped the phone back in her pocket and looked at me. "Axel Tredstone wants to meet you. Tomorrow."

"Tomorrow?"

"He'll be on the west coast next week, then Germany. Gone a few months. And who knows where we…" Madeline swallowed. "Where we will all be in a few months." Madeline didn't seem the kind of person who contemplated the future often. She walked into each moment and lived it. But, apparently, the thought of the future had just scared her. Hypothetically—more than hypothetically, if we didn't figure out who was stalking her and stealing her work—her gallery could be closed in a few months.

Corrine Breslin took a step back and looked me up and down. "Axel Tredstone wants to paint you?"

"That's right," Madeline said.

The Fex didn't take her eyes off me. "Jeremy told me you did the Pyramus. Did you?"

"Yes," I said. "With Syd." I figured I might as well use Syd to my advantage when I could. From what I'd heard, he had a great reputation in the Chicago art world.

Corrine looked at Madeline, impressed. "*Syd,* as in your former assistant Syd?"

Madeline nodded.

Corinne looked back at me, a sort of musing expression on her face. "I'm surprised he didn't mention you to me."

"Are you close?" I asked.

"We're dear friends."

Oh, really? Suddenly a whole new array of suspects opened up. And maybe it wasn't just one person, maybe it was two. Both Corrine and Syd had reasons to steal and forge the artwork—Corrine to keep it for herself or maybe to screw over her husband. Syd to get back at Madeline for their breakup. Although it sounded like they were back together now, Syd seemed obsessed enough with Madeline to stalk her. If the emails and letters stopped now, would that implicate Syd?

"I will say—" Corinne continued "—and I'm not necessarily talking about you—but both Syd and my ex-husband have excellent taste."

I wondered, *Should I point it out or not?* The blonde in me decided to go for it. "You just called him your 'ex' husband..." I said. I let my words die off when no one responded. I looked from her to Madeline and back. Neither of them were moving, and for a moment I felt as if I had stepped into another art installation.

Corrine Breslin blinked fast, and something changed on her face. Then she burst out laughing. "Oh, my God, you're right." She smiled. Her attitude toward me was suddenly different. "*Thank* you," she said. I liked her a little then.

The phone rang in Madeline's office. "Excuse me," Madeline said, "I need to take that." She looked at me. When I nodded that I could take over, she turned toward her office.

"I apologize, Izzy," Corrine said. "Let's start over. So what's new around this place?" Corrine glanced around the gallery.

"Well, we got this sculpture in this week." I led her to the other side of the room.

The sculpture itself was inside one of the large plate

windows. Unlike the one we'd moved, Madeline had placed it there for a sunny day just like today so the light could hit the yellow glass tiles of the sculpture.

As we neared it, I blinked at the sun coming in. Outside, I saw, again, a glimpse of orange. Maybe a security guard wearing an orange Bears scarf?

I told Corinne what I knew about the sculpture. The yellow tiles had been selected and placed in a particular pattern to represent a scientific idea. I also told her about the artist and his background in DNA science. "According to the artist, the tiles are like a cellular wall—light moves through them naturally."

"Yes," Corinne said. "And the bright yellow reminds me of youth and childhood."

We talked more about it, and I found I liked Corinne.

Twenty minutes later, she had a delivery date of next Friday for the sculpture. And I was elated.

When Corinne left, Madeline came back into the gallery. "Feel good? Your first sale."

"Yes!" For the first time, I truly felt a part of the art world.

Madeline was a tiny person, but she was strong. And she hugged with a ton of emotion. When we pulled away, she said, "So I have to call Axel back. Are you in for tomorrow?"

I didn't think about it this time. "I'll do it."

49

Madeline had her Japanese weaving class on Fridays, so she headed there after she closed the gallery.

At home, I read about the blizzard on the computer, watched coverage of it on TV and cleaned my condo. As I did, I tried to mentally prepare myself for being painted by Axel Tredstone. But how in the hay was one supposed to do that?

I was running high on energy. I was still elated by my first art sale, and intrigued by the thought of working for—with?—Axel Tredstone. My emotions about that were equal parts of excitement and hesitancy. But my mind kept returning to Corinne Breslin.

And the question that had arisen when she first came into the store. *Could Corinne be the thief or the forger?*

I decided to drop Corinne for a moment and rewind all I'd been learning. I'd been assuming that the art was stolen during the move from one gallery to the other at any time. There were just so many danger points, so many ways the heists could have gone down. As a second thought, I'd been considering someone who had access to either of the galleries. Madeline had confirmed that Syd was the only one who had had keys to both. At the old gallery, some construction people might have had keys, or some artists working on installations, but Madeline was pretty sure those keys had been returned. No matter what Madeline thought, Syd was still high atop my list.

Jeremy was also on that list. I'd been doing research on the black market for art, and it was clear that identities were protected and the money was huge. Jeremy had mentioned money a number of times—money Corinne was insisting he give her. Having the paintings forged, and allowing the forgeries to be discovered, would allow him to pay Corinne less and sell the pieces on the black market.

But what if it was Corinne? What if she'd had those paintings forged before Jeremy took them in for appraisal? What if she'd been planning to get divorced and had arranged for the paintings to be taken from the house, faked and replaced? Or what if she realized that money was going to be an issue in their divorce and had them copied after they began splitting up? Madeline had said that Corinne initiated the divorce. What if she'd planned the timing to allow her to forge the art?

She would have needed assistance, though, if she wasn't an artist herself. Which brought me back to Syd. And then someone else's name appeared—Margie Scott. The art moving specialist.

I found her name on the internet and called. I figured I'd leave a message and try to meet with her next week to see what I could find out. I was surprised when the phone was answered quickly.

"Margie Scott," a low, serene voice said.

"Oh, hello. This is…" I hadn't even planned out a fake name yet. "Isabel Hollings." That would have been my name now if I'd married Sam. I'd tried it on so often, that even though we were no longer together, it rolled off the tongue.

I told Margie that I was moving, from a Gold Coast apartment to an Uptown home, and needed assistance moving my art.

"Of course," she said. She described the process she went through to assist in moving art from one residence to another. "We'll even install for you in your new home," she said. "Now, how many pieces are we talking about?"

Shazzer. I should have thought about this before I jumped into it. If I gave too high a number she might wonder why she hadn't met such a collector. If I gave too low a number she might tell me she didn't do that size job.

"About twenty," I said, taking a stab.

She murmured, "Okay, okay." Then, "What type of art or artists?"

Shazzer again. I dredged up a few artists I knew from Madeline's gallery. "I received your name from Madeline Saga actually." I threw that in for good measure.

"Oh, Madeline," she said in a happy-sounding voice. "She's wonderful. Such a pro."

I decided to throw out another name. "I believe Corinne Breslin also mentioned you."

"Hmm. I don't recall her. But we've done so many jobs."

"Of course." I asked if we could meet the next week, and within minutes, I had an appointment for Tuesday morning.

I got off the phone, my mind returning to Corinne. Margie Scott didn't know her, but Jeremy had said that

Corinne knew the art world well, and that was clear from my dealings with her that day. If she was responsible for the forgeries, she could have had her ear to the ground. And she said she was dear friends with Syd, who now knew my real identity.

Could Corinne Breslin have heard about me being a part-time private investigator? Was that why she came into the gallery today, using my date with her husband as a ruse?

The thought didn't sit well.

And I didn't sleep well that night.

When I got up the next morning, before I headed to Axel Tredstone's studio, I knew who to call for help. "Mags," I said when she answered. "I'm coming over."

"Come in, come in," Maggie said, opening the door to her high-rise apartment. From down the hallway, I heard a full, soulful sound. I cocked my head that way. "Is that Bernard practicing?"

She nodded. Bernard played the French horn for the Chicago Symphony.

"It's beautiful."

"Yeah, well." Maggie rolled her eyes. "It's not that beautiful when you have to hear it all the time. We'll soundproof the room eventually, but in the meantime, sometimes I think I'm losing my mind."

A haunting yet lovely note snuck down the hallway, then grew louder.

We went into her kitchen. "You're still not drinking coffee?" she asked over her shoulder.

"Actually, I'm dabbling," I said.

"Good." She poured me a cup, then put sugar and milk in front of me. "It's decaf."

"Pregnancy thing?"

"Yeah." She sighed, leaning against the counter. "And you cannot believe all the physical stuff that happens when you're doing this." She pointed at her belly. "I'm a human science experience. I can't believe women have been doing this forever. It's freaky!"

Maggie's face was growing animated, and it made me laugh.

"Seriously, Iz," she said. *"Seriously."*

She held up her hands. She looked like a stand-up comedian about to tell the best part of the bit. "I woke up the other night, middle of the night, and I forgot I was pregnant, you know? I was half asleep, and I thought I was the old Maggie. And then I heard this snore, and I looked around and my first thought was, *Holy shit, there's a huge Asian guy in my bed.* But you know, that happens all the time, that's not necessarily pregnancy related. My brain still doesn't always realize right away Bernard is here."

I leaned back on Maggie's counter, ready for the rest of the story. I *loved* Maggie's stories. It was like actually being in her life. The way she told them made you feel you were down the hallway, in the middle of last night, waking up to your new boyfriend, a big Filipino French horn player who'd gotten you pregnant quite quickly.

Ten minutes later, she ended with, "Only then did I remember I was pregnant. I had completely forgotten while I was sleeping!"

I was laughing again, imagining tiny Mags, naked in her bathroom, shocked at her swollen belly.

"Aside from that, how do you feel being pregnant, about to be a mom?"

We both fell silent at that.

"A *mom*," I repeated.

"I know. Can you believe it?"

"I've always said you'd be a good mom."

"And I've always thought that. But now, it's just speeding toward me, and I don't know anymore. I'm realizing I really don't know anything!" She got up and poured herself another coffee. When she sat down again, she gave me a look I didn't see too often. One that said, *I'm nervous. Help.*

"Mags," I said. "You've helped your sisters raise their kids. You've been there for all of it, from the birth to the near teenagers."

"Yeah, but except for those first few weeks, I always got to go home to my bed. Ultimately, I wasn't responsible."

More silence.

"That is intense," I admitted. Maggie wouldn't accept clichéd platitudes from me.

"Right?" She nodded. "And my sisters have gone through it so long ago that they're all, 'Don't worry about it! No big deal!' But it is a big deal."

"You'll knock it out of the park."

"I'd settle for a single."

"Not a problem."

She looked at me plaintively. "You're sure?"

"Positive. And hey, you've got a friend who is both an associate *and* a babysitter."

"Thanks, Iz."

"So I've got a question for you. How's your bullshit detector?" I asked Maggie. "Is it off because the pregnancy?"

"No. It's better than ever," she said.

In their business as criminal defense lawyers, Maggie Bristol and her grandfather, Martin, had intensely investigated and ruthlessly cross-examined many detectives and prosecutors. They'd accused them (in addition to many other sins) of judging people based on hunches.

The truth was, Maggie believed in her own hunches just as much.

I told Maggie, as vaguely as I could, about Madeline's situation. I told her that an unnamed gallery might have unintentionally sold forged artwork, and the gallery owner had been followed. I told her some of the players, rounding around to the Fex. The title came in handy, since I wasn't using real names.

"So it's likely our client has had her work space invaded and the paintings stolen, then forged," I said.

"Or it happened somewhere in the moving process," Maggie said.

"Right. Or there could be something else going on altogether. For example, our client just told me she occasionally keeps artwork in her house if it hasn't sold yet but she believes that somewhere down the line it will. The internet comments and emails she's gotten might be from the thief or maybe not." I told her then about the difference in opinion as to whether the author of those comments and emails was female. Vaughn was sure it was. Mayburn, who knew more about the case as a whole, wasn't so certain.

Maggie blinked. I waited for some brilliant shot of insight. "Did you say Vaughn?" she asked. "As in Detective Damon Vaughn?"

"Yeah."

She shook her head, like, No. No. I can't believe that. Maggie knew my whole history with Vaughn.

I took a deep breath. "Yeah. And you won't believe what I have to tell you about him."

"Oh, I think I will. Nothing that asshole does would surprise me."

"He arrested me Friday night."

That one stopped even Maggie Bristol in her tracks.

50

When I got to Axel Tredstone's studio, I was distracted. I was still mulling over Maggie's pronouncement that I should watch out for the Fex, although Maggie didn't think Corinne had anything to do with the forgeries.

"Your basis for the opinion that the Fex isn't the thief?" I'd asked her, getting into witness examination mode.

"My gut. Isn't that what you wanted?"

More than anything, once she got over her shock, Maggie wanted to talk about Vaughn. She wanted to rail about Vaughn, and how awful he was, "like most cops." "They just decide what justice should look like," she said. "And then they put it into play. They're the judge *and* the jury."

I pointed out to her that she had essentially done the same thing by declaring the Fex someone to watch out for, but not someone who necessarily had committed the crime.

"Yeah!" she'd said. "That's a gut instinct. You're right! But I'm not about to go out and arrest someone over it."

"Technically, I did break the law by not paying the cover."

"That's not something you arrest someone over. Certainly not a member of the Illinois bar."

"His buddy owns the club."

"Why are you sticking up for him?"

"I have no idea."

Maggie waved her tiny arms in the air. "And then he gets you stuck in a blizzard!"

I had left the apartment a few minutes later, laughing, after Maggie had declared Vaughn an "immense and gaping asshole."

So when I arrived at Axel Tredstone's studio, I was in a good mood. It was large, with old hardwood floors, brick walls and black-painted ductwork overhead.

The first person I met was his assistant, a small guy dressed in skinny jeans and a studded leather belt who scurried around putting up lights and big shaded things on sticks, barely paying attention to me except to point me to another guy, the makeup artist.

"Hi, honey," the second guy said. He grabbed me and hugged me like we'd been friends for twenty years and he hadn't seen me in ten. "Sit here." He directed me to a high chair in front of a big mirror surrounded by lights. Next to that station was "the stand up area," as the makeup artist described it, where I could be painted while I stood.

"Okay," he said. "Now I'm going to base you."

"You're going to what?"

"I'm going to the lay down the base coat of paint." He raised a finger, then ran it through the air, pointing up and down the front of my body. "All at the direction of Axel, of course. And then he does the details, the creating."

"Okay," I said. It sounded reasonable enough.

He directed me to a modest, all-white bathroom, where I undressed. I felt…fine. A plain, white cotton robe hung there, and I put it on. I was surprised (and a little impressed) by my nonchalance.

But then Axel Tredstone arrived at the studio.

At first, the experience wasn't as strange as I'd anticipated. After working with Forester Pickett, my former client, and a lot of his compatriots, I found I communicated well with men in their fifties and sixties.

But Axel Tredstone was a rock-star/artist guy in his fifties. He had been graced with a lot of blondish-brown hair that crested back from his forehead and hung right below his ears. He grazed it with the fingers of one hand and tossed it to one side, a trait that was not without its charm.

He was lean. He dressed casually in jeans and an untucked shirt, with a jacket over that and a great crimson scarf, both of which he tossed over a chair as soon as he saw the makeup artist beginning to set up the base paints.

"Stop," he said to the makeup guy. "I need her."

Need. I rather liked the sound of that.

He was German, but he sported (if this were possible) a British-y/Chicago accent—lovely, at least to my ears. The photo assistant and makeup artist scattered, and Axel and I sat on two stools in a middle of an open studio, nothing else around, just me in a robe, no big deal.

Strangely, that's how it felt—casual. Normal.

"Tell me about you," he said. "Where were you born?"

And we were off. I talked and talked, and Axel listened. He was an inviting listener. Every reaction to my sentiments seemed not just authentic but thrilled. He actually appeared rejuvenated by my words, fascinated by me. And I wasn't even giving him the whole story. I left out my last name and the fact that I was an attorney. And that I was a part-time private investigator. I did mention—without facts or names—that my fiancé had taken off a few months before our wedding, that we'd patched things up but never gotten married and that I'd been in a relationship since then but that was over, as well.

"And yet *you* are not over," he said.

"What do you mean?"

"You haven't lost your spirit or your fight."

"No, of course not."

"Why do you say it like that?"

"Well, what else would I do but move on?" I looked around, as if searching. "Really, what else is there to do?"

He threw his head back and laughed, then raked his hands through his blond hair. "There are many things. I like that you choose to reinvent."

We talked for about an hour. He told me about his process, how he'd come to it.

Finally, he nodded, falling silent. "If you are, I think I'm ready to begin."

And now I was naked. I'd been base-painted black by the makeup person—deep black, Axel had said, which I found curious.

While that took place, there was still a lot of activity. Axel issued orders to his photo assistant in that slightly gravelly accent. The makeup person occasionally asked Axel about certain blacks he was using, which would affect later paint. For example, whether my right shoulder would be painted. And what about my quads? If so, what colors was he considering?

It was all done so quickly and with such a business-like manner, that I was surprised when the makeup artist, said, "Voilà," and pulled out a bunch of fans and a hair dryer.

And now, and now, and now…

And now Axel Tredstone was sitting in front of me on a stool, a palette of vivid colors in one hand, brush in the other. His brush touched me. I looked down at my breast. The dot was blue, like part of my arm, which boasted curls around the bicep, reminding me of Theo's tattoos. There was also blue on my belly, high on my ribs. Below that was a circle. A circle of flesh that Axel had achieved by washing off some of the black and painting a black tree in the circular space he'd created. It was as if I'd ingested the tree.

"Does that feel okay?" he said, in a distracted kind of voice, dabbing the paint on my nipple.

"Sure, sure." *What else to say?*

"I see a lot of blue in you."

"You do?"

"Yes. Not necessarily *blue* like you Americans say, like sadness. I don't find you sad."

I nodded. I didn't see myself as sad, either, at least not on a regular basis.

"I see blue as a mysterious color," Axel said. "I see you as having a lot of mystery."

"Hmm. Do you think that's because you simply don't know everything about my life?" *Like the fact that I'm investigating the invasion of Madeline Saga's gallery and the forging of her artwork?* I looked down at the peach-colored heart shape on my left shoulder. It struck me that this body painting was a kind of art that would be impossible to forge.

"No," Axel said. "It's true that I've only had the briefest amount of time with you, so of course, I don't know even a fraction of you. Yet, I believe you don't know everything about yourself, either."

That one stopped me. But he was right. I was discovering new things about myself all the time. My quickly changing life kept shifting things around, causing random revelations and never-before-imagined passions.

I had certainly never imagined being part of the art world before, not like Pyramus, not the gallery and certainly not like this. Axel kept painting my breast. A cloud was there now, blue and lit with white. A plain red banner ran over the other side of my chest and twisted past the tree on my stomach, and down my right leg. One of my feet resembled a tangle of vines, laden with green grapes. My other was still black.

"You seem like you know yourself very well," I said. "You know what art you want to create, what it means, who you will work with."

He paused, brush in the air, the tip now coated white. Then he laughed. "I don't feel that way."

"You don't?"

"Not most of the time. I worry that my artwork will begin to be viewed differently. I worry my best work is behind me."

I cleared my throat. "Excuse me, but you have your

paint brush on my, um, breast. Please don't say your best work is past you."

He laughed and laughed. So much, he had to put his palette down. He clapped his hands and looked at me. "No, this…" He drew a hand toward me. "This is going to be some of my very, very best."

He looked at me then. "You know *you* are an artist."

"How do you figure?"

He pointed to my face. "You had done your own makeup before you got here. I saw it. You did that makeup. You selected colors, determined how much or how little. You shaded, you blotted. You made certain aspects of your face stand out."

I thought about it. "I guess that's true."

He nodded, then pointed at my hair. "And you did this."

After the base painting was done, Axel had said he wanted my hair "massive and fiery."

Since I was always trying to tame my hair, I knew exactly what would pump it up. I'd teased and teased, and now it stood about six inches away from my head.

A comfortable pause. I smiled at him. We started talking again, and we didn't stop.

51

When it was over, it was a shock, as if a door had been opened fast, forcing cold to barrel inside. In reality, nothing about the studio or the physical surroundings had changed. But after finishing the painting, after Axel had been snapping with different cameras for two hours, it was simply over.

I said as much to Axel. "This is just the death of *this* particular experience," he replied. "At this point in time. That is all."

Still, a wave of sadness overcame me, then the feel of cold. Axel handed me a present wrapped in shiny silver paper. Inside was a thick, silk robe that bore a tag, *Made by hand in Germany.* The color was a burnt orange.

"I always get these for my subjects. But I've never bought this color. I chose this for you before I knew too much about you. Only what Madeline had told me on the phone. But I see now the color is perfect."

I thanked him and slipped it on. "The color *is* perfect. Funny that you didn't use this color at all in your painting." I waved a hand up and down my body.

"Too obvious."

We smiled at each other.

"So you have some options," Axel said to me. "We can take the paint off now or tomorrow or the next day. We can give you a special soap and you can do it yourself at home. Whatever you want."

Under the robe, I could still feel the paint, and strangely, I enjoyed it. Somewhere in the hours of the painting and the shoot, I had grown into the paint like a second skin. It felt like me—like all of me was represented in the images (even the parts, Axel had pointed out, that I didn't even realize I had).

I decided I wanted to show Madeline the painting. She was the one who had gotten me into this, after all.

I told Axel I'd take the soap home. Eventually, I went back into the restroom, took off the robe and put on the dress I'd worn to the studio. I slipped on my long, black cashmere coat and my boots. I pulled my hair back. However, my face was painted black, covered in tiny stars. It would have to go. Using Axel's soap, I took off the facial paint, then wound a scarf around my neck. When I was done, the body painting was completely covered.

Before I left, Axel stood in the doorway and faced me. "May I say something?" he asked.

I looked at him, nodded.

"You are all these things," he said, pointing to my body, referring to his painting. "You are all those things. And we must not be afraid of ourselves." He said "our" and "selves" distinctly like two separate words. "*You,* Izzy, should certainly never be afraid or ashamed or angry at yourself. You are remarkable."

"So are you," I said.

We hugged and I thanked him. It was one of those

goodbyes that might be the last or might be the beginning of many in a friendship.

Outside, the city was abuzz with activity—many people still digging cars out of the snow, others ready to let off stress, packed the bars and restaurants.

It took me a while to find a cab. Once inside, on the way to Madeline's gallery, I kept thinking of Axel's words. *We must not be afraid of our selves.*

When I reached the gallery, it was dark. I looked at my phone and realized that it was more than an hour after closing time.

"I didn't realized how late it was," I said to the security guard. He was there five nights a week. His brother took the other shifts. Because he was the evening guy, I didn't know him except to say hello and listen to talk about his wife's tamales (which sounded delicious).

"She just came back, actually," he said, jerking a thumb toward the gallery.

"Madeline? Oh, great. Thanks." I felt the paint then, and I wondered if he sensed something different in me, some shift, something lurking below the surface. But he just clicked the button under the desk to open the gallery door.

When I stepped inside the gallery, I saw a light in the back. I walked toward it, feeling strange and wonderful in the dark gallery—a painting myself.

When I reached the back room, Madeline was standing at the drawers where she kept various canvases. Unlike her usual daywear, Madeline was dressed in black jeans, black shirt and vest.

When she looked up, she seemed surprised to see me.

"I know it's after hours," I said, "but I just finished with Axel."

"Axel," she said, blinking.

"Axel Tredstone."

"Yes. Of course." She didn't seem as enthusiastic as before about my being painted.

"So anyway, I just wanted to thank you," I said. "It was such an incredible experience. I don't know what the final images will look like, but the process was… it was exquisite."

Madeline nodded. "Exquisite. That is good."

She said it in a flat way. I didn't know where her excitement for the project had gone. But then again, Madeline had more to worry about than her assistant's fun-and-sexy foray into body painting. Suddenly my impulse, to show her Axel's work, seemed silly and self-centered.

"Are you okay, Madeline?" I asked.

"Yes. I'm okay." She looked back at the drawer, avoiding my gaze. She was speaking a bit strangely, using few words.

"I'm sorry you're going through this, Madeline," I said. "I know the thefts and forgeries have been very painful for you."

Her eyes stared intently into mine now. "Painful. Yes."

"Well, let me know if you want to talk about it." I made my voice as welcoming as possible, but in truth, I was feeling the same way as I had when she told me she'd given Syd information about the forgeries and our investigation—like I had less faith in her than before.

She said nothing.

"I'll get going," I said.

She nodded. "Yes. I'll go soon, too."

52

The next morning, Sunday morning, I lounged in bed thinking about my time with Axel Tredstone. But often my thoughts returned to Madeline. *Was she cracking under the pressure? Was she all right?*

Yet, as I thought of her in her back room after hours, at the drawers where canvases were kept, that image kept striking me, or maybe it was that fact that she was in her gallery, after hours, with canvases that could be rolled up and easily taken away.

What if...what if...what if Madeline, herself, had something to do with the paintings going missing and being forged?

Maybe she needed money. Or maybe she loved art as much as Mayburn said she did, and she wanted to keep the real things for herself. I'd never even been to her home. It was near the lake, I knew, somewhere around Astor Street. Were the walls in those rooms laden with the most amazing collection of original art, stolen from her own gallery? What if the inheritance money was gone, or she had exaggerated the amount? Or made up the whole thing? Did she need money? If so, had she quickly rid herself of the originals on the black market?

I got up, padded into my kitchen and called Mayburn.

"It's not Saga," he said, even before I could get out my potential theories.

"No, listen to me." I laid out my thoughts.

"She absolutely does not need the money," he said. I kept talking.

He interrupted with a sigh, frustrated and, I sensed, disappointed in me. "I can't believe you don't see it," he said.

"See what?" I asked.

"That she would never do what you're saying. And I can't believe that you don't see her love for the art."

"I have seen it. And I wonder if it's so strong it could cause her to do something she wouldn't usually."

He said nothing. He didn't refute me. "I can tell you that she wouldn't send herself a sculpture of a knife in flesh, or whatever that shit was."

"Well, we know the sculpture was created by someone with talent, right? Madeline and Syd both said as much—that it required skill to make."

"So?" Mayburn said.

"So someone either commissioned it or made it."

"It's not…" He paused, and then that pause went on, as if he were seriously considering something. "It's not Saga."

I said nothing. I didn't have to. I'd heard the pause. And he had, too.

"Hang with her," he said. "As much as you can."

53

I called her cellphone.

"Okay," Madeline answered, without any other greeting. "Tell me about the shoot."

She sounded like her good mood was back.

"Feeling okay today?" I asked.

"Great," she said definitively.

She sounded so different from her remote mood of last night. I was happy to feel the connection I had thought was building between us again. I summarized the experience as best I could, and as she responded I felt excited, too, at being able to share the experience, especially with someone who understood it well. Maybe better than I did, myself.

"Are you still wearing the paint?" she asked.

"I am. I slept in the silk robe that Axel gave me and it doesn't seem to have rubbed away."

I thought about Mayburn telling me to spend as much time with Madeline as possible. I also thought about that pause of Mayburn's. What if this whole "investigation" Madeline had brought to him was an elaborate hoax to cover up the fact that she was the thief?

But aside from the suspicions that had slowly grown, I didn't need Mayburn telling me to hang out with Madeline. In fact, the more time I spent with her, the more I realized how much more I wanted to know about her. I really liked her.

"You really should see Axel's work," I said.

"I absolutely want to see it. Meet me at the gallery?"

The gallery was closed on Sunday, so I'd have time to talk with Madeline for a while.

"Sure," I said.

"I'll see you in an hour."

When I got there, Madeline was in the front of the gallery, and I could tell immediately that she was truly back in her usual form.

"Tell me all the details," she said. She was dressed in orange jeans, boots and a gray sweater. She was smiling. She asked question after question, wanting to know more about the painting and the shoot.

I had worn a long skirt with a sweater and my silk scarf. Finally, Madeline gestured at my outfit. "Are you going to show me?" Something about her voice was sultry, fun.

I laughed.

"You don't have to, you know," she said. "You really don't."

"I want to show you," I said. Living in the skin Axel had painted had grown more and more art. And maybe viewing it would draw out something in Madeline, something that would help me determine if she was part of the theft.

"Come on back," Madeline said.

In the back room, in the far left corner, was a green-lacquered screen that sometimes hid equipment and installation props. Madeline nodded at it.

I stepped behind the screen, moving aside a large,

round photography light. I slipped off my boots then my skirt. I pulled the sweater over my head. I hadn't worn a bra for fear it would rub off the paint. I had brought the robe from Axel, and I hung it over the screen.

When I was nude, I covered my painted breasts with one arm in a half-hearted show of modesty, then stepped from behind the screen.

Madeline turned. She gasped, her hands flying to her heart and took a few steps toward me. "This is some of his best work." She took my hand gently, and the movement seemed to cause my own hand and arm, those that covered my chest, to slowly unfurl from my body.

Madeline studied the arm she held, taking in everything. "These," she pointed at a series of lavender teardrops. I hadn't quite figured out what those meant. "These are..." She sighed, seemingly unable to find words.

She peered at the painted blue ribbons that wound around my biceps. "And these," she said, cocking her head. "Do these mean anything to you?"

I laughed. "I didn't tell Axel anything about him, but my boyfriend...ex-boyfriend...Theo—"

Madeline nodded. I'd mentioned Theo the first night we went out.

"Well, Theo had red ribbons tattooed on his biceps. It was one of the things that fascinated me about him."

Madeline shook her head in wonderment. "Theo is a part of you," she said.

I nodded. "He is."

Slowly she went through the other parts of Axel's painting—murmuring *brilliant* about the circle of flesh on my stomach and the black tree painted inside. She exclaimed over the vines on my foot, the peach heart on my left shoulder.

I pointed at that heart. "This color reminds me of the way the light sometimes comes in the studio. You know when it gives off orange-ish flashes."

"I *do* know what you mean. I thought I was the only one who noticed. It only started happening in the last few months."

"Maybe that's because you got your first snow at your new gallery, and it reflects the sun differently."

"Exactly," Madeline said, and I felt proud that I had contributed to the discussion.

Madeline took a step back. "Truly one of Axel's best works," she said, sighing happily. "How long are you going to keep the paint on?" she asked.

"I don't know. What's the protocol?"

"There isn't any. But you know..." Her voice was mischievous. "Some women have said they've left the paint on. *And* had sex."

I felt my eyebrows shoot to my forehead. "That would require the right kind of guy, I think."

"Yes, a worthy and interested recipient." She nodded. "What about Jeremy?"

I shook my head. "We're not there yet. And after Corinne's visit..." I told Madeline what I'd been thinking about yesterday, that maybe Corinne could have been the cause of the forgeries and thefts.

Madeline paused. For a long time. "Perhaps. We're not friends," she said. "She, not her husband, has been the driving force behind their purchases here. She has an excellent eye. But it was Jeremy I became friends with."

It struck me then that Corinne might have another

motive. "Do you think she was angry about your friendship with him?"

"I don't know." Madeline's brow furrowed. Her lips pursed. "On one hand, it would make me feel better if that were the case, because I'm under the impression that someone I know did this to me. And yet, as I told you, to my knowledge, *none* of my friends would do this."

But would you do it, Madeline?

Madeline shook her head, taking short, fast breaths. "Let's return to the topic at hand." She smiled, glanced up and down my body. "So Jeremy is out."

"Right. In addition to everything else, I wouldn't want to be wearing this—" I waved a hand up and down my body "—the first time I was intimate with someone." I noticed that I still felt entirely comfortable nude, discussing the paint on my body.

"I see what you mean," Madeline said. "The sex would be fabulous, but you'd never be able to get it out of your minds."

"Never. And it could be difficult to top. I mean, where do you go from there?"

"Yes, I see." We were both quiet for a second. "Theo?" she said. "Could you reach back into the past?"

"Theo would be *perfect*," I said. The idea of it was so powerful I almost swooned. I would have fantasy material for the rest of my life with that one. "But he's out of the country."

Out of habit, I thought of Sam and mentioned him. "But I don't think this is his thing," I told Madeline. "And we're not friends with benefits like some exes are." *Like you and Syd are.*

Then, for some bizarre reason, I thought of Vaughn.

Body art? Definitely—*definitely*—not his thing. And why was I even thinking about Vaughn in this context? Apparently, Axel's work had opened me to even more possibilities than I thought.

Madeline studied me again. She crouched and looked at a flag that covered one of my calves. She spent some time behind me, studying my back, most of which was covered with stars.

I checked in with myself to see if I was starting to feel awkward, but I felt nothing of the kind. One of the reasons for art—I'd learned from Madeline—was to open up your universe to those different planes. On me, Madeline was seeing something different, and in the act of her appreciating me, I was doing that, as well.

"It is too bad," she said, when she'd reached the front of me again. "That Theo is out of town."

"Oh, it is. It *really* is." I almost couldn't let myself think about what that experience would be like. I might self-combust.

"You do not seem angry," she said, "to have had him move away?"

"No. I understood why he had to move." I slid my arms back into the robe that Axel had given me as I talked, but left it open. I told Madeline more about Theo, that he was a wanderer right now, a seeker, moving from Australia to Thailand. I told her that he was an only child and mentioned that he'd been betrayed by his parents.

Madeline listened, very carefully, an ear sometimes leaning toward me as if to soak up my words as much as she could.

"He's been through a lot of things that are going to leave their mark," I said.

"Yes," Madeline said. "Of course. I loved my adopted parents very much. I am even glad that I did not grow up in Japan—I love America—but I have always felt something was missing. Always."

She stopped and looked at me. "But perhaps everyone feels that way as a child?"

I thought about it. I had grown up without my father, and yet I'd never felt that something was missing from *me*. I told Madeline as much.

"Now, my mom," I continued, "she always had this..."

"...this sense," Madeline finished for me. She nodded deeply.

"I don't know that Theo felt that missing element," I said.

"I not only knew something was missing," Madeline said, "but I felt betrayed by my Japanese parents, too. At least until the inheritance."

"What happened then?"

"That gift made me realize that I *was* someone who had mattered to my biological family. They just couldn't be with me when I was born."

"Yeah." I nodded. "I understand why my father left." I shrugged. "It's complex."

Madeline's mouth lifted in a small smile, her eyes meeting mine. They were deeply brown, but they had a ring of hazel. They were like pieces of art.

"Yes, Isabel," she said. "It's complexity you speak of. And you're right. I believe that we, as humans, have more capacity for this trait than we think. We have evolved to the point where, with practice, we are able to hold all those things—love, lack of trust, disgust, wild-eyed surprise and more—at the same time."

I thought about it. "I agree. But that's pretty hard."

She nodded again. "Of course. You must stay open."

I thought about that, too. "I keep parts of me open, I suppose. I love both Sam and Theo, for example, and yet if I look deep and I admit it, I am still a little angry at each of them."

"Precisely," she said. "It might have been easier to have shut Sam or Theo out of your life."

I nodded. "I could have just lopped them off, told both of them that I didn't want to speak to either of them."

"Like cutting off a big hunk of meat," Madeline said. "And with it so might have gone that anger."

We both paused then. I think we were both thinking of the sculpture with the knife in it that she'd received at the gallery.

"But it is so much more interesting to test the limits of what you can handle," Madeline said. "And so you chose the harder road, by staying open to experience. And yet that is the experience that, I hope for you, is more enjoyable."

I didn't have to think about it long. "Yes, that's true."

"You do not have to kill a part of your life in order to pass by it. Or enjoy another part of your life. In my estimation," she said, "tolerance is an honorable guest to have at the table in your world."

I smiled at her. I'd grown fond of the way Madeline spoke in images, fashioning them and other concepts from whatever raw material was around her.

She caught my smile and returned it. Once again, I could see who Mayburn had fallen in love with—a beautiful woman who, when she wanted, turned every bit of her energy onto you. And bathing in that felt good. It was an alive feeling—fierce but gentle, private but all-inclusive, as if you could somehow feel all of yourself, all of her. And really? All of everyone in the city at the same time.

Madeline glanced down for a second and a shiny pane of black hair swung over her face, momentarily hiding her from view.

She took a step toward me, one barely perceptible.

Even if I hadn't seen Madeline step closer to me, I would have felt the nearness of her. My body tingled suddenly, as if every cell had realized that we were here for a reason. For something special. Another step and another and suddenly Madeline was immediately in front of me. She was shorter than me, but wore high-heeled, patent-leather booties. And so we were nearly eye to eye.

What is happening here?

I closed my eyes for a moment, and felt Madeline's hair brush my cheek. It felt like the softest silk, the most fragile strands of life. She smelled exotic and delicate at the same time. I decided not to open my eyes.

The next thing I felt was her mouth. On mine.

54

I had never kissed a woman before.

I was used to men—men like Jeremy, who placed his hands on my face, bringing me to him. And Theo, who would use his own hands to raise me up as we kissed, my legs wrapping around his waist. But this kissing with Madeline? It was curious, young, fun, sweet, new. In a way, it felt like I did when I was thirteen and I kissed a boy for the first time in his parents' closet.

The experience had the same surreal qualities— *What is this? Is it really happening? Why?*

That last question was one I hadn't actually thought the first time I kissed a boy. That thought—*why?*—was only here. With Madeline.

Somehow we were drawn into the front room of the gallery. She kissed me again. Again, I had some ringing bell that said, *Why is this happening? Why now?*

I pulled back from her, looking at her face, wanting to be suspicious and yet feeling strangely comfortable, the way a dream is when you know it's just a dream and it's okay to enjoy it while it lasts.

And then the light shifted, introducing a tangerine color from outside. We both pulled back, a little surprised. We both turned and blinked at the window.

"That's it!" I said. "That's the orange flash of color we were talking about."

"Exactly," Madeline said. But then she frowned, peered. She moved quickly to the glass and put her hands and face to it. "Jacqueline?"

"Jacqueline?" I repeated, not knowing who or what she meant. Then, when it hit me, "Jacqueline Stoddard, the owner of the gallery across the street?"

Madeline nodded.

When I looked closer, it was apparent. Jacqueline Stoddard, wearing her orange-peach coat, was standing outside the gallery. She looked startled. She spun around.

That was when Madeline broke the spell, when she turned away from me and walked outside.

55

After Madeline went outside, I stood in the gallery, wearing only the robe, pulled closed now over the paint. Perhaps I didn't want the artwork to end. Perhaps I knew, as Axel Tredstone had described it, that this was the death of a particular experience.

But I could not get myself to the same point as Axel when he'd said, "At this point in time. That is all." It was harder to get my head around the thought that it was not something momentous.

For maybe five minutes, I watched Madeline and Jacqueline. I stood like a statue, as if I really were an art installation. I didn't move but I watched Madeline for SOS signals. She gave none.

She was, in fact, doing a lot of talking. Which, as a lawyer, made me nervous.

I ran into the back and threw on my clothes. When I returned, Madeline and Jacqueline were in the same positions, like two actors on the stage. Jacqueline occasionally shook her head.

I put on my coat and boots and went outside.

When I reached the two of them, they looked at me.

As if I'd been in the conversation all along, Madeline said, "Jacqueline admits that she's been...spending some time—" Madeline seemed to be choosing her words carefully "—outside of the gallery. My gallery. Watching us."

I glanced at Jacqueline.

Something like pain crossed her face.

I felt bad for her, felt empathy for whatever was causing that pain. And then, as if I'd moved to the next part of the installation, I suddenly knew something else about Jacqueline Stoddard.

"You wrote the comments," I said.

She kept shaking her head.

"The comments on Madeline's website."

She stopped shaking her head. She looked at me. Her eyes searched mine. They seemed to say, *Please understand.*

I nodded. *I'll try.*

56

Jacqueline Stoddard's gallery was open on Sundays. It was much more traditional than Madeline's, with lots of gold-leaf frames. The woman behind the front desk, however, was dressed in a striking, contemporary red dress. She nearly tripped trying to get around the desk to shake Madeline's hand, making comments of praise that showed she clearly thought of Madeline Saga as someone very big in the Chicago art world.

Madeline was cordial but not effusive. She greeted the receptionist, then waved her hand toward the back. "Just stopping in to see Jacqueline."

As I followed Madeline through the gallery, I tried to catch my breath from all the activity of the past hour.

Jacqueline's office was also traditional—molded ceilings and bookshelves, maroon couches.

She gestured at the couches.

We sat together. Madeline and Jacqueline stared at each other while I looked back and forth, noticing that Jacqueline's stare went from fearful to stern and back again.

"Okay, ladies," I said, breaking up the staring contest. "Jacqueline, from what I heard outside, you wrote the Dudlin comments. The ones implying they were fakes."

"Yes, that's right." Jacqueline Stoddard's voice was soft but the words flew from her mouth. Then she admitted that she'd started writing the comments because of hatred toward Madeline Saga, a hatred born of intense envy.

"I just wanted to keep an eye on her when she moved to Michigan Avenue," Jacqueline said, addressing me. "At first, I truly wanted to see how I could *help*."

"And did you *help* me," Madeline said, "with your insinuations of forgeries from my gallery?"

Another steely stare. "Insinuations that turned out to be true."

"Why do you say that, Jacqueline?" I asked. In other words, *What do you know?* I didn't want Madeline inadvertently telling Jacqueline more than she needed to.

Jacqueline's face took on a cast of sadness. "I hate someone other than you," she said. She pointed at herself. "This hatred is turned inward. Because I betrayed someone."

I assumed she'd meant she betrayed Madeline, and was about to launch into an apology, but then Jacqueline said, "Jeremy."

Jacqueline put her face in her hand, as if she couldn't bear to take in our gazes.

"What?" Madeline said, sounding unsure she'd heard correctly. "Jeremy told me he had spoken to *no one* about the forgeries."

"He told one other person," Jacqueline said, raising her face. "Me. I've known Jeremy since he was first in the city. And we'd become friends over the years."

"As did I," Madeline said.

Jacqueline nodded. "He and I were different. I've sold him and his wife a lot of art, as you have. And over those years, he and I became friends who confided in each other."

"Did you have an affair?" *Oops.* That was out of my mouth before I could stop it. The blond part of my personality just kept popping up every so often.

Jacqueline brusquely shook her head. "Just wonderful friends. And technically I was true to my word—I never really broke his confidences. I was anonymous in those comments, never gave any specific facts, very vague…"

"What about the email?" Madeline asked, incredulous. "Was that *vague?*"

"What email are you referring to?" Jacqueline said.

"The one where you threatened to have me 'cut and stretched'?"

"Excuse me." Jacqueline's voice was disgusted. "I did *not* write you any such email. The only email I've sent you in the last few months was about that Bobby Branch opening next week."

She had been forthcoming with her confessions, but she vociferously denied sending Madeline any threatening emails. And the more she talked, the more I believed her. Maybe the author wasn't Jacqueline.

"What about the wording in the comment?" I asked, returning to territory we could all agree on. "The one you put on the website when you said, 'she obliterates'?" I asked.

"That's how I feel," she said, her voice small, her eyes darting to Madeline and then back to her desk. "That's how you make me feel."

"What have I obliterated?" Madeline asked, her voice getting loud.

"Me. In a way."

"What way?"

"It's hard to describe."

"Please, try!" Madeline's voice was beseeching.

A silent few seconds passed. The energy, thankfully, went down a notch.

"Have you seen the movie *F is for Fake?*" Madeline asked.

I had not.

"Of course," Jacqueline said.

"*Our works in stone, in paint, in print are spared,*" Madeline quoted. "*Some of them for a few decades or a millennium or two, but everything must finally fall in war.*"

Jacqueline joined in. "*Or wear away into the ultimate and universal ash.*"

"*The triumphs and the frauds,*" Madeline said.

"*The treasures and...*"

The moment stretched, as if we were in a permanent installation.

But then, something seemed to crystallize for Jacqueline. Her eyes went wider, she cocked her head a bit and some clarity came into her expression. "The treasures...and the fakes," she said. The moment seemed to allow her to see something clearly. She pulled back her head a bit.

"Madeline," she said. "You don't think I'm responsible for the forgeries, somehow?" Her voice was incredulous.

I tried to dial back the conversation, but then Jacqueline Stoddard stood. "It appears I should get myself an attorney." She gestured at the door. "If you'll leave now."

"Jacqueline," I said. "I—"

"Leave," she said intensely. "Now."

The confession was clearly over.

Madeline and I left under the gaze of Jacqueline's assistant and a few others who had materialized outside the office.

But they didn't bother me. I couldn't help but feel pleased, because we knew Jacqueline had played a *part* in all this. We finally caught something in the net we'd cast. Now we needed to understand whether or not someone else was working with her.

Outside, the sun had gone down and the city was dead again, one of those Sundays when everyone stays in, no fight left after dealing with the snow.

I pulled my scarf tighter around me. Madeline pulled up the fur collar of her coat.

"Izzy, you're amazing," Madeline said to me. The Tribune Tower was behind her, and it lit her black hair with a blue glow. She looked, right then, like an angel.

"Congratulations," I said. "We're figuring this thing out."

"We are."

I'd never been on a team in school. Even when I was a litigator at a big firm, I was sort of a lone wolf. But now, standing in the snow with Madeline Saga, I felt like I was on a team.

Where to go from here?

"I'll talk to Mayburn tonight," I said. "I'll let you know what he says."

She nodded. She smiled, her eyes luminous. "I'll see you tomorrow?"

"I'll see you tomorrow," I repeated.

Madeline leaned forward and kissed me on my cheek, so softly if felt like an angel's touch.

"Tomorrow," she said again, giving me another smile before she turned away.

57

Jacqueline. It was Jacqueline.

Madeline Saga felt terrible for her. To have made Jacqueline feel so badly was awful.

In bed that night, sleep nowhere to be found, Madeline thought of how Jacqueline called her "Lina." She saw now that the name was Jacqueline's way of trying to get close to her. And she'd been unimpressed with the nickname, dismissive even.

Across the bedroom, she heard a tiny beep from her phone.

She stood and crossed the room to a tall nautical chest she used for her lingerie. On top was her cellphone. She was relieved when saw a text from Izzy, saying she'd spoken to Mayburn. He wanted them to pull all the shipping records again tomorrow morning, the ones dealing with moving from the old gallery to the new, so that Izzy could review them.

Madeline wondered what else John had told Izzy when he'd heard about Jacqueline. She thought of calling Izzy or John, but decided instead she'd go to the gallery now and get those records ready. She wanted to contribute to the solution. She didn't want anyone to hurt anymore.

Madeline looked at her watch. Eleven o'clock. She'd take a cab, then make sure she had all the records Izzy needed and leave them out in case Izzy was in earlier. Then, maybe, she'd be able to sleep.

She found a taxi. It reached the corner a block away from her gallery and stopped at a red light. Madeline was impatient, so she gave the driver a twenty and jumped out, heading toward the Wrigley Building.

Someone was coming out of the gallery, someone familiar.

They stopped when they saw each other.

And that was when Madeline Saga's world stopped.

Wasn't she was always telling people— *If you just look, life happens like art. Perspectives shift, new planes appear?*

She had never before understood those concepts the way she did then.

And she knew there was no going back to the place she was in before—the perspectives or the planes. They would all shift now. For good.

58

I felt as if I'd gone to bed during one, long, dark, magical January night…and awoken, hours and hours later, to the same evening.

I looked at my bedside clock. Six-thirty in the morning. I opened my window shade. In the light of the streetlamps, I saw white orbs of snow dotting the trees, as if hundreds of kids had stood under them and thrown snowballs heavenward.

I went up to my roof deck, the easiest way to check the temperature. I opened the door and squinted as the sun just began to coat the city.

I saw a dog and his owner step out of an apartment building on Eugenie, and *wham!*—both of them fell. The dog's paws sprawled on the ice, shooting out four different ways. The owner went down on his back. They promptly went back inside.

The temperatures had apparently risen just a little, enough to turn the snow into black ice. It covered the sidewalks like glazed shellac, like the gloss over Madeline's Dudlin piece.

Madeline.

Truly, I didn't know how to feel about my… What to call it? My *interactions* with her? I only knew that I

felt different. *I* felt magical because of what Madeline
had involved me in—the art world and the installations
and, well, some of her.

I started to shiver in the orange robe that Axel had
given me. It was time, I knew, to wash off the paint.
And not just because the weekend was over, but because what had occurred to me during the painting process was true, I realized—this piece of art could not
be lost. I was part of the art, not just because I'd been
painted, not just because Axel had listened to me, tried
to learn about me, but also by engaging in it, by spending time with Madeline yesterday, by clearing some of
the mysteries about her case. *Some of the mysteries.*
Unfortunately, not all; the complete picture was growing more and more hazy the more I thought about it.

Jacqueline Stoddard had worked with both Jeremy
and the Fex. She'd sold many artworks to them, and
she had become friends with them. Particularly Jeremy.
Had she helped him—or Corinne—forge and then replace the paintings? She could easily have sold them on
the black market, from the research my dad had done.

But Jacqueline had seemed genuinely shocked as
she realized we were suspicious of her for more than
writing a few web comments.

Mayburn had grunted when I told him that, not
wanting to concede one way or the other whether Jacqueline could be responsible for more. He was, I knew,
telling me to keep my mind open.

I had learned that well enough. And my open mind
had led to those "interactions" with Madeline.

But if I kept my mind open…could Madeline and
Jacqueline had been working together? Yet, if that
was true, why bring John Mayburn in to investigate? I

thought about something Madeline had said one of the first nights we were out—something to the effect that she hadn't asked Mayburn to work for her, he'd insisted.

I shook my head to twist away any mental cobwebs. Despite the still-rising sun, my mind continued to swirl.

I closed the door to the roof deck and went back into my apartment. I drew a bath of the hottest, most foamy water, mixing a number of bath salts and Axel's soap. When I got in, the tub felt like a happy water haven, heavenly scented, a place to slide into, to give in to. *To just be,* as Madeline would say.

So that's what I did.

59

Madeline did nothing that morning to quell my suspicions. She was certainly acting different. Again.

She seemed nervous, sometimes confused, sometimes surprised. What she was surprised about, I didn't know. She was distracted when I came in. Barely said hello. *Where was the team?* I wondered.

"So," I said, following her into her office and leaning on the door as she sat at her black lacquer desk. "I spoke with Mayburn again before I came in. He thinks it's time to bring in the police."

He hadn't actually insisted or anything, just mused that maybe some official art authorities—if there were any—should be consulted eventually. But I wanted to see what Madeline's reaction would be.

Madeline looked at me, blinking, then at something on her desk—an invite from another gallery, it appeared.

"In fact," I said, trying to catch her attention. "He thinks it should be soon. Jacqueline Stoddard must know more about the forgeries than she's telling us. After all, she has a lot of contacts in the art world. And you know that detective who arrested me? Vaughn. We could use him. I actually believe he can be discreet." I thought about being in the back of that car during the blizzard, the plastic seat. "And I figure he owes me."

Madeline had appeared mildly amused the last time I mentioned Vaughn, but now she looked fearful. She looked at me directly. "No."

"No?" I stood a little straighter.

"Not yet. No."

I tucked a lock of hair behind my ears. "Then when?"

"I'm not sure." She returned her eyes back to the invitation, but she didn't seem to be truly reading it. She cocked her head a little.

My thoughts turned to where Madeline was—the Madeline of yesterday, the one who had kissed me. Were we even going to deal with that? Truthfully, I was okay with a little avoidance on that issue, but what was going on here?

Was it possible that the whole kissing thing was just a ploy? A way to play me, and draw any suspicions from her?

Madeline picked up her phone. "Izzy, I have to talk to someone," she said. "I printed out the shipping manifests. Could you review those at home?"

"I could…" I said, hesitantly. "Why?"

"I've got a designer coming in. He'll be in the back room here, and I don't want him to see them and start asking questions."

Sounded reasonable enough.

Madeline looked at the door. And her meaning was clear. *Time for you to go.*

I left. Not because she wanted me to, but because I had to talk to someone, as well.

60

The Belmont Police Station had to be one of the ugliest stations in the country—brown and squat, it sat beneath a highway underpass, as if the city found its presence distasteful and had dumped it there to keep it out of sight.

The station was near the secret club that Madeline had taken me to, the one haunted by the art crowd. As I'd seen Maggie do before, I pulled into a parking space marked *Police*. Apparently (ironically) such spots were known as the few places in the city from which they never towed.

Plus, I was there to *see* the police. That visit to the station was the first time I noticed a sculpture, big, colorful and rounded, that had been installed in front of the station. I'd never given it much notice before, but now I stopped and tried to take it in and appreciate it.

But I kept thinking of Madeline and her strange behavior that morning.

I took a breath, tried to open my eyes and really see the sculpture, its curves.

Still, Madeline—suspicions, questions and a growing feeling of distrust. I thought about Syd. *Did he have anything to do with Madeline's change of heart? Had*

*she seen him last night after we'd spoken to Jacque-
line?* According to a plaque, the name of the sculpture was...

Nope, I couldn't do it. I needed some help.

I turned away and headed toward the entrance of
the station.

Then, I stopped again and texted Mayburn to let
him know where I was—just in case Vaughn decided
to randomly arrest me again.

But this time, I was the one coming to find Vaughn.
When I'd called from my car, I'd been told by the front
desk that Vaughn was in the office and would see me.
But ten minutes later I was still tapping my fingernails
on the counter.

The uniformed officer glanced at my hand, then
at me.

"Sorry," I said, taking a step back.

Finally, Vaughn sauntered into the lobby. He wore
a blue buttoned-down shirt, pressed brown pants and
a shoulder holster. I looked down and noticed surprisingly attractive brown boots.

He gestured across the hallway, where there was a
small conference/interview room. "In here okay?" He
sounded surprisingly nice.

When we were in the room, he nodded toward a
small desk. I sat. A closed laptop was bolted to the top.
I leaned my elbows next to it. "Thanks for seeing me.
I need you to answer a hypothetical. That's the main
reason I'm here."

"And the other reason?"

"Figuring out what in the hell happened the other
night."

I stopped, sat back, so he could jump in and apologize.

He didn't say anything.

"Okay, let's start there. With the other night," I said. "On one hand I get it—you Chicago cops are always looking out for your own, and you have buddies who are bar owners. And they had some girl who didn't pay the cover. Fine. Why did *you* have to handle it? I don't know."

He coughed, seemed like he was going to say something, but stopped.

"What?" I prompted.

He sighed.

"What?"

"I do have a lot of buddies who are bar owners, and they have been calling me more frequently."

"Why?"

He shook his head; he wouldn't meet my eyes. "You know, since the breakup."

"Oh, I see. Are they trying to get you *in* the bars so you can pick up chicks?"

He glared at me. But he didn't correct me.

"So you could meet women," I said, revising.

This time he nodded.

"Ah," I said. "How's that going?"

He shook his head again.

"Okay, fine," I said. "So they call with the excuse that a blonde didn't pay the cover. They get you away from your beat where you can maybe meet some girls, and then…"

He didn't explain.

"What were you thinking?"

"Initially? That the blonde was hot."

"Oh. Well, that's nice." I shifted on the chair. "Thanks."

"You're welcome."

"But then you realized it was me."

"Yeah."

"And you got this disgusted look on your face. What was that about?"

He sighed. "I was thinking that you get to have all the fun."

"*I* get to have all the fun? Like last year when you were accusing me of murder? That was a big bowl of fun cherries."

He paused. Glared. "I guess it's just that everything works out for you."

"Oh, that's rich. Did you notice I'm not engaged like I was when I met you last year? That the boyfriend I had after that relationship is now out of the country? Did you notice that I'm not employed by that huge law firm anymore?" Truthfully, I was glad I wasn't at Baltimore & Brown, but I wasn't about to tell Vaughn that.

He said nothing.

"So, why arrest me, when you realized it was me?"

His head was hanging low now. "It's so fucked up. I'm embarrassed."

I was about to say, *You* should *be embarrassed*.

"It's like I don't know how to date anymore," he said, speaking faster than I'd heard. "I don't…" He looked around the room as if searching the walls for words. "Okay, here it is…" He exhaled, didn't look at me, but he kept going. "It's like I don't know how to talk to women without the shield of my badge and my marriage."

My eyebrows drew together, thinking of something.

"Oh. You said you thought I looked hot that night. You arrested me, when you knew it was me...so we could spend time together?"

A mere nod.

"Dude, that is *so* flubbed up." The swear word replacement wasn't working. "*So* fucked up," I corrected.

Nothing from Vaughn.

"Look," I said, feeling bad for him. "I have a buddy, Grady, from my old law firm. He's got a girlfriend now, but he's always been quite the ladies' man. Maybe I can put you two together for a beer, and he can give you some tips."

More glaring, more head hanging. Why, *why,* had I said that?

"Why don't we table this part of the discussion?" I suggested.

"Please."

"Great. So let's get to the hypothetical I want you to answer." I sat up straighter. "What do you do—as a police officer—when you have a victim of a crime, but the victim doesn't want to press charges?"

Vaughn looked at me for the longest time. "This isn't about me?"

"No."

"In any way?"

I thought about it. "No."

His body relaxed. He leaned back in the chair across from me and pointed. "Well, as a lawyer, you know that it's not up to the victim if he wants to press charges."

I nodded. "So what's the protocol? How do you handle it?" Vaughn seemed to be mulling over the situation, so I kept talking. "Do you just move forward?" I asked. "Do you just process the charges, start the ball rolling?"

"No." Vaughn shook his head in ponderous arcs. "No."

"What then?"

"The first, and only, thing I'd do right now?"

I nodded.

"Make damn sure you have the right guy."

Or right *girl,* I thought.

I debated whether or not to tell Vaughn about Madeline's case. But Madeline had seemed insistent this morning that the authorities not be contacted yet. She was my client, via Mayburn. I had to listen, at least for now, to what she wanted me to do.

But then something else occurred. I stopped thinking about Madeline, and about Madeline and Syd. And suddenly, I wondered— *Why does Madeline Saga not want to turn in Jacqueline Stoddard?*

61

"No," Jacqueline Stoddard said, interrupting my introductory spiel. "I will not talk to you. I've hired one of the best lawyers in the city."

I couldn't help but wonder whom she'd retained.

"I've been instructed," she continued, "not to talk to you or Ms. Saga."

No more *Lina,* I noticed.

"Or to the police." She hugged her arms around herself.

"May I sit?" I asked gently, pointing to the office couch where Madeline and I had sat yesterday. I needed more time. Despite her words, I could tell she had something to say. And I really, really wanted to hear it. She paused, her lips pursing. Finally, she nodded.

When I'd sat, she said, "I did not write that email you referred to. I did *not*."

"And the sculpture?"

"What sculpture?" Her brows, perfectly waxed and arched, raised.

I got out my phone and showed her a photo of the knife in the flesh.

She looked at me. "That? You think that's *me?* God, no." Her words were adamant. She wanted me to believe her. And that was helpful, because I needed her to talk to me. I needed her help figuring some things out.

I leaned forward and put my elbows on my knees, letting my hair hang toward my face, giving what I hoped was a calm, kind smile. "You were the one who was keeping an eye on her, right?" I asked her. "It started out as a good thing. You really *wanted* to help her."

"God, yes." She covered her eyes with her hands as she had last time, but her voice sounded strangled. "I am mortified at my behavior, and how…out of control it's gotten. The comments, the constant watching her gallery—it really did start as an altruistic endeavor." Her hand dropped away from her eyes. She looked into mine. "I swear."

Sitting in front of Jacqueline Stoddard then, following my discussion with Vaughn, I thought I knew right then how it felt to be a Chicago police detective—one whose true desire was to find the people who were doing the wrong, at least part of the wrong. I wanted to pin her down to the truth. That was why the police had procedure.

Since I wasn't on the police force, I had no duty to explain anything to Jacqueline Stoddard before I asked her any more questions. But it struck me as wrong to hold the detectives, and Vaughn, to a different standard than myself in the same situation.

So I sat up straighter on the maroon couch. I asked Jacqueline Stoddard a couple of questions— *You realize I am not your lawyer? You realize you don't have to talk to me? You're going into this conversation to tell me your side of the story?*

To all, she answered *yes*.

62

"So, you started keeping an eye on her?" I settled back in the couch to make Jacqueline feel more comfortable.

I put on my figurative deposition hat. I was happy to be able to practice the skills, since there were few or no deps in criminal work. I pulled a notepad out of my bag. "Do you mind?" I asked Jacqueline. "I can show you everything I write."

"That's fine," she said quickly, softly, as if to say, *Let's just get this over with.*

"When you first started to 'keep an eye out for' Madeline, when exactly was that?"

Jacqueline Stoddard leaned back in her chair, as well. She wore a soft blue scarf around her neck. It struck me as the same as the faint color under her eyes today. If I were an artist, that's how I'd have painted Jacqueline Stoddard—with the scarf and all around the eyes as the primary color, blue. The rest would be dove gray, like Jacqueline's outfit, her mood.

"I really did want to make sure she was okay." Jacqueline let her chair swivel and she looked out the window. Across the street was the Wrigley Building, where Madeline's gallery was on the first floor. Now, our view was the gray and sculpted stone surrounding the higher windows of the building. In that light, everything inside those windows looked black, soulless.

"I don't know how to describe this," Jacqueline said with a mirthless laugh. "It's absurd, but I truly wanted to be friends with her. I started calling her Lina, because I felt like that was a girlfriend's thing to do." She looked away from window, at the side wall of her office, as if telling her sins to a priest in a confessional, preferring not to see the listener. "I'll correct something. I didn't necessarily want to be her friend. I wanted to be her mentor. And I thought…" A pause, the heavy scent of pain in the air. "I actually thought she would *want* to be my protégé."

She paused, and I let the silence stay there, sensing she would fill it.

"I constantly get requests from art and design schools. *Become a mentor!* they say. *Give back to the art community!* But to be honest…" She took a breath. "I felt like *I* needed a mentor. No one had helped me in this business. I taught myself, then I went to art school, then I did studio work for a few years. When I realized I wanted to be on the other side of the business—the business side—I went back to school, and I had to learn a whole other scene, a whole other network of people. And it was exhausting."

At this, she turned to me. Her eyes were open wide, pleading for understanding.

"I know what you mean. I do," I said honestly. "You're so scared you're failing that it's hard to imagine what wisdom you could impart to someone else. You're not sure yet that you're doing anything right."

"Exactly." She looked at me. "You fear that you might, in fact, give the *wrong* advice to a mentee."

I nodded.

"I'd followed Madeline's career from afar since she got to Chicago," she said. "I thought she was brazen, really smart, fascinating. I really was, career-wise, ahead of her at the time. As I grew more successful, I thought, *Now I feel ready. Now I feel ready and contented enough to share what I have.*" Her eyes dipped.

"She rejected you?" I said.

Jacqueline returned her eyes to me. "Madeline was friendly with my overtures, but yes, she rejected me. And I took it personally."

Jacqueline clasped her hands, as if praying, and put them in her lap. The confession continued. "To make it worse, it seemed like Madeline hogged the PR spotlight, always being featured in one magazine or another, even national magazines, even when she didn't have an exhibition or an opening to publicize," she said. "Every magazine covered her. *Her,* not just her gallery—*Michigan Avenue, CS, Chicago Magazine,* the *Trib,* the *Sun-Times, Architectural Digest, Vogue, New York Times.* The list went on and on."

"Wow," I said. I didn't know Madeline had garnered such professional respect for herself. But I understood why.

"Wow," Jacqueline repeated. "Exactly. She represented something to me. In her love and appreciation for art? I saw that she was on an entirely different level than me. Professionally and personally. I knew enough to see that much. But I also knew…" Jacqueline's body seemed to shrink and hunch over all at the same time.

"I knew," she said, "that I would never reach the state that Madeline was at. Not in my lifetime."

"That's what you meant by 'she obliterates,'" I said, keeping any judgment out of my voice. The truth was, I really didn't have any judgment.

"Yes." A beat went by. "She showed me what could be, and at the same she time obliterated any hope that I could be that way myself."

"I don't think you're analyzing this correctly," I said. "Madeline is simply a different person than you are." I leaned forward again, wanting to give Jacqueline Stoddard, who looked so very defeated right now, some kind of comfort. "Isn't that all you recognized in that situation? Aren't we all different?"

She shook her head. "I distinctly saw her as *above* me. That's how I viewed it—she showed me what could be, and at the same time, she showed me that I would never be that. I could not get those impressions out of my head, and I starting resenting her." Jacqueline was talking louder and faster. "And then I started *disdaining* her, and meanwhile, I'm acting so...inauthentic. I'm acting like all is fine, because why would a professional and accomplished and creative person like me be envious, jealous, of *anyone?* Hadn't I accomplished enough not to have to deal with that kind of burden?" Her words just stopped for a while. Finally, she continued, but in a softer voice. "And that made me hate Madeline."

"Sounds like a vicious circle," I said.

Her eyes met mine. They were exhausted again, defeated.

I hated to do it, but I had to ask. "The knife," I said. "The sculpture in that picture. Was that yours? Was that a threat, reminding Madeline that you could return the 'obliteration'?"

Jacqueline shook her head. "No." She appeared definitive and I was inclined to believe her, given the statements that had been pouring from her mouth. I put aside the knife sculpture for the moment.

"You said you did studio work," I said.

"Yes."

"So you had the skills to forge the Dudlin. And the other piece."

"Ha. No. I left studio work because I didn't have the chops. I wasn't a great artist by any stretch."

"You don't have to be a good artist to copy, do you?"

"On the contrary, you have to be *gifted*. And I was definitely not gifted. Or even good."

She shook her head again. But this time her look was different. This time, if I was correct, she was scared.

I looked a little inside myself. And what I saw was that I was scared, too.

Because if Jacqueline was telling the truth, and she hadn't been responsible for the knife sculpture, if she hadn't sent that email and stolen the artwork, then who had?

63

I got back to my condo and I was *frustrated.*

I paced around. I made a fire and sat in my yellow-and-white chair. I gazed into the fire, searching for stillness and clarity. But my thoughts bounced from Jaqueline Stoddard to Syd, to Jeremy and the Fex, to Amaya and everyone else I'd met while working on this case. And to add to the list, tomorrow morning, I had a meeting with Margie Scott, the art-moving specialist.

I was getting nowhere, so I decided to put the case out of my mind for a while. Instead, I got up and cleaned out some closets. I found all sorts of Theo's adventure gear. Currently, I possessed a wind-surfing vest, a bike pump, a tent and a lot of nylon straps.

Would Theo ever want these things in the future? Had he discarded them, in his mind at least? Would he ever be back for them? I left those ideas to sift around as I unloaded the closet, discovering more of Theo's stuff.

When that was done, I paced some more. I left a message for my dad. Maybe I would talk to him about… what? The case? But he hadn't worked on it since its inception. Dating? I would tell him that I had gone out a few times with a guy named Jeremy? That I hadn't heard from him since his wife was in the gallery? Or the fact that I really didn't mind that much. Jeremy was charming. Beyond. But I didn't miss him when he wasn't around.

I looked longingly at Theo's gear. I was struck with the feeling that I hadn't appreciated him enough when I had him. Was that right? Or was I simply missing someone around the house to talk to?

Who else could I call? Maggie had told me that she and Bernard were having a date night, introducing him to more of Chicago.

I tried Charlie. No answer. I tried my mom and Spence. Same thing. My dad preferred texts, so instead on calling again, I sent him one, which was quickly answered with *Love to see you. Tomorrow?* I stared at the word—*love*. My father hadn't said he loved me since he returned. He wasn't the type. But that word meant a lot to me.

I sighed, sat down in the yellow chair again.

I thought of another person to call.

Bunny Loveland answered immediately. "Yeah?"

"Bunny, it's Izzy," I said.

"Yeah," she said, but this time there was the slightest touch of excitement in her voice. "Whatcha got goin' girl?"

"Umm, I'm…"

"What are you calling me for?" Classic Bunny Loveland. And her hostility, based in love I knew, always made me feel better.

"I just wanted to say hi," I said. "See what's going on."

Bunny Loveland was the housekeeper my mother hired when we moved to Chicago. I was eight and my brother, Charlie, five. My mom thought Bunny was going to be the maternal type. She certainly looked the type with her curled gray hair. She seemed a sturdy woman who didn't fluster easily. Well, she was that, but she certainly wasn't the maternal type. Bunny was one of those people to whom you didn't ask a question unless you *really* wanted an answer.

And for decades, nothing much had been going on in Bunny's life since an inheritance from a distant relative allowed her to quit cleaning and doing "other peoples' child caring." Her home in West Lincoln Park—a squat, old brown cottage on Schubert Avenue—was overgrown with trees and hadn't been painted since the early seventies. It was one of those places the neighbors wanted to torch in the middle of the night.

"I bought a bar," she said.

"What?" Bunny was in her late seventies and rarely left her house. Bunny didn't go to bars, much less own them. "You bought a bar?"

"Yep. You know that place a few blocks from me on Southport?" Her voice bore its usual strongly graveled tone.

In my mind, I strolled Bunny's neighborhood. "You mean the place next to the vacuum cleaner store?" I asked. That bar was a decrepit old place, with a bulletproof frosted window. There was no way to look inside from the street.

I liked dive bars—really, really liked them. But even I was a bit freaked out by that particular place. It had never had a name that anyone knew. And not in the way that Saga's secret place didn't have a name. If I was thinking of the right one, the bar only had a sign that said *Old Style,* as if *Really, what else is there to say?*

I described the sign to Bunny.

"That's the place," Bunny said. "And I need some customers. Bring some suckers in tonight."

64

I didn't know any suckers, but I needed to get my mind off Madeline's case and I knew someone who probably felt guilty enough to meet me at a really crappy bar on a Monday.

"Hey," Vaughn said when I called the station. I almost said, *We answer my calls, do we?* But I realized it was a good sign that he'd done so.

I gave him the basics of Bunny and her new bar. "What time do they let you leave there?" I used the word *let* in order to stir up what I now knew was a dislike for his job.

And it worked.

"I leave when I want to," he said.

"Great. I'll see you there at seven."

I stepped into Bunny's bar at six forty-five. I'd gone early to catch up with Bunny. She was behind the bar, her gray hair looking like she might have had it colored and set at the shop recently. And Bunny was laughing.

Now that was something I'd seen only a few times before.

It took one or two steps for me to realize who she was laughing with—Vaughn.

She saw me, waved at the bar stool near Vaughn and kept talking. "Sure, I knew Gacy!"

I gripped the bar when the stool's rickety legs felt like they might give away.

"I went to a few parties at his place," she said.

"Hi," Vaughn said to me, smiling, then looking back at Bunny. "C'mon," he said.

"Seriously!" Bunny said.

"You guys aren't talking about John Wayne Gacy, are you?" I asked.

"Yeah, my husband and I knew him."

She and Vaughn chatted a little more—just light, Chicago bar chat about one of the most prolific serial killers in history. Bunny put an Old Style draft in front of me, without asking what I wanted, then went to the end of the bar to help a lone patron. Vaughn had a mug of the same beer in front of him.

"Cheers," I said, raising my drink.

He clinked glasses with me. "Cheers."

Two hours later, there was barely a lull in the conversation. Who knew how fun it could be to hang with Vaughn? He had a million stories, of course, about criminals, both stupid and chillingly smart. We now knew a number of the same people since I worked in criminal defense. We traded stories and laughed our asses off.

"You know," I said to him, "you're exhibiting another trait of a lawyer."

"What's that?" He looked interested.

"War stories. We love telling 'em."

"Ah, that's a cop thing, too."

"I don't know," I said. "A lot of the stories you've been telling me end up in the same place."

"Where's that?"

"With you in court."

Vaughn thought about it. "Huh," he said. "I guess that's true." He took a sip of beer. "Huh." He looked at me. "You're pretty smart."

"Thanks."

"And you're pretty cool."

"Thanks."

A pause.

"Is this your way of hitting on me as an alternative to arresting me?" I asked.

He looked like he might be pissed off, then decided to let it go. He laughed. "Yeah. How's it going for you?"

I thought about it. "Good," I said. "I'm giving you good reviews."

"Yeah? And so what would you recommend I do now?"

I looked at him. And I can't believe what I said next. "I'd recommend that you kiss me."

65

Bunny eventually kicked us out.

"This is not why I opened a bar," she said, exasperated.

We'd been smooching on and off at the bar for at least thirty minutes by then. Time had taken on a weird quality, and I had to distract myself from pondering the bizarro-ness of it all. I'd never kissed three different people in the span of only a few weeks, and who would have thought one of them would be a woman. Or that I would *ever* kiss Vaughn?

I knew part of me was feeling rejected by Madeline's cold behavior after what we'd shared. But damn, the guy could *kiss,* and so Vaughn was definitely helping matters.

"And you," Bunny said, disapprovingly, shaking her head at Vaughn, as if to say, *I expected more.*

"Hey," he said to her. "Now that we're friends, I'm always at your service. Always."

"Yeah," I said, standing and slipping my arm into my coat. "He's got a lot of friends who own bars, and he'll do anything for them. Like arrest people for really ridiculous reasons." I laughed.

But Vaughn didn't. Oops. I had taken it too far.

But then, slowly, like it was difficult for him, he smiled. He leaned down, mouth to my ear. "I want to get you out of here."

He put a fifty-dollar bill on the bar for Bunny.

"Congratulations on the bar," I said to her.

"Thanks, girl." When Vaughn turned his back to pick up his coat, she pointed at him, winked, smiled and nodded.

Vaughn had been granted the rarely seen Bunny stamp of approval.

66

Vaughn had a laserlike focus for finding cabs. Outside Bunny's bar, in a little-traveled block of Southport, it was like Vaughn could smell them.

"There!" he said, pointing two blocks away to a cab with its lights on. He took my hand, as if it were natural for him to do so, and pulled me to walk faster toward the cab. When the cabbie blinked his lights to let us know he'd seen us, we slowed.

In the cab, Vaughn said, "Where?"

And I don't know if it was the blonde or redhead in me, or some combination of the two, but somebody leaned forward and gave my address to the driver.

It took forever to get inside my condo. Because we kept making out on the stairs.

I'd take a few steps up, he'd make an inappropriate (and really sexy) comment about my ass. I'd take a few more and his hand might touch the back of my thigh. Just for a moment. I'd take a few steps more and I would cave.

I would turn, lean down and kiss him. And soon he was leaning over me. One time I sat on his lap. Each time we kissed and kissed and held ourselves together in a tight knot of arms and legs. Then one of us would be an adult and say, *Okay, let's go.*

But then the cycle would begin all over again.

Finally, we were inside my living room. I playfully pushed him onto the couch. He landed, his mouth open, his eyes looking at me like this was the best night of his life.

I fell on the couch next to him, letting myself lean into his weight, and *God* did that feel nice.

This time our kissing was going somewhere. There was nothing but us now—no bar or cab or stairwell. Nothing but our mouths and our faces and our necks, and, of course, our bodies, nearly twitching for each other.

My phone had rung inside my purse a few times on our way up the stairs. Now someone was calling again. And again. And again. It was messing with my beer buzz and the completely unexpected delight named Damon Vaughn.

The phone rang *again.* I growled. "Sorry," I said.

I stood, noticing my sweater was halfway up my rib cage. I looked at the phone. *Mayburn.*

"What?" I said.

"Why are you answering like that?" he said.

"Please tell me what you need." I glanced back at Vaughn. He was panting ever so slightly.

"I need you to go to the gallery. Tonight."

"Why?"

"I'm starting to wonder if you're right. I'm starting to think it could be Saga."

67

Flushed and flustered, I'd smoothed my hair and gave Vaughn an *I'm sorry* look while I listened to Mayburn talk.

He summarized some things we'd learned about the case. "We need to know why she's been in the gallery at night," he concluded.

"To see if she had opportunity to get things out of there."

"Yeah. It's been bugging me. You said she was in there on a Saturday night, wearing different clothes from earlier. That's been scratching at me, so I looked at the video."

"And?"

"Remember how I told you that the back entry doesn't appear on the video feed from the security cameras."

"Yeah. Madeline said the previous owners installed it, mostly to show cars that were blocking access to the delivery door."

"Right."

"You think Madeline knows that, and knows how to leave the building with a piece of art without being picked up by her cameras?"

"Maybe. But I'd guess the security guard has a whole different set of shots."

"From the building's video system."

"Right. He probably sits there in the foyer and watches all sorts of video from different angles. We need to know what he knows. You gotta talk to him while Madeline isn't there."

"What if this is one of the nights she is in there? Should I say I wanted to review the shipping manifests again?" I'd had no luck reviewing those documents yet, but I hadn't gotten to explain that to Madeline since she'd essentially told me to leave the gallery.

"Yeah, exactly."

I hung up and turned to Vaughn. "Duty calls."

"What kind of duty?"

"Just work," I said, because I wasn't about to confide anything in Vaughn, and also I liked the way he seemed to think of me as mysterious.

I said goodbye to him on the front stoop of my place. There was no wind, and Eugenie Street felt perfectly still—a snow globe with no snow.

"So this…" He nodded at me. "This is pretty good."

"Yes."

We hugged. He held me very close.

"I'm going to want to see you," he said.

"Yes," I said.

I got in a cab. And when he was gone, when I could no longer see his form on the corner, I missed him.

68

The security guard was nice, like always. I brought up his wife's tamales; he told me that she'd won a cook-off contest with them. I tried to channel Vaughn. Now that I didn't hate him, I could actually see and imagine good things about him. How would *he* get this guard to talk?

It wasn't as easy as it sounded. Doormen (and women) are prized for their ability to remain friendly and seem open without divulging anything about their residents.

I figured Vaughn would be straight with him. What had he told me about talking to gangbangers? *Everyone deserves respect,* or something to that effect. I could almost hear him saying, *Tell it to the guard straight, but give as little information as you have to. Don't contaminate the scene. Use your brain.*

After we chatted about the tamales, I got out my keys and made like I was going to open the gallery door, reminding the security guard that I had a certain amount of cred there. "Hey," I said, turning back to him. "Thanks for being so great with us while we've been so busy lately."

"Sure, that's my job." He smiled jovially at me.

"It must be hard to do the night shift."

He shrugged. "Well, I got a family. Kids. You know. And I miss them. But this is my job."

"Yeah, sure. I just know Madeline really appreciates it."

He nodded at me, pleased.

"Madeline works really hard, too," I added.

"Oh, yeah," he said. "She's a businesswoman. You got to."

"I know, but I always tell her, don't work so much at night, you know? I don't want her to run herself into the ground."

The guard made an agreeable face, as if to say, *Maybe you got a point.*

I was thinking of a way to ask him if Madeline had been coming to the gallery at night, other than this past Saturday, but he spoke again. "Hey, there she is now."

He was looking down. I took a few light steps toward him. I craned my neck to see that he was pointing at live video feeds. As Mayburn had said, they showed different areas around the building. The one he specifically was pointing to showed the back entrance. And sure enough, on the screen, there was Madeline Saga, pulling keys out of a fur coat she was wearing. She opened the door and stepped inside.

Oh, my gosh. What should I do? My thoughts ran around in circles.

But then I halted the scrambling mental activity. Wait a minute. This all seemed too easy. I'd come to see if Madeline spent much time at the gallery at night, and now there she was? Why did I feel like I was being set up?

I was about to make up some excuse and leave,

maybe try calling Madeline from a cab and see if she willingly told me she was in the gallery.

But something on the screen caught my eye. *Someone*.

Someone was following Madeline in the back entrance of the gallery.

My eyes darted to the Madeline on the screen. She wasn't looking back, just moving forward as if unaware of the presence so close behind her.

Madeline! I wanted to yell.

I leaned forward. Who was that behind her? The person was small, about Madeline's size.

Still, I wanted to yell out, *Madeline! Be careful...*

I looked at the guard. He cocked his head, but his gaze shifted again to a different screen, clearly not alarmed.

I returned my gaze to the screen. And what I saw made me blink a few times.

What I *appeared* to see was...

I leaned in farther.

What my eyes thought they saw was that the person following Madeline inside was...Madeline?

The security guard buzzed in another business owner and greeted them.

I leaned in again, peering.

I knew I'd just seen Madeline open the back door and step inside. But there she was on the screen, taking hold of the open door and stepping inside again. And she wasn't wearing a fur coat.

What was going on here?

There were, I realized then, two of them.

69

"Uh, yeah, good," I said to the security guard, moving fast to the gallery's front door again. "There's Madeline. Right on time to meet me. Good to see you."

I slipped the keys in quietly and opened the door. I closed it behind me and a silence settled over the place. In the back room, a light went on.

I heard no sounds.

I took one step, then another. I noticed absently how different the artwork was in the dark—some pieces losing their power, others containing a deep creepiness that hadn't been there before.

I took another few steps. I heard something.

I stopped. Faint murmuring.

I took a few more steps. Two women talking. But then I knew that—two women. Yet why did both of them appear to be Madeline Saga?

The murmuring grew louder as I crept toward the back.

When I peeked in from the front room, the only person I saw was Madeline. In her fur coat.

I bent over farther and saw someone else holding a wood crate, the kind people sent paintings in. And that person...again...that person was...Madeline?

"What in the hell?" I said.

When they both looked at me, I realized I'd said it out loud.

70

"We are twins," Madeline said.

I looked back and forth between the two of them. The other woman was quiet as Madeline spoke.

Madeline told me she'd come to the gallery the night before. She had been thinking about Jacqueline, feeling bad that Jacqueline was so twisted up about this—about her—and yet not quite believing that Jacqueline could have sent the knife sculpture. Or really wanted harm to come to Madeline.

Madeline had gotten out of bed. She'd left her house. She planned to pull out the shipping manifests for me and leave them in case I came in early. She was glad that Mayburn and I wanted to go over the information again. Madeline knew, she said, that we hadn't quite seen the whole of the situation yet.

And although, as a lover of art, she'd gotten adept at noticing perspective and vantage point, she had a distinct sense that our view and hers was too narrow.

She'd found a taxi but got out of the cab before it reached the building, wanted to walk, to do some kind of activity.

She'd been somewhat distracted as she walked toward the Wrigley Building.

So, when she saw someone near her building, it took her a moment to focus.

The person was leaving her gallery foyer. The person was someone she thought she recognized.

"That was as far as I got in my thoughts," Madeline said. "I thought I recognized her."

"And?" I prompted.

Madeline looked at the woman next to her. "We stopped when we saw each other."

Both women were quiet now; they stared at each other in a comfortable, yet adoring way that gave no sense of urgency. It was as if each felt they could stay that way forever.

"Okay, ladies," I said softly, not sure how to address them.

Still, they stared at each other.

"Madeline," I said, a bit louder now.

She looked at me.

"Are you saying that you met your twin sister outside your gallery? A twin you didn't know you had?" I wanted to add, *Oh for Christ's sake, c'mon!*

"Please," the twin said then. She looked at me. "I will tell you how it started." Her words had an empowered tone, as if she had a very good reason for what she'd done and very much needed to tell me.

It had begun as an accident, the twin said.

She spoke with a light accent, from where I wasn't sure. Yet oddly, it was at the same register, the same volume as Madeline's.

The twin kept talking. She said she had come to Chicago to see how Madeline lived, to see what she'd been denied.

"What *you* have been denied?" I said, pointing to the twin.

She nodded. Madeline did, too, I noticed.

She had been in Chicago for almost a year now, the twin continued.

I blinked at her, confused. When she didn't slow down, I stopped formulating questions and just tried to keep up with her words.

She had found part-time work, she said, at a dry cleaner's. And in her spare time, she practiced her own art and watched Madeline. She studied what she wore, she grew her hair so it looked the same and started to adopt her wardrobe. She found herself in a whirl of emotions—at once mesmerized by Madeline, full of hatred for the sister who had everything, and yet hating herself most of all.

The twin shared Madeline's sheets of long black hair and Madeline's intense eyes.

"What is your name?" I said to the person who claimed to be Madeline's sister. The woman had gone from looking empowered a few moments ago to looking stricken now.

She didn't say anything at first. I saw her turn her head to Madeline for approval.

"Please," I said. "Please tell me your name."

"Ella," she said. "It is a shortened version of my Asian name. But that's what everyone calls me. Ella."

She continued telling her story.

She often wandered outside Madeline's gallery on Michigan Avenue, she said. "I liked when Madeline wasn't there."

It was then, she said, she could really study the gallery, noticing what she had already suspected—that

Madeline had everything. And flaunted everything. As if others weren't entitled to that level of success, that degree of passion, that obvious amount of money.

"The money," I said.

Both women nodded. They dipped their chins and then raised them again at the exact same pace.

"The money was supposed to be hers, as well," Madeline said.

"Are you speaking about your inheritance?"

Madeline squeezed her eyes shut. Ella's gaze grew hard.

"Yes." No further explanation.

Eventually, she started tempting fate, Ella said. "And then one night, I followed Madeline into a party at another gallery."

I looked at Madeline, whose eyes were still shut as if physically hurt by hearing the words.

What would Vaughn do?

Be gentle. That's what I thought. But when had Vaughn ever been gentle? That was easy—*when he was with me.*

"So what happened?" I said, my voice low. "At the party?"

Still, Madeline's eyes were closed.

"No one noticed me," she said. Devastation. That's what I heard in her voice.

Madeline exhaled loudly.

"Maybe you only felt like that?" I said.

She and Madeline shook their heads simultaneously.

Ella continued to talk. She wanted to see how far she could go, she said. "I kept doing it."

She went to the same restaurants, the same bars, she said. Only she found that she was invisible.

"Okay, wait a minute?" I said, my voice nice, but stopping her, this time holding up my hand. Enough of gentle. Enough prodding. "One of you needs to start at the beginning, and tell me the whole story," I said, I looked at Madeline.

Madeline joined in the tale again.

71

"Our mother's family," Madeline said, "was Taiwanese, but moved to Japan shortly after our birth. Ella was told they went to seek work."

Ella shot Madeline a look.

"And they were embarrassed about our mother's pregnancy," Madeline added.

I thought of Vaughn again. *What would he do now?*

The answer came quick. *He would know when to shut up.*

"What Ella has told me," Madeline said, "is that our father's family was wealthy. And when they found out he'd gotten our mother pregnant, they funded her family to go to Japan to have the babies. Then they set up a trust fund to care for us, without knowing our mother would eventually give us up for adoption."

"They didn't expect me to come back," Ella said.

"What?" I didn't understand now and wasn't afraid to show it.

"Our grandmother—our mother's mother—decided that our mother was too young to take care of us, and we were put up for adoption. Madeline was adopted first, by a couple in the United States," the twin said. "Our mother agreed that we could be split up, if necessary. I remained behind, and our mother waited for me to be adopted, as well."

She spoke again. The family wasn't doing well in Japan, and no one came forward to adopt Ella. Desperate, her mother went against her grandmother's wishes and contacted the twins' father. Their father, she said, was humane enough to realize his child shouldn't be left abandoned. Against his family's wishes, he picked Ella up from the airport. His family disowned them, cutting off all ties. Including removing Ella's name from the trust fund so the father would never get a piece of it.

"You've confirmed this?" I asked her. I couldn't help it. My wariness about the whole thing crept into her tone.

I wanted to say, *c'mon!* Because Madeline sounded very sure, like she was accepting a lot that this woman told her. And to my ears, it sounded like she might be accepting a whole lot of bullspit.

"Yes." Madeline took me in with her eyes. I saw them moving from my scalp to my face and down to my toes. "Izzy, meeting Ella last night was as shocking to me as it is to you now."

She looked at her twin then, as if in awe, faced with the most amazing artwork she would ever see. "This morning, I called the law firm that represented me when I got my inheritance. There wasn't anyone there who had worked on the file, but I made them pull it from the archives."

"And?" I said.

"They need to look further into it, but they confirmed that although the trust fund had originated in

Japan, it had been funded by a bank account in Taiwan."

She and Ella glanced at each other, like two sides of the painting in Madeline's gallery. If I let my cautiousness die away, it struck me that she was speaking a tale that had been waiting within both of them.

"I often dream about it," Ella said. "The flight home—did I feel happy? A little lost?"

"She was raised by our father," Madeline said, "who was just a teenager himself. He tried, I imagine, but he did not know enough to raise Ella with any kind of love."

"He didn't try *that* hard." Ella's words were biting. When I said nothing, she continued. "My father was wealthy."

Again, silence.

"He threw money at the issue," I said, prodding. I had a feeling that issues like these were universal in some ways, dealt with in similar fashion.

They both said, "Yes," at the same time.

"I grew up thinking of him as an awful man," Ella said.

"He left her to be dealt with by different women he dated," Madeline said.

"I adored them," Ella said, her voice softening.

"Yes, but they resented you," Madeline said.

"Deeply," the twin said.

I decided to drop out of the conversation, to let the energy of the topic drop.

Madeline and Ella, their words overlapping each other, told me the rest of the story. Like Madeline, Ella had always found joy in art, spending her time alone, painting. She had some talent, but her father had no interest in her work. Neither did the women who had cared for her. But it was one of those women who opened up her world when she was in her mid-twenties. She had told Ella about her sister—the one who had been taken to America. The one who had been acknowledged by their father's family in a trust fund.

Then Ella learned everything she could about the United States. She fantasized about what Madeline was like—carefree and rich and able to do anything she wanted. Everyone knew you could do anything you wanted in the United States.

When she started learning more about Madeline, she found she was right. And that, she said, was the beginning of an obsession.

For years, she researched Madeline's world any way she could. As they grew older, she studied and she learned. Ella could quote, by heart, bios of Madeline's artists, the names of the artworks, the inspirations behind them. She programmed her computer to send an alert every time Madeline's website was updated.

I exhaled and looked away from the two women. The sight and the story was overwhelming, and my thoughts no longer knew where to land.

Finally, it was Ella who spoke. "Madeline."

We all looked at her.

"Madeline," Ella said, as if testing her voice. "You claimed on your website that you believe everything is an art form."

"Yes," Madeline said simply.

"But really, you only focus on what is right in front of you." There was an accusatory tone to her voice.

"Yes," Madeline said again.

"Your life is viewed in pieces."

Madeline threw her head back, flipping one side of her hair over her shoulder, as if wanting to clear anything that might obstruct her thoughts.

"You are right," Madeline said. "But I only see such pieces because I can't bring too much content into focus. I am not that emotionally capable. I get confused. So I focus in." She raised one of her small hands and lightly tapped her chest.

"Yes," her twin said. "And then you focus *in*. Always away from everyone else."

Madeline dropped her gaze, and I couldn't tell if she was ashamed or trying to restrain herself.

The twin kept talking. At first, she said, she had watched Madeline at a distance.

But her desire to get close to her sister, to slip into Madeline's world undetected, grew intense and brought her the most pain. Because hiding in plain sight meant she was not noticed by Madeline. And eventually, the pain turned into anger.

72

The night it really began, Ella said, she decided to walk by the gallery one more time.

"It was last summer, a beautiful night," Madeline said. "I remember that night." It seemed as if she was trying to help her twin, by telling part of her story.

It was balmy that night, Ella said, but dark black, the street lights making only shallow wells around themselves. When Ella reached the end of the block she turned around and walked past the gallery again. When she reached the end of that block she did it again.

Back and forth she walked in front of the gallery, going only as far as the block's end each time. She had done this many times. But suddenly, that night, she couldn't stand it anymore; she had to at least peer through the inside glass at some of the artwork while Madeline wasn't there.

"Did you know there was a security guard?" I asked.

"Yes," Ella said. She figured she would keep her head down, tell the security guard that she was one of the gallery's customers, that she was debating about a piece and wanting to look in the windows. She'd been ignored so many times before.

To her delight—and shock—the guard had mistaken her for Madeline.

"Forget your keys?" he'd said to her.

She'd put her hands in her jacket pockets and moved them around as if searching for something and nodded.

"Need to be let in?"

"Yes," she had said.

She had gotten in. And every time she went back, it got easier. They didn't blink when she took artwork out through the back alley. She only removed pieces that were made with acrylic or charcoal, materials that didn't require long drying times.

The pieces fell into place for me.

"And then I saw you," I said. "After I'd been with Axel Tredstone." I pointed at Madeline. "I thought *you* were at the gallery that night. I came here around eight at night, and I found you in the back room. You were distant to me." The twins nodded in unison.

"Izzy, do you understand why I couldn't tell you this morning?" Madeline said. "You know why I couldn't let John Mayburn go outside our circle?"

"You mean, to call the cops?" I asked.

"Yes. I had just found Ella, last night."

Madeline looked at me. "Do you want to know the strangest thing for me?"

"Yes," I said quickly. It was hard to imagine a time when I didn't want to get a glimpse inside Madeline Saga's mind.

"I've been fascinated by sisterhood, by women at other times in their lives," Madeline said

I nodded with my head toward the gallery. "Hence the painting with two women in two different time periods."

"Exactly." She smiled. She faced me, her whole body. "And then you came into my life, Izzy. And I have been fortunate to know you. I feel like we will always be friends. Sisters."

I smiled back.

Madeline looked from me to Ella.

Ella said nothing.

"Then, on my way into the gallery last night," Madeline said, looking at me, "I ran into not only my sister. I felt I met myself, the rest of me."

"We looked into each other's eyes," Ella said.

"Right there," Madeline said.

Madeline smiled then, an open, light, almost playful smile I'd never seen before. She was a passionate woman, of course, but also an intense one.

"We stood there for a long time," Madeline said, about the moment she and Ella met. They had entered the gallery together, as if in a womb.

Madeline looked at her sister. "I never knew. But I always sensed you." A few silent moments passed.

Then Ella began to cry.

The sounds were small at first. And I thought, *Finally,* because how was she containing all this emotion that she must have?

Then she started to cry harder, to wail really.

As her cries got louder something in the room seemed to become unmoored, as if the back room of the gallery was a ship whose ropes had been cut loose.

I reached out my hand to the nearest counter to steady myself.

Madeline did the same. But then she launched herself at her sister. And hugged her fiercely.

73

At Bunny's bar the next month, Mayburn and I did our final debrief, as Mayburn liked to call it, of the Madeline Saga case.

When Madeline joined us, Mayburn asked, "Are you sure you don't want to bring in the authorities?"

Madeline made a face, disapproving. We were seated at a booth in the back, the walls decorated with shellacked photos of musicians from the early '80s—Duran Duran, George Thorogood, Flock of Seagulls.

I looked across the bar. Bunny Loveland, God love her, was talking to Ella. Sort of. Actually, she was yelling at her. "You haven't been to Murphy's?"

Poor Ella just shook her head.

"The bar by Wrigley?" Bunny yelled. She was astounded; you could hear it in her voice. "Then you haven't been to Chicago! Just scratch off the last year."

Ella glanced over at us. Mayburn and I gave her a thumbs up, while Madeline smiled her assent.

"I do not want to talk to anyone about this," Madeline said. "I will not."

There was no misjudging the tone in her voice, either. Madeline knew what she wanted.

I thought of that night again, just Madeline and me

in her gallery, me entirely painted. Now I was at peace with it. Mostly, when I thought about it now, I remembered what we talked about—how Madeline believed that as human beings we could hold many different experiences, maybe even more than one person, in our mind and our hearts, and still be complete.

If that was true, then I could be livid at Ella for what she'd done to Madeline—stealing, stalking, making her feel unstable and terrified. I could despise her for the heartache she'd brought my friend.

Yet, I suppose, I could also feel happy for the two of them. Because Madeline was no longer scared. Not in the slightest. And if there had been a hole in my friend's heart, as Madeline said—a place that was empty, that knew something was missing—that hole seemed repaired now. Some part of Madeline's heart and life had flowered. The twins were so elated together.

I glanced around. If I continued to believe in this concept of multifaceted emotional acceptance, I could feel many things about the man who had just walked up to our table.

"Hi, Dad," I said.

My father smiled under his copper glasses. He shed a wool coat and nodded at Mayburn. He shook hands with Madeline, whom he'd met once before, and then my father slid into the booth next to me.

I felt the warmth of him, even through his clothes, as his forearm touched mine. If I believed in that multi-emotional concept then I could, I realized, hold many things about him in my mind, never having to go with only one. I could feel a little conflicted about the fact that my father was growing close with my mother's best friend, Cassandra. (I felt a little like a piece of him was being taken away before I had a chance to enjoy it.) And yet I could be happy for him, too. I could be happy for the kids in me and Charlie, who were both thrilled that our father was around and that, for now, he wasn't leaving Chicago.

"Hello!" I heard Bunny bellow. My eyes shot to her behind the bar.

When Bunny bellowed, it was rarely in a jovial way. But two of the few people Bunny loved—my mom and Spence—had entered the bar.

Bunny introduced them to Ella. My mother took to her immediately, even though I'd told her nothing about the case. I could hear her murmuring, *How are you? Lovely to meet you.* I watched them begin to talk.

In true Spence fashion, he began praising Bunny's new property, pointing out aspects that were "Great! Just great!" He gestured toward the wood molding (it was truly molding, turning green), toward the jukebox (that held no songs past the 1980s), to the dusty wineglasses behind the bar. "Great!" he declared again. "Excellent!"

My mom and Spence—they were two people whom I felt a fountain of fondness toward. Nothing too conflicted about them right now, and for that I was grateful.

Another bellow. This time, Bunny moved around the bar, facing the entering patron, throwing her arms open like Evita Peron.

Vaughn.

The sight of Detective Damon Vaughn last summer? It would have slayed me, slit me open with fear.

But now he slayed me in a different way.

He searched the room for me with his eyes. I could tell by the way he looked, so anticipatory, so excited.

"Douchebag," I heard Mayburn mutter.

"He's gorgeous," Madeline said.

He found me. Vaughn smiled a sly, sexy smile that I was starting (just a little bit) to adore. Who would have known that smile existed under the old exterior of him?

He stepped farther into the bar. "Hey, Iz," he said, in a soft, familiar way. I let the thrill charge up my spine.

He held a wrapped package, the paper green and yellow. When I looked closer, I saw that it bore the Green Bay Packers logo.

"What is that?" I said, pointing.

"It's a present for you."

"That's for me?"

"Yeah." He sounded a little exasperated.

"You wrapped it in freaking Green Bay Packers paper?" Mayburn snarled. But when I glared, he had the decency to leave. Madeline smiled and went to her sister and my mom.

Vaughn sat and handed it to me.

"Thanks," I said. I looked down. "But I have to go with Mayburn for a second. Why would you wrap this in Packers paper when you know I love the Bears?"

What had we been doing this past month, I wondered, if not learning each other's likes and dislikes? He knew, for example, that I followed the Bears and the Cubs. Vaughn? Packers (some twisted version of childhood revenge).

"I love the Packers," Vaughn said.

"I *know* you love the Packers." Was I supposed to climb on board with the archenemy of the Chicago Bears just because Vaughn and I were sorta dating?

He pushed it farther toward me across the table.

I twisted it around. The thing was maybe a foot-and-a-half by a foot, covered in brown paper.

I opened it. It was a painting.

Framed in an old wood frame, the painting was done in oils or maybe acrylics. It was about sixteen inches tall by twelve inches across. Depicted was a woman with long red hair, sitting in a bathtub, leaning forward over blue bath water, wringing out her hair.

I didn't know what to say. I looked up from the painting into Vaughn's brown eyes, the hazel rims seeming to almost glow.

"It looks like you," Vaughn said. "Right?"

I looked back down at the painting. The woman, the way she was depicted in bold yet tiny lines of paint, made her seem avant-garde, and yet the image of her in the bathtub could have been from any decade. "Yeah. Where did you get it?"

"A garage sale." He described the house on California Avenue he had stumbled across one Saturday when he was supposed to be working. "The guy said his aunt painted it years ago."

When I didn't reply right away, too surprised to know how to form words right then, he said, "I guess she was a high school art teacher."

I thought about Madeline.

She would not, in the past, I knew, have approved of this piece of "street art." But Madeline had grown into an even more accepting person, humbled by what few would ever know—that her twin sister was responsible for all her trouble.

Madeline wasn't concerned the way Mayburn and I were. She reached out to Jeremy and Corinne, replacing the artwork they lost, and they agreed to be quiet about the matter. Jacqueline Stoddard, too. She would stay silent about the forgeries, she said, once she knew Madeline had forgiven her and would be silent, too— about Jacqueline's obsession.

In the month that had followed the discovery of her twin, Madeline welcomed her sister into her life. The more time Madeline and her twin spent together, the harder it was to tell the difference between the two.

Life is art, Madeline had said to Mayburn and me just ten minutes ago. She had looked between the two of us and back again. *And so every moment, one has to do what one feels truly and in their heart.*

I looked at the painting now. *What was my heart telling me?* I thought about the other piece of art. Vaugh. That I wanted to see where that would go—that piece of art.

I looked at Vaughn. And then I kissed him.

* * * * *

Acknowledgments

Thank you to Amy Moore-Benson, an author's shining light, and my fantastic editor, Miranda Indrigo. Thanks also to the amazing team at MIRA Books, especially Donna Hayes, Margaret Marbury, Lorianna Sacilotto, Valerie Gray, Craig Swinwood, Pete McMahon, Stacy Widdrington, Andi Richman, Andrew Wright, Katherine Orr, Alex Osuszek, Dianne Moggy, Erin Craig, Margie Miller, Don Lucey, Gordy Goihl, Dave Carley, Ken Foy, Erica Mohr, Darren Lizotte, Reka Rubin, Margie Mullin, Sam Smith, Kathy Lodge, Laurie Mularchuk, Michelle Renaud, Sean Kapitain, Kate Studer, Stephen Miles, Malle Vallik, Tracy Langmuir, Anne Fontanesi, Scott Ingram, Diane Mosher, Sheree Yoon, Alana Burke, Margie Mullin, John Jordan and Brent Lewis.

Thank you so much to everyone in or around the Chicago art community who answered myriad questions, especially Richard Hull, Madeline Nusser, Andrew Rafascz, Shannon Stratford, Megan Carroll, Pam Carroll and Bill Zehme. Special thanks to Chicago artist, Jason Lazarus, for putting me in his art installation, *The Search*.

Thank you, thank you to Carol Miller for holding

down the fort. Thanks also to Tom Kinzler for his knowledge of Japanese law. Lastly, gratitude to all the members of the Chicago Police Department who graciously answered my questions about protocol as well as the joys and difficulties of their jobs.

NEW YORK TIMES BESTSELLING AUTHOR

KAT MARTIN

Millions of lives are on the line. But for him, only one matters.

It's not in bodyguard Jake Cantrell's job description to share his suspicions with his assignments. Beautiful executive Sage Dumont may be in charge, but Jake's not on her payroll. As a former special forces marine, Jake trusts his gut, and it's telling him there's something off about a shipment arriving at Marine Drilling International.

A savvy businesswoman, Sage knows better than to take some hired gun's "hunch." And yet she is learning not to underestimate Jake. Determined to prove him wrong, Sage does some digging of her own and turns up deadly details she was never meant to see.

Drawn into a terrifying web of lies and deceit—and into feelings they can't afford to explore—Jake and Sage uncover something that may be frighteningly worse than they ever imagined.

AGAINST THE SUN

AVAILABLE NOW WHEREVER BOOKS ARE SOLD.

www.Harlequin.com

MKM1350R2

REQUEST YOUR
FREE BOOKS!

2 FREE NOVELS
FROM THE SUSPENSE COLLECTION
PLUS 2 FREE GIFTS!

YES! Please send me 2 FREE novels from the Suspense Collection and my 2 FREE gifts (gifts are worth about $10). After receiving them, if I don't wish to receive any more books, I can return the shipping statement marked "cancel." If I don't cancel, I will receive 4 brand-new novels every month and be billed just $5.99 per book in the U.S. or $6.49 per book in Canada. That's a saving of at least 25% off the cover price. It's quite a bargain! Shipping and handling is just 50¢ per book in the U.S. and 75¢ per book in Canada.* I understand that accepting the 2 free books and gifts places me under no obligation to buy anything. I can always return a shipment and cancel at any time. Even if I never buy another book, the two free books and gifts are mine to keep forever.

191/391 MDN FEME

Name	(PLEASE PRINT)

Address	Apt. #

City	State/Prov.	Zip/Postal Code

Signature (if under 18, a parent or guardian must sign)

Mail to the **Reader Service:**
IN U.S.A.: P.O. Box 1867, Buffalo, NY 14240-1867
IN CANADA: P.O. Box 609, Fort Erie, Ontario L2A 5X3

Not valid for current subscribers to the Suspense Collection
or the Romance/Suspense Collection.

Want to try two free books from another line?
Call 1-800-873-8635 or visit www.ReaderService.com.

* Terms and prices subject to change without notice. Prices do not include applicable taxes. Sales tax applicable in N.Y. Canadian residents will be charged applicable taxes. Offer not valid in Quebec. This offer is limited to one order per household. All orders subject to credit approval. Credit or debit balances in a customer's account(s) may be offset by any other outstanding balance owed by or to the customer. Please allow 4 to 6 weeks for delivery. Offer available while quantities last.

Your Privacy—The Reader Service is committed to protecting your privacy. Our Privacy Policy is available online at www.ReaderService.com or upon request from the Reader Service.

We make a portion of our mailing list available to reputable third parties that offer products we believe may interest you. If you prefer that we not exchange your name with third parties, or if you wish to clarify or modify your communication preferences, please visit us at www.ReaderService.com/consumerschoice or write to us at Reader Service Preference Service, P.O. Box 9062, Buffalo, NY 14269. Include your complete name and address.

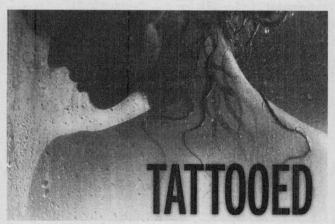

LAURA CALDWELL

32932	CLAIM OF INNOCENCE	___ $7.99 U.S.	___ $9.99 CAN.
32666	RED, WHITE & DEAD	___ $7.99 U.S.	___ $8.99 CAN.
32658	RED BLOODED MURDER	___ $7.99 U.S.	___ $8.99 CAN.
32183	LOOK CLOSELY	___ $6.99 U.S.	___ $8.50 CAN.

(limited quantities available)

TOTAL AMOUNT	$ _____
POSTAGE & HANDLING	$ _____
($1.00 for 1 book, 50¢ for each additional)	
APPLICABLE TAXES*	$ _____
TOTAL PAYABLE	$ _____

(check or money order—please do not send cash)

To order, complete this form and send it, along with a check or money order for the total above, payable to Harlequin MIRA, to: **In the U.S.:** 3010 Walden Avenue, P.O. Box 9077, Buffalo, NY 14269-9077; **In Canada:** P.O. Box 636, Fort Erie, Ontario, L2A 5X3.

Name: _____
Address: _____ City: _____
State/Prov.: _____ Zip/Postal Code: _____
Account Number (if applicable): _____

075 CSAS

*New York residents remit applicable sales taxes.
*Canadian residents remit applicable GST and provincial taxes.

HARLEQUIN® MIRA®
™ www.Harlequin.com

MLC0912BL